Takeoff!

Randall Garrett writes in his introduction: "A pastiche attempts to tell a story in the same way that another author would have told it.... A parody, when properly done, takes an author's idiosyncracies — of style, content, and method of presentation — and very carefully exaggerates them. You jack them up *just one more notch.*" When a master does it, few things in literature are more delightful. Here are Asimov, Lovecraft, Russell, van Vogt, Sprague de Camp, Anderson and many others, so well done that you may have difficulty believing it. *Takeoff* is a rare phenomenon, and one of the most delightful books in science fiction. And it is more than that. It also speaks of, from A. E. van Vogt's introduction: the "elegance of his style" and "the beauty of his imagery," and the "easy insertion of difficult technical information. No matter what he writes, the style flows poetically." But most of all, it's just plain fun.

Takeoff!

by Randall Garrett

Cover illustration by Phil Foglio
Interior illustrations by Kelly Freas
Edited by Polly and Kelly Freas

THE
DONNING COMPANY
PUBLISHERS
Norfolk/Virginia Beach 1986

Takeoff! is one of the many fantasy and science fiction titles published by The Donning Company/Publishers. For a complete listing of our titles, please write to the address below.

The Donning Company/Publishers
5659 Virginia Beach Boulevard
Norfolk, Virginia 23502

10   9   8   7   6   5   4   3   2   1

Library of Congress Cataloging in Publication Data:

Garrett, Randall.
   Takeoff.
   (Starblaze editions)
   1. Science fiction, American 2. Parodies.
I. Freas, Polly. II. Freas, Kelly. III. Title.
Pz4.G2388TAK [PS3557.A7s38] 813′.5′4   79-9140
ISBN 0-915442-84-1
Cover copyright © 1986 by Phil Foglio
Interior illustrations © 1979 Frank Kelly Freas
Printed in the United States of America
Editor for Starblaze Editions/Graphics, Kay Reynolds

DEDICATION

This book is dedicated to Jerry Moore, without whose indefatigable research it would not have been possible.

Table of Contents

Introduction 1
Foreword 5
Gentlemen: Please Note 9
Backstage Lensman 30
The Cosmic Beat 76
Despoilers of the Golden Empire 96
The Horror Out of Time 132
Look Out! Duck! 144
Master of the Metropolis with Lin Carter 180
Mustang 187
No Connections 193
On the Martian Problem 209
Prehistoric Note 215
Reviews in Verse 217
Isaac Asimov's "The Caves of Steel" 219
Alfred Bester's "The Demolished Man" 223
L. Sprague DeCamp's "Lest Darkness Fall" 227
A.E. van Vogt's "Slan" 230
Poul Anderson's "Three Hearts and Three Lions" 235
John W. Campbell's "Who Goes There?" 240
The Adventures of "Little Willie" 243
Introduction to Benedict Breadfruit by Grendel Briarton .. 244
Through Time and Space with Benedict Breadfruit 245

INTRODUCTION

By A. E. van Vogt

In my opinion, the author of *Takeoff* should have been under official surveillance from the day he was conceived. At some distant future time, when we really know how to do things right, such as Randall Garrett will be watched closely from a very early age.

Why?

About 10 years ago I read a new work by the famous Russian psychologist, A. R. Luria (whose book *The Nature of Human Conflicts* made him world famous many decades earlier). The new work, possibly Luria's last, was about a man with the "greatest" memory in all of Russia.

Well!...I don't know whether Randall Garrett has in his time possessed the greatest memory in North America, or if he still possesses it. But I am sure that he has been right up there with the finalists.

I cannot recall anyone ever mentioning Randall's super ability. No American Luria sought him out, tested him periodically, and finally wrote him up as a case history of eidetic recall.

Actually, the Luria account of the Russian memory wizard was not up to the standard of this scientist's earlier work—from my point of view. It gave the numerous tests and their results. It described to a small extent some of the memory aids the Russian had worked out all by himself. (There were some elements in these of the Roth memory-by-association system.) But it failed to describe any of the commonplaces of, or the side effects of the

1

ability on, the man's daily life.

The commonplaces of Randall's life shall come under closer scrutiny—let me assure you—right here in these pages. Though neither I nor anyone else has apparently ever received direct replies from him on basic aspects of his life. When was Randall born? The only printed clue I have been able to find is given in the editor's introduction to the original magazine version of *Masters of the Metropolis*, as follows:

> "Randall Garrett and Lin Carter had not been born when Hugo Gernsback created RALPH 124C 41+. To stress their youth further (for one can, like me, be far from young and still have been born after the first appearance of RALPH in Modern Electrics), they had not even been born when Gernsback founded *Amazing Stories*, the first all-science-fiction magazine...."

Yet, sitting across from me and my Russian princess at the L.A. airport Mariott Hotel Capriccio Restaurant recently, Randall made the statement that he had known me for 30 years.

He is the one with the eidetic memory. So, since Gernsback founded *Amazing* in 1926 (and Randall wasn't born by then), and thirty years ago was 1948, we can put two and one together into twenty-one, or two and zero together into twenty.

Randall, did you emerge into this cruel world in 1927? Or was that strange party you gave in the spring of 1978 a celebration of half a hundred years of life?

Where was I in 1948 that our paths crossed? I have many memories of Randall over the years. But that '48 meeting is a blur to a memory—mine—that cannot even recall the title of Luria's book on Russia's greatest observed rememberer.

(Alas, I bought the book. Read it. Gave it as a gift to a friend. And have never been able to locate another copy.)

Are Randall's parents still alive? Where was Randall born? Where did he go to school? What was the title of his first published work? Does he have brothers and sisters? Was he born a Catholic? Or did he convert?

These last two, particularly, are relevant questions. Because Randall for ten years (after his initial foray into SF) attended seminary training, and became a Catholic priest.

Did his Russian alter ego experience some similar moral concern? There is no record of such details in Luria's work.

It is interesting that the Russian with the supermemory was a newspaper reporter when Luria first met him. I mean, both men—Randall and the Russian—became writers automatically. Since Luria does not mention it, and because newspapermen do not normally have their works collected, we cannot examine the writings of the Russian mental marvel for clues about his personal life.

Fortunately, that is not our problem with Randall. He has a body of literature to his credit. Of which you, dear reader, hold a portion in your hands. And a very revealing portion it is.

In these pages you will find...pastiches. Stories written in the styles of other writers. Here you will find E. E. Smith, Ph.D. and H. P. Lovecraft and Eric Frank Russell as if returned from the dead, etc. Randall remembers each author's style exactly. In the case of the E. E. Smith "takeoff" he actually, after more than thirty years, repeated an entire paragraph of E. E. Smith's without having seen the story in the interim. Since he had made no conscious effort to memorize the story at the time he read it, he subsequently realized by vivid recall what he had done, and rewrote the offending item. Rewrote it because there are unknowing people who would have considered it plagiarism if it had ever come to light.

The pastiche, though not called such, is a well-known phenomenon of the Hollywood film game. It is an act of paralleling someone else's work, using a new concept. So far as I know, no psychologist has ever made a serious study of the TV writers—particularly—who do this well. (Do they also have exceptional memories?)

Each week these men and women write the exact same format for a continuing series, but with a different story. If you think this is easy, try it some time. (The writers who find such paralleling sheer agony are the ones you hear screaming about TV censorship. The others collect their $10,000 or so for an hour script without a peep of protest. And in fact they seem to wonder what all the fuss is about.)

Randall is a mimic in voice, also. Like an actor, he can duplicate the way other people talk, and imitate the exact intonation of a foreign language. I am personally, currently, in process of learning 200 languages, and, not being the mimic type, am learning them on the hearing level only, to start. As a consequence of this study, I have observed that less than 5% of the populace are mimics.

One of the first things to notice about a Randall Garrett story, pastiche or otherwise, is the elegance of his style. The beauty of his imagery. The easy insertion of difficult technical information. No matter what he writes, the style flows poetically.

Which reminds me that in England, until recently, students were required to memorize thousands of lines of poetry during a school year. Shakespeare, in the days of Elizabeth I, had to do the same. Virtually all the men and women who gave England such a rich poetic heritage were forced memorizers.

So it is interesting that we find our Randall of the marvellous natural memory writing his reviews in poetic form. Entire novels are condensed, and commented on—poetically. Think about that. And when you read the reviews in this collection bear in mind that no one ever told Randall to do it that way.

Undoubtedly, perfect memory has its drawbacks. For example, one is bound to recall—perfectly—the unpleasant along with the pleasant. Once again, Luria—from whom we could have learned so much that would be useful—fails us. He does not mention that aspect of the greatest memory in all the Russias.

Indeed, toward the end of his book we suddenly find him referring to the man as having died several years before. How did he die? From what? Was the death memory-related? Not a mention of such in Luria's work.

At this point let me apologize slightly for these criticisms of the great Russian psychologist. I believe he was over eighty years old when he wrote this final book. Also, we have to credit him with having done anything at all. So far as I know, it is the only work of its kind ever published by a psychologist.

But it's true, alas, that he has no advice for Randall as to what to watch out for as he grows into his second half century.

I do have one comment. It is significant that Randall, when he drinks, takes his liquor straight—no water, no 7-Up, no dilution with ice. What is significant about this is that liquor is the one thing that can temporarily dim vivid unpleasant memory images.

We live in an intermediate stage of history. The great scientific millenium is still ahead of us. When that millenium arrives, both special and unspecial—an even more difficult type to evaluate or help—people will be noticed early for what they are, or are capable of.

And the correct action will be taken.

Until then, here's Randall who, in doing the best he could on his own with a perfect memory, has given us a few glimpses of that strange, wonderful world of the human mind. Question: is it possible that all people with good memories have a need to write pastiches?

Which brings us back to what I said earlier: somebody in authority should be looking into Randall Garrett. And maybe even looking after him.

4

FOREWORD
By Randall Garrett

In the first chapter of Tolkien's *Fellowship of the Ring*, the venerable Bilbo Baggins makes a speech at the party he is giving to celebrate his eleventy-first birthday. In that speech, he tells the assembled hobbits that he does not know half of them as well as he should like, and he likes less than half of them half as well as they deserve.

Most of his guests sit around trying to work it out and see if it comes out a compliment.

I am still doing exactly the same thing with Van's introduction to this book.

Van vastly underrates his own memory and even more vastly overrates mine. I remember our first meeting well, but—

Why should A. E. Van Vogt, who has been a glittering star in the science fiction firmament since 1939, remember an unimpressive, awestruck fan who had one very minor story published under another name four years before? That summer of 1948, I found his name in the L.A. phone book and trepidatingly called him up. I must have said something right, for he invited me to his home.

I showed up, but I have the feeling that Van was far more impressed by the blue-eyed honey blonde I brought with me.

Van's working out of my age is a marvel of mathematical exactitude. I *was* born in 1927. Unlike Bilbo, I have never liked birthday parties, especially my own. Just for the novelty, I decided to celebrate my fiftieth, but only after it had passed.

You are all invited to my next such party, to be held sometime after my eleventy-first birthday.

By that time, I may have enough material to put together another book like this, but that is problematical. You see, I only do them when I bloody well feel like it. If the right idea for a pastiche or parody hits me, I do it, but that doesn't happen often. This book represents some twenty years of that kind of work.

The difference between a pastiche and a parody is, perhaps, a subtle one.

A pastiche attempts to tell a story *in the same way* that another author would have told it. In this book, *The Best Policy* is a pastiche, not a parody. I used, to the best of my ability, Eric Frank Russell's style of writing and his way of telling a story.

A parody, when properly done, takes an author's idiosyncrasies—of style, content, and method of presentation—and very carefully exaggerates them. You jack them up *just one more notch*. The idea is to make those idiosyncrasies *blatantly* visible. Thus, *Backstage Lensman* is a parody. Doc Smith would never have—very probably *could* never have—written it. It is very difficult indeed for a writer to see his own idiosyncrasies; they are too much a part of him.

But the line between parody and pastiche is not hard and thin; it is broad and fuzzy. Is *The Horror Out of Time* a pastiche or a parody? I don't know. You tell me.

I do not decide to write a pastiche or parody just for the sake of writing one. The story idea comes first. In 99.44% of the cases, I write my own story in one of my own styles. But once in a very great while it seems to me that the idea belongs in someone else's universe. Then I write a pastiche. See, herein, *No Connections*.

And when the idea belongs in another's universe—except that it is patently ridiculous—I write a parody. The idea for *Backstage Lensman*, for instance, you will find in the next-to-last scene, in a simple mathematical formula. All the rest of it came from that.

The "Reviews in Verse" are a different breed of mutant. They are quite deliberate. The idea is to tell the plot with reasonable accuracy—*and leave out the entire point that the author was trying to make!* So even if you do not heed my warning at the beginning of that section, you will still not know what the story is really about. For that, go to the originals.

The "Little Willies" are takeoffs of an Englishman named Harry Graham, who originated them. Since he was a retired officer of Her Majesty's* Coldstream Guards, he wrote under the name "*Col. D. Streamer.*"

---

*Victoria, that is.

The Benedict Breadfruit stories need no introduction from me. My very good friend, Reginald Bretnor, got *his* very good friend, Grendel Briarton, to do an introduction for them. And Mr. Briarton, apparently, had to go to Ferdinand Feghoot for the final copy.

I have not, by any means, given what might be called The

Garrett Treatment to *all* the writers I admire. Although Van's *Slan* is in here, his distinctive style is ripe for story treatment. Ted Sturgeon would be fun. Fritz Leiber is on my little list. Bob Silverberg is begging for it. Lester del Rey is going to get his one of these days. Cordwainer Smith has it coming. Frank Herbert will not go unscathed. Mack Reynolds is overdue. Avram Davidson will not be neglected. Neither will Michael Kurland. There are others. Just wait.

Maybe *before* my eleventy-first...

Wait! Don't go away! This book is like a tapestry. I supplied the basic material, and Frank Kelly Freas supplied the lovely embroidery.* When this book becomes an expensive collector's item *(when, not if)*, it will be because of Kelly's work, not mine.

---

*Is that a crewel remark?

(Kelly, if you or Polly cut what follows because of some false feeling of modesty, may your pencils break, your inkpots run dry, your typewriter clog, your paints become gelatinous, and your canvas rot. Truth, dammit, is *truth!*)

This book is Kelly's work in more than one way. Let me give you some background, and then I'll tell you a true story.

I met Kelly in the early fifties at a science fiction convention. I don't remember which one; they all begin to blend into one another after all this time. (See, Van? I told you!) I don't remember the con, but I remember Kelly. At that time, he sported a large red mustache and a smile which kept it turned up at the ends. I loved the man immediately.

Kelly is witty, outgoing, friendly, gregarious, and articulate. He is shrewd, careful, intelligent, and analytical. He is sensitive, understanding, warm and compassionate. And he knows the science and technique of art as few people in history have known it.

He is, of course, a science fiction fan of the highest caliber. It shows in every illustration he does. He *cares* about science fiction. And he cares about the people who write and read it.

That's not all the background I could give you on the man, but it will have to do for the nonce. Now comes the story.

A while back, I was talking to Kelly on the phone about a book of mine that didn't quite measure up to his and Polly's specifications. Suddenly, he said: "Hey! What about a book of your parodies and pastiches?"

"Is the world ready for this?" I asked.

"Damn right it is!" and he mentioned several stories he liked. He got me enthusiastic, and I went to work finding them.

About a week later he called me. "I've got it! I've got it!" he shouted into my tender ear.

Carefully easing the receiver back toward that offended organ, I said: "You do? Is it contagious?"

"No, no! I've got the title for your book!"

Nero Wolfe once said: "I have no talent. I have genius or nothing." The thing about Kelly is that he has *both*.

His talent lies in his ability to use any and every artistic medium that exists. His genius lies in the *way* he uses them. And that genius shows through every medium.

Let me give you an imaginative example—what Albert Einstein called a "thought experiment."

I am fond of churches as works of art; I am a church buff, among other things, and I go absolutely ape over the Gothic style. The great Gothic cathedrals of Europe really turn me on, and if I were going to build a church, it would be in that style. Suppose I had enough money to build the church of my dreams. It would take many tens of millions of dollars today.

With that vast sum in my pocket, I would go to Frank Kelly Freas and say: "Kelly, build me that church. Hire engineers, hire architects, hire artisans of any kind you need. Money is no object, but build me that church."

He could do it; you damn well betcha he could. The spires, the gargoyles, the statues, the stained glass windows—all. And when he was through (assuming a lifespan of some three centuries), it would be the most beautiful church in all Christendom. That is his talent.

And those who know his genius would take one look at it and say, in no irreverent tone: "My God! *That's a Frank Kelly Freas Church!*"

Selah.

8

GENTLEMEN: PLEASE NOTE
By Randall Garrett

This might be considered an "alternate history" story, and in a way, I suppose it is. But not in the sense that, say, the Lord Darcy stories are. This is a takeoff, not on history, but on the way certain self-important know-it-alls do their best to put down the gifted person just because his notions don't agree with theirs. And, far too often, they succeed.

This is a study in "how to stomp on the crackpot."

With the exception of General B-f, all the characters mentioned in this story were actual historical persons, but, with the possible exception of King Charles II, were nothing like I have depicted them.

My apologies especially to Isaac Barrow, who, as far as my historical reading has led me to believe, was a much nicer guy.

18 June 1957
Trinity College
Cambridge

Sir James Trowbridge
No. 14 Berkeley Mews
London

My dear James,

I'm sorry to have lost touch with you over the past few years; we haven't seen each other since the French War, back in 1948. Nine *years!* It doesn't seem it.

I'll tell you right off I want a favour of you. (No, I do *not* want to borrow another five shillings! I haven't had my pocket picked again, thank you.) This has to do with a little historical research I'm doing here. I stumbled across something rather queer, and I'm hoping you can help me with it.

I am enclosing copies of some old letters received by Isaac Newton nearly three hundred years ago. As you will notice, they are addressed to "Mr. Isaac Newton, A.B."; it rings oddly on the ear to hear the great man addressed as anything but "your Grace," but of course he was only a young man at the time. He hadn't written his famous *Principia* yet—and wouldn't for twenty years.

Reading these letters is somewhat like listening to a conversation when only one of the speakers is audible, but they seem to indicate another side to the man, one which has not heretofore been brought to light.

Dr. Henry Blake, the mathematician, has looked them over, and he feels that it is possible that Newton stumbled on something that modern thought has only recently come up with—the gravitational and light theories of the Swiss mathematician, Albert Einstein.

I know it's fantastic to think that a man of even Newton's acknowledged genius could have conceived of such things three centuries before their proper place in history, but Blake says it's possible. And if it is, Blake himself will probably do to Newton's correspondents the same thing that was done to Oliver Cromwell at the beginning of the Restoration—disinter the bodies and have them publicly hanged or some such thing.

Actually, Blake has managed to infect me with his excitement; he has pointed out phrases in several of the letters which tally very well with Einstein's theory. But, alas, the information we have is woefully incomplete.

What we need, you see, are Newton's letters—the ones he sent which provoked these answers. We have searched through everything here at Cambridge, and we haven't found even a trace;

evidently the Newton manuscripts were simply discarded on the basis that they were worthless, anyway. Besides, records of that sort were poorly kept at that time.

But we thought perhaps the War Office did a somewhat better job of record-keeping.

Now, I realise full well that, due to the present trouble with the Austro-Hungarian Empire, the War Office can't take a chance and allow just anyone to prowl through their files. It wouldn't do to allow one of the Emperor's spies to have a look at them. However, I wondered if it wouldn't be possible for you to use your connexions and influence at the War Office to look for Newton's letters to one of the correspondents, General Sir Edward Ballister-ffoulkes. You can find the approximate dates by checking the datelines on the copies I am sending you.

The manuscripts are arranged in chronological order, just as they were received by Newton himself. Of them all, only the last one, as you will see, is perfectly clear and understandable in all its implications.

Let me know what can be done, will you, old friend?

With best wishes,
SAM
Dr. Samuel Hackett
Department of History

12 November 1666
London

Mr. Isaac Newton, A.B.
Woolsthorpe

Dear Mr. Newton:

It was very good of you to offer your services to His Majesty's Government at this time. The situation on the Continent, while not dangerous in the extreme, is certainly capable of becoming so.

Your letter was naturally referred to me, since no one else at the War Office would have any need for the services of a trained mathematician.

According to your précis, you have done most of your work in geometry and algebra. I feel that these fields may be precisely what are needed in our programme, and, although you have had no experience, your record at Trinity College is certainly good enough to warrant our using your services.

If you will fill in the enclosed application blank, along with the proper recommendations and endorsements, we can put you to work immediately.

Sincerely,
Edward Ballister-ffoulkes, Bart.
General of Artillery
Ballistics Research Dept.

12 November 1666
Cambridge

Mr. Isaac Newton, A.B.
Woolsthorpe

My dear Isaac,

I am sorry to hear of your decision to remain at home for a while longer instead of returning to the College, but if you feel that your health is delicate, by all means rest until you are in better spirits.

I think, however, that you should attempt to return as soon as possible; you have a great deal of work ahead of you, my boy. Mathematicians—like Rome—are not built in a day—nor in four years.

If, however, you would like to do a part of your studies by post, I see no objection to it, under the circumstances, although, of course, it will be necessary to spend a part of your time in residence here, and the final examinations will have to be taken here.

Later on, when you are feeling better, I will send an outline of some work I intend to do on conic sections; I think it would be of great benefit to you to work with me on this. I have always had confidence in your ability. You are young yet, but, given time and plenty of study, you should make a place for yourself in the world of mathematics.

I think that the work I have in mind for you should prove stimulating.

Most sincerely,
Isaac Barrow, Ph.D.

16 November 1666
London

Dear Mr. Newton:

It would most certainly be quite convenient for you to do your work there at Woolsthorpe.

An explanation of the work we are trying to do and some of

the problems we are up against will be despatched to you as soon as possible.

Sincerely,
Ballister-ffoulkes

21 November 1666
Cambridge

My dear Isaac,

Your paper has arrived. I haven't had time to look it over yet, but I shall find time to peruse it during the forthcoming holidays. I am, of course, very interested in what problems concerned you during the summer.

A very merry Christmas to you, my boy.

Is. Barrow

22 November 1666

FROM: Ballistics Research Dept.,
 British Army Artillery
TO: Isaac Newton, A.B.,
 Woolsthorpe
SUBJECT: Ballistics research data.
ENCLOSURE: Range table sample for 9 lb. artillery.
2nd ENCLOSURE: Outline and general discussion of ballistics

1. In order to better understand the problems facing this Department, you will familiarise yourself with the enclosed material.

2. This material is confidential, and is not to be allowed to fall into unauthorised hands.

By order of the Commanding General

SECOND ENCLOSURE

The purpose of this project is to determine, with as great a degree of precision as possible, the range of artillery used by His Majesty's Armed Forces, and the methods of accurately firing upon targets at various distances from the cannon.

After a great deal of research, the following factors have been found to affect the distance which a cannon ball may be hurled by exploding gunpowder:

1. Weight of the cannon ball.
2. Weight of powder used.
3. Angle of elevation of cannon.
4. Length of cannon barrel.

The first two factors are obvious; the heavier the cannon ball, the more powder it will take to blow it a certain distance, and contrariwise.

The third is somewhat unwieldly to work with and definitely problematical in its effects. Up to a certain point, increasing the angle seems to increase the range, but after that point is reached, an increase in elevation decreases the range of the weapon. In view of this, it has been decided that all cannon will be fixed at the best angle for maximum range and the other factors varied to change the actual distance the cannon ball is fired.

(Here it may be noted, incidentally, that the angle of elevation is of no use in the Royal Navy, since that angle is indeterminate, due to the roll of the ship.)

The fourth factor, too, may be discarded, since a barrel of too great a length would make it unwieldy on the battlefield, although those of fixed fortresses could be somewhat greater. And, in view of the fact that changing the length of a cannon barrel on the field is out of the question, we may safely say that the fourth factor is a fixed quantity in each cannon and thus ignore it.

It has, therefore, been decided to test each of the various types of cannon presently in use by Army Artillery and publish for each a range table for various cannon balls and charges of powder, and to furnish a copy of such table to the battery leader of each field piece.

This programme, as may well be imagined, has required a great deal of cannon testing in the past year, and will undoubtedly require a great deal more before the project is finished. We hope, however, that it will be of at least limited use in the very near future, and will eventually greatly advance the science of cannon-firing.

2 January 1667

My dear Isaac,

Your Christmas was, I trust, a pleasant one? I hope your mother is in good health, and I hope your own is improved.

My dear boy, I have some advice for you; I do hope that you will take it as it is intended—as from an old friend and tutor who wishes you only well.

It has come to my attention that you are—shall we say—prostituting your talents. A friend of mine who works at the War Office tells me that you are doing some mathematical work by correspondence—something to do with cannon, I believe?

Now, I quite understand that you are in a somewhat precarious financial position, and believe me, I deeply sympathise with you. I know that the earning of a few pounds can mean a great deal to you in furthering your education.

I do not say that such work is menial, either. I would not have you think that I deplore your choice of work in any way; it is necessary work, and money is certainly necessary for life.

However, let me warn you: a simple task like this, which pays rather well, can become soporific in its effect. Many men of talent, finding themselves comfortably fixed in a mediocre position, have found their minds have become stultified through long disuse. *Please*, dear boy, don't fall into that trap; don't throw away a fine career in mathematics for the sake of a few paltry pounds. You are young and inexperienced, I know, and have a great deal yet to learn, so please take the advice of one who is somewhat older and wiser.

No, I haven't gotten round to reading your paper yet; I'll do it this evening, my boy, I promise.

Most sincerely,
Isaac Barrow

3 January 1667
Cambridge

My dear Isaac,

I read your paper, and I am, I must confess, somewhat nonplussed. What *are* you doing?

I see that my letter of yesterday was somewhat premature; I should have waited until I had read your paper, since it is in exactly the same category.

You ask: "What is the optimum shape for a wine barrel? Should it be tall and thin, or squat and broad?"

And I ask: "What on Earth difference does it make?"

Surely you are not thinking of becoming a wine merchant? If so, what need is there to waste your time studying mathematics? On the other hand, if you intend to become a mathematician, why should you debase a noble and lofty study by applying it to wine barrels?

As I told you, I have no objection to your making a few pounds by doing minor calculations for the Army, but this is foolishness. You have gone to a great deal of trouble for nothing; as you gain more experience, you will realize the folly of such things.

As to your theory of "fluxions," I admit myself to be completely at a loss. You seem to be assuming that a curve is made up of an infinite number of infinitely small lines. Where is your authority for such a statement? You append no bibliography and no references, and I cannot find it in the literature.

Apparently, you are attempting to handle *zero* and *infinity* as though they were arithmetical entities. Where did you learn such nonsense?

My boy, please keep it in mind that four years of undergraduate work does not qualify one as a mathematician. It is merely the first stepping stone on the way. You have a great deal of studying yet to do, a great many books yet to read and absorb—books, I may say, written by men older, wiser, and more learned than yourself.

Please don't waste your time with such frivolous nonsense as toying with symbols derived from wine barrels. No good can come out of a wine barrel, my boy.

I hope you will soon find yourself in a position to aid me in some of the calculations on conic sections as I outlined them to you in my letter of the 28th December last.* I feel that this is important work and will do a great deal to further your career.

With all best wishes,

Sincerely,

Isaac Barrow

This letter was either lost or returned to Dr. Barrow.—S.H.

5 January 1667
London

Dear Mr. Newton:

Thank you for your tabulations on the seven-pounder. I must say you were very prompt in your work; there was no need to work over the holidays.

Your questions show that you are unacquainted with the difficulties of manufacturing military arms; I am not at all surprised at this, because it takes years of training and practical experience in order to learn how to handle the various problems that come up. It is something that no university or college can teach, nor can it be learned from books; only experience in the field can teach it, and you have had none of that.

I can, however, explain our method of approach thus:

Each cannon to be tested is fired with several balls—some of iron, some of lead, some of brass, and some which have been hollowed out to make room for a charge of gunpowder in order that they may explode upon reaching the target. With each type of ball, we find the amount of powder required to drive the ball five yards from the muzzle of the piece; this is considered the minimum range. (Naturally, with the testing of hollow, explosive missiles, we do not fill them with gunpowder, but with common earth of equal weight. To do otherwise would endanger the cannoneer.)

After the minimum range is found, more balls are fired, using greater amounts of powder, added in carefully measured increments, and the distance achieved is measured off.

This process is kept up until the safety limit of the weapon is reached; this point is considered the maximum range.

Naturally, the weights of different balls will vary, even if they are made of the same metal, and the bores of cannon will vary, too, but that can't be helped. What would you have us do? Make all cannon identical to the nearest quarter-inch? It would not be at all practical.

I am happy to see that you are enthusiastic over the work we are doing, but please, I beg you, wait until you have learned a great deal more about the problem than you have done before you attempt to make suggestions of such a nature.

As to the paper which you enclosed with your tabulations, I am afraid that it was of little interest to me. I am a military man, not a mathematician.

Thanking you again for your excellent work, I remain.
Yours sincerely,
Edward Ballister-ffoulkes, Bart.

9 January 1667
Cambridge

My dear Isaac,

I have known you for more than five years, and I have, I might say, a more than parental interest in you and your career. Therefore, I feel it my duty to point out to you once again that your erratic temper will one day do you great harm unless you learn to curb it.

You take me to task for saying to you what is most certainly true, viz.: that you are not yet a mathematician in the full sense of the word. You are young yet. When you have put in as many years at study as I have, you will understand how little you now know. Youth is inclined to be impetuous, to rush in, as the saying goes, where angels fear to tread. But better men than yourself have come to realise that the brashness of youth is no substitute for the wisdom of maturity.

As to your other remarks, you know perfectly well what I meant when I said that no good can come out of a wine barrel. To accuse me of sacrilege and blasphemy is ridiculous. You are twisting my words.

Please let us have no more of this name-calling, and get down to more important work.

Sincerely,
Isaac Barrow

12 January 1667
London

Dear Mr. Newton:

Thank you again for your rapid work in tabulating our results. It is most gratifying to find a young man with such zeal for his work.

As I have said before, I am no mathematician, but I must confess that your explanation makes very little more sense to me than your original mathematical formulae.

As I understand it, you are proposing a set of equations which will show the range of any weapon by computing the weight of the ball against the weight of the powder. (Perhaps I err here, but that is my understanding.) It seems to me that you are building a castle-in-Spain on rather insubstantial ground. Where is your data? What research have you done on cannon-fire? Without a considerable body of facts to work with, such broad generalisations as you propose are quite out of order.

Even if such a thing could be done—which, pardon me, I take the liberty to doubt—I fear it would be impractical. I realise that you know nothing of military problems, so I must point out to you that our cannoneers are enlisted men—untutored, rough soldiers, not educated gentlemen. Many of them cannot read, much less compute abtruse geometrical formulae. It will be difficult enough to teach them to use the range tables when we complete them.

Indeed, I may say that this last point is one of the many stumbling-blocks in the path of our project. More than one of the staff at the War Office has considered it to be insurmountable, and many times I have fought for the continuance of research in the face of great opposition.

I greatly fear that using any but methods known to be practicable would result in our appropriation being cut off in Parliament.

Again, however, I thank you for your interest.

Most sincerely,
Ballister-ffoulkes

24 January 1667
Cambridge

My dear Isaac,

I am truly sorry I didn't get around to looking over your second manuscript until now, but, to be perfectly truthful, I have been outlining our course of work on conic sections, and had little time for it.

As it turns out, it was all for the best that I did so; it would have been sinful to take valuable time away from my work for such trivialities.

You are still harping on your wine-barrel fluxions and your Army cannon balls. Am I to presume that the whole thing is a joke? Or are you seriously proposing that the path of a cannon ball is related to the moon? That is rank superstition! Sheer magic! One would think that even a lad as young as yourself would have grasped the basic concept of the Scientific Method by this time.

How have you tested this absurd thing experimentally? Where are your measurements, your data? Your references?

Do not think, my boy, that fame and fortune in the sciences can be achieved by pulling wild hypotheses out of your imagination. There is no short-cut to mastery of a difficult subject like mathematics; it requires years of hard work and study.

As an example of what can happen when one has not learned enough of the subject, look at your own work. You appear to be handling Time as though it were a spatial dimension. You even end up, in several equations, with square seconds! Now, a yardstick will show that a foot up-and-down is the same as a foot East-and-West or a foot North-and-South. But where can you find a foot of time?

Please, dear boy, use your time to study the things you have yet to learn; don't waste it exploring a nonsensical cul-de-sac.

I will send you the outline on conic sections within the week.

Sincerely,
Isaac Barrow

1 February 1667
London

Dear Mr. Newton:

In reference to your letter of 14 January 1667, on the simplified algebraic formulae for the prediction of the paths of cannon balls, our staff has considered the matter and found that not only is your mathematics incomprehensibly confusing, but the results are highly inaccurate. Where, may I ask, did you get such data as that?. On what experimental evidence do you base your deductions? The actual data we have on hand are not at all in agreement with your computations.

Men with more experience than yours, sir, have been working on this problem for several years, and nothing in our results suggests anything like what you put forth. Finding data is a matter of hard work and observation, not of sitting back in one's armchair and letting one's mind wander.

It would, indeed, be gratifying if our cannon would shoot as far as your equations say they should—but they do not. I am afraid we shall have to depend on our test results rather than on your theories. It is fact—not fancy—which is required in dealing with military operations.

Sincerely,
Edward Ballister-ffoulkes, Bart.
General, Army Artillery

3 February 1667
Cambridge

My dear Isaac:

I feel it would clear the air all round if we came to an understanding on this thing. Your continued insistence that I pay attention to theories which have no corroboration in the literature and are based on, to say the least, insufficient confirmatory data, is becoming tedious. Permit me, as a friend, to show you where, in your youthful impetuosity, you err.

In the first place, your contention that there is a similarity between the path of a cannon ball and the moon is patently ridiculous. I cannot imagine where you obtained such erroneous information. A cannon ball, when fired, strikes the earth within seconds; the moon, as anyone knows, has been in the sky since—according to Bishop Ussher—4004 B.C. Your contention that it remains held up by a force which pulls it down is verbal nonsense. Such a statement is semantically nothing but pure noise.

You state that the path followed by a cannon ball is parabolic in nature. How do you know? Can you honestly say that you have measured the path of a cannon ball? Have you traced its path, measured it, and analysed it mathematically? Can you prove analytically that it is not an hyperbola or part of an ellipse? Have you any data whatsoever to back up your statements, or any authority to which you can refer?

You make broad generalisations on the assumption that

"every body is attracted equally to every other body;" that the earth attracts the moon in the same way that it attracts an apple or a cannon ball. Where is your data? You have not, I dare say, measured the attraction between every body in the universe. Have you checked the variations in apples according to sugar content or the variations in cannon balls with reference to their diameters? If not, have you checked with any reliable authority to see if such work has already been done?

And where did you learn that anyone can just sit down and make up one's own mathematical systems? I am certain that I taught you no such thing. Mathematics, my boy, is based on logical interpretation of known facts. One cannot just go off half-cocked and make up one's own system. What would happen to mathematics as a science if anyone should just arbitrarily decide that two added to two yields five or that two multiplied by two equals one hundred?

You said that the whole thing came to you "in a flash" last summer when you were sitting under an apple tree and one of the fruit fell and struck you on the head. I suggest that you see a good physician; blows on the head often have queer effects.

If you have the data to prove your contentions, and can show how your postulates were logically deduced, then I will be very happy to discuss the problem with you.

As soon as you feel better, and are in a more reasonable frame of mind, I hope you will return to Cambridge and continue with the studies which you so badly need.

Sincerely,
Dr. Isaac Barrow

P.S.: It occurs to me that you may have meant your whole scheme as some sort of straight-faced pseudo-scientific joke, similar to that of another gentleman who bears our common Christian name.* If so, I fail to comprehend it, but if you would be so kind as to explain it to me, I will be only too happy to apologise for anything I have said.

Is. Barrow

---

*I have no idea who this might be. The reference is as obscure as the joke.—S.H.

8 February 1667
London

Dear Mr. Newton:

I have tried to be patient with you, but your last letter was sulphurous beyond all reason. I may not, as you intimate, be qualified to judge the mathematical worth of your theories, but I can and do feel qualified to judge their practical worth.

For instance, you claim that the reason your computations did not tally with the data obtained from actual tests was that the cannon ball was flying through the air instead of a vacuum. By whose authority do you claim it would act thus-and-so in a vacuum? Do you have any data to substantiate your claim? Have you ever fired a cannon in a vacuum? For that matter have you ever fired a cannon?

What would you have our cannoneers do—use a giant-sized Von Guericke Air Pump to evacuate the space between the cannon and the target? I fear this would be, to say the very least, somewhat impractical and even dangerous under battle conditions. I presume a tube of some kind would have to be built between the enemy target and the gun emplacement, and I dare say that by that time the enemy would become suspicious and move the target.

You speak of "ideal conditions." My dear Newton, kindly keep it in mind that battles are never fought under ideal conditions; if they were, we should always win them.

If you wish to spend your time playing with airy-fairy mathematical abstrusities which have no basis in fact, that is perfectly all right with me. This is a free country, and no one proposes to dictate one's private life. However, I would appreciate it if you would do me the honor of not burdening my already overtaxed mind with such patent nonsense.

Otherwise, your work with the tabulations has been most excellent; I am enclosing a cheque for £ 20 to cover your work so far.

> Sincerely,
> Edward Ballister-ffoulkes,
> Bart.

12 February 1667
Cambridge

My dear Newton:

You have stretched the bonds of friendship too far. You have presumed upon me as a friend, and have quite evidently forgotten my position as head of the Department of Mathematics at this College.

The harsh language in which you have presumed to address me is too shocking for any self-respecting man to bear, and I, for one, refuse to accept such language from my social inferiors. As a Professor of Mathematics in one of the most ancient of universities, I will not allow myself or my position to be ridiculed by a young jackanapes who has no respect for those in authority or for his elders.

Your childish twaddle about glass prisms producing rainbows—a fact which any schoolboy knows—is bad enough; but to say that I am such a fool that I would refuse to recognise "one of the most important advances in mathematics" is beyond the pale of social intercourse.

Repeatedly during the last few months, you have attempted to foist off on me and others implausible and unscientific theories which have no basis whatever in fact and which no reputable scientist would be foolish enough to endorse. You are not a mathematician, sir; you are a charlatan and a mountebank!

You have no data; you admit working from "intuition" and hypotheses cut out of whole cloth; you cannot and will not give any reliable authority for any of your statements, nor will you accept the reliable statements of better men than yourself.

This unseemly behaviour forces me to exercise my prerogative and my authority in defence of the college and the university. I shall recommend to the authorities that you be refused readmission.

Isaac Barrow, Ph.D.
Department of
Mathematics
Trinity College

16 February 1667

FROM: Ballistics Research Department,
                 Army Artillery
TO: Mr. Isaac Newton,
                 A.B., Woolsthorpe
SUBJECT: Reduction in personnel
ENCLOSURE: Cheque for   2/10s/6d

1. In view of the increased personality friction between yourself and certain members of this department, this department feels that it would be to our mutual disadvantage to continue retaining your services as mathematical consultant.

2. As of 16 February 1667 your employment is hereby terminated.

24

3. Enclosed is a cheque covering your services from 8 February 1667 to date.

By order of the Commanding General
Major Rupert Knowles,
Adjutant for
General Sir Edward Ballister-ffoulkes

12 March 1667
Whitehall

My dear fellow,

I am making this communication quite informal because of your equally informal method of—shall we say—getting my ear.

I have been nagged at day and night for the past three weeks by a certain lady of our mutual acquaintance; she wants me to "do something for that nice young Mr. Newton." She seems to think you are a man of some intelligence, so, more in order to stop her nagging tongue than anything else, I have personally investigated the circumstances of your set-to with the Ballistics Research Department.

I have spoken with General B-f, and looked over all the correspondence. Can't make head or tail of what you're talking about, myself, but that's beside the point. I did notice that your language toward the general became somewhat acid toward the last. Can't actually say I blame you; the military mind can get a bit stiff at times.

And I'm afraid it's for that very reason that my hands are tied. You can't expect a man to run a kingdom if he doesn't back up his general officers, now, can you? Political history and the history of my own family show that the monarch is much better off if the Army and Navy are behind him.

So I'm afraid that, our little lady notwithstanding, I must refuse to interfere in this matter.

CAROLUS II REX

19 March 1667
Whitehall

Newton:
No! That is my final word!

C II R

21 May 1667
Cambridge

My dear Isaac,

Please accept the humble apologies of an old friend; I have erred, and I beg you, in your Christian charity, to forgive me. I did not realise at the time I wrote my last letter that you were ill and overwrought, and I have not written since then because of your condition.

As a matter of fact, when your dear mother wrote and told me of your unbalanced state of mind, I wanted desperately to say something to you, but the blessed woman assured me that you were in no condition for communication.

Believe me, my dear boy, had I had any inkling at all of how ill you really were, I would have shown greater forbearance than to address you in such an uncharitable manner. Forgive me for an ungoverned tongue and a hasty pen.

I see now that the error was mine, and it has preyed on my mind for these many weeks. I should have recognised instantly that your letters to me were the work of a feverish mind and a disordered imagination. I shall never forgive myself for not understanding it at the time.

As to your returning to the College for further study, please rest assured that you are most certainly welcome to return. I have spoken to the proper authorities, and, after an explanation of the nature of your illness, all barriers to your re-entrance have been dropped. Let me assure you that they are well aware of what such an unhappy affliction can do to unsettle a man temporarily, and they understand and sympathise.

I can well understand your decision not to continue your studies in mathematics; I feel that overwork in attempting something that was a bit beyond one of your tender years was as much responsible for your condition as that blow on the head from that apple. It is probably that which acounts for the fact that serious symptoms did not appear until late in March.

I feel that you will do well in whatever new field you may choose, but please do not work so hard at it.

Again, my apologies.

Isaac Barrow

3 April 1687
York

To His Grace,
The Most Reverend Dr. Isaac Newton,
By Divine Providence the Lord Archbishop of Canterbury
  My Lord Archbishop,
      May I take this opportunity to give you my earnest and
heartfelt thanks for the copy of your great work which you so
graciously sent; I shall treasure it always.
      May I say, your Grace, that, once I had begun the book, I
found it almost impossible to lay it down again. In truth, I
could not rest until I had completed it, and now I feel that I
shall have to read it again and again.
      In my humble opinion, your Grace is the greatest theo-
logical logician since the Angelic Doctor, St. Thomas Aquinas.
And as for beauty and lucidity of writing, it ranks easily with
"De Civitate Deo" of St. Augustine of Hippo, and "De Imita-
tione Christi" of St. Thomas a Kempis.
      I was most especially impressed by your reasoning on the
mystical levitation of the soul, in which you show clearly that
the closer a human soul approaches the perfection of God, the
greater the attraction between that soul and the Spirit of God.
      Surely it must be clear to anyone that the more saintly a
man becomes, the greater his love for God, and the greater
God's love for His servant; and yet, you have put it so clearly
and concisely, with such beautifully worded theological rea-
soning, that it becomes infinitely more clear. It is almost as
though one could, in some mystical way, measure the distance
between an individual soul and the Holy Presence of God by
the measure of the mutual love and attraction between the soul
and the Blessed Trinity.
      Your masterful analysis of the relative worthiness of
those who have come to the Kingdom of Heaven on the Day of
Judgement is almost awe-inspiring in its beauty. Even those
souls which have been cleansed as white as snow by the
forgiving Grace of God differ, one from another, and your
comparison between those souls and a ray of pure white light
striking a prism of clearest crystal is magnificent.
      The Church has always held that those whose entire lives
have been lived in holy purity and in the Grace of God would hold
a higher place in heaven than those whose lives have been sinful,
even though God, in His graciousness, has forgiven them their
sins. But no one had shown how this might be so. Your analogy,
showing how the white light of the sun may be graded into the

colours of the rainbow, ranging from red to violet, illustrates wonderfully how Our Lord will grade His chosen servants on the Last Day, when the sinful souls of the damned are cast into Darkness.

There are other instances, almost too numerous to mention, which show your immense theological understanding and deep thought. So thought-provoking are they that I would not dare to comment on them until I have re-read and studied them carefully, for fear I should show my own shallowness of mind.

It is my belief that your "*Prinicpia Theologica*" will be read, honoured, and loved by Christians for many centuries to come.

I shall, of course, write to you further and at greater length on this monumental work.

Praying for God's blessing on you and your work, and for the fullness of God's grace during the coming Eastertide,

I am,

Most faithfully yours,
William Sancroft
By Divine Permission
Lord Archbishop of York

BACKSTAGE LENSMAN
By Randall Garrett

The Lensman series, comprising, as it does, some six hundred thousand words, is still, to my mind, the greatest space opera yet written. It has, to use one of Doc Smith's favorite words, "scope."

E. E. Smith, Ph.D., had more scope, more breadth and depth of cognizance of the Cosmic All, than anyone before—or since.

He had his flaws; we all do. But the grandeur of his writing overpowered those flaws, made them insignificant.

I first wrote Backstage Lensman nearly thirty years ago. The original is long lost. There was no market for it in those days, and my moving about...well, it got lost. This is a re-creation from memory. It was a test of memory in another way, too: not once, during the writing, did I look into the Lensman for descriptions or phraseology or situations to parody. I've read those books so often over the years that there was no necessity for it. The style came naturally.

Only once did my memory fail me. I was too accurate. I had to rewrite one paragraph because, when I checked with the original, it was word-for-word. And that's plagiarism.

Doc saw the first version of Backstage Lensman in 1949, and laughed all through the convention. It was his suggestion that I call the spaceship Dentless.

On a planet distant indeed from Tellus, on a frigid, lightless globe situated within an almost completely enclosing hollow sphere of black interstellar dust, in a cavern far beneath the surface of that abysmally cold planet, a group of entities indescribable by, or to, man stood, sat, or slumped around a circular conference table.

Though they had no spines, they were something like porcupines; though they had no tentacles, they reminded one of octopuses; though they had no wings or beaks, they seemed similar to vultures; and though they had neither scales nor fins, there was definitely something fishy about them.

These, then, composed the Council of the Meich, frigid-blooded poison-breathers whose existence at temperatures only a few degrees above zero absolute required them to have extensions into the fourth and fifth dimensions, rendering them horribly indescribable and indescribably horrible to human sight.

Their leader, Meichfrite, or, more formally, Frite of the Meich, radiated harshly to others of the Council: "The time has now come to consider the problem of our recent losses in the other galaxy. Meichrobe, as Second of the Meich, you will report first."

That worthy pondered judiciously for long moments, then: "I presume you wish to hear nothing about the missing strawberries?"

"Nothing," agreed the other.

"Then," came Meichrobe's rasping thought, "we must consider the pernicious activities of the Tellurian Lensman whose workings are not, and have not been, ascribed to Star A Star.

"The activities and behavior of all members of the never-to-be-sufficiently-damned Galactic Patrol have, as you know, been subjected to rigid statistical analysis. Our computers have come to the conclusion that, with a probability of point oh oh one, the Lensman known as Gimble Ginnison either is or is not the agent whom we seek."

"A cogent report indeed," Meichfrite complimented. "Next, the report of Meichron, Third of this Council."

"As a psychologist," Meichron replied, "I feel that there is an equal probability that the agent whom we seek is one whose physical makeup is akin to ours, rather than to that of the fire-blooded, oxygen-breathing Tellurians. Perhaps one of the immoral Palanians, who emmfoze in public."

"That, too, must be considered," Meichfrite noted. "Now to Meichrotch, Fourth of the Meich..."

And so it went, through member after member of that dark Council. How they arrived at any decision whatever is starkly unknowable to the human mind.

On green, warm Tellus, many megaparsecs from the black cloud which enveloped the eternally and infernally frigid planet of the Meich, Lensman Gimble Ginnison, having been released from the hospital at Prime Base, was talking to Surgeon-Major Macy, who had just given him his final checkup.

"How am I, Doc?" he asked respectfully, "QX for duty?"

"Well, you were in pretty bad shape when you came in," the Lensman surgeon said thoughtfully. "We almost had to clone you to keep you around, son. Those Axlemen really shot you up."

"Check. But how am I *now?*"

The older Lensman looked at the sheaf of charts, films, tapes, and reports on his desk. "Mmm. Your skeleton seems in good shape, but I wonder about the rest of you. The most beautiful nurses in the Service attended you during your convalescence, and you never made a pass—never even patted a fanny."

"Gosh," Ginnison flushed hotly, "was I expected to?"

"Not by me," the older man said cryptically.

"Well, am I QX for duty? I have to do a flit."

Surgeon-Major Macy handed Ginnison an envelope. "Take this to the Starboard Admiral's office. He'll let you know. Where are you flitting for?"

"I'm not sure yet," Ginnison said evasively, taking the envelope.

"Right. Clear ether, Gimble."

"Clear ether, Macy."

True to an old tradition, these two friends never told each other anything.

The Starboard Admiral slit open the envelope and took in its contents at a glance. "According to Macy, you're fit for duty, son. Congratulations. And, in spite of everything, that was a right smart piece of work you did on Mulligans II."

Ginnison looked at the tips of his polished boots. "Gee whiz," he said, blushing. Then, looking up: "If I'm fit for duty, sir, I'd like to make a request. That mess on Cadilax needs to be cleaned up. I'm ready to try it, sir, and I await your orders."

The Starboard Admiral looked up into the gray eyes of the young, handsome, broad-shouldered, lean, lithe, tough, hard, finely-trained, well-muscled, stubborn, powerful man who stood before him.

"Gim," he said firmly, "You have disobeyed every order I have ever given you. It always came out all right, so I can't gripe, but, as of now, I'm getting out from under. I've talked to the Galactic Council, and they agree. We are giving you your Release."

The Release! The goal toward which every Lensman worked

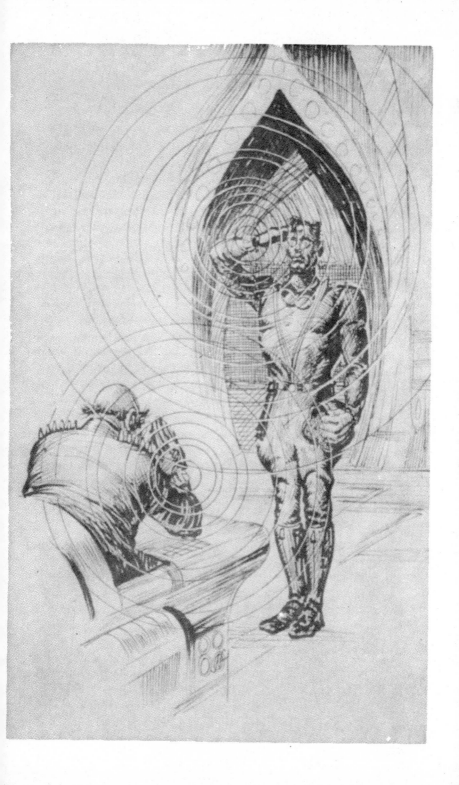

and so few attained! He was now an Unattached Lensman, responsible to no one and nothing save his own conscience. He was no longer merely a small cog in the mighty machine of the Galactic Patrol—

He was a Big Wheel!

"Jeepers!" he said feelingly. "Goshamighty!"

"It's all of that," the Starboard Admiral agreed. "Now go put on your Grays, take the *Dentless,* and get the hell out of here!"

"Yes, *sir!*" And Ginnison was gone.

He went to his quarters and took off his black-and-silver uniform. Then he proudly donned the starkly utilitarian gray leather uniform which was the garb of the Unattached Lensman. And as he did so, he made that curious gesture known as Gray Seal. No entity has ever donned or ever will don that Gray uniform without making that gesture. It is the only way you can get the zipper closed.

In his office, solidly sealed against both thought and spy-ray beams, the Starboard Admiral sat and stared at the glowing Lens on his wrist, the Lens which was, and is, the symbol of the rank and power of every Lensman of the Galactic Patrol.

But it is far more than merely a symbol.

It is a lenticular structure of hundreds of thousands of tiny crystalloids, and each is built and tuned to match the ego of one individual entity. It is not, strictly speaking, alive, but its pseudo-life is such that when it is in circuit with the living entity to whom it is synchronized, it gives off a strong, changing, characteristically polychromatic light. It is a telepathic communicator of astounding power and range, and kills any being besides its owner who attempts to wear it.

Thus, it is both pretty and useful.

Manufactured and issued by the mysterious beings of dread and dreaded Arisia, it cannot be counterfeited, and is given only to those entities of the highest honor, integrity, honesty, and intelligence. That knowledge made the Starboard Admiral, as, indeed, it did all Lensmen, feel smug.

The mighty *Dentless,* from needle prow to flaring jets, was armed and armored, screened and shielded as was no other ship of her class and rating. Under the almost inconceivable thrust of her mighty driving jets, she drilled a hole through the void at her cruising velocity of a hundred parsecs per hour.

Not in the inert state could she so have done, for no body with inertial mass can travel faster than the velocity of light, which, in the vast reaches of the galaxy, is the veriest crawl.

But her Bergenholm, that intricate machine which renders a spaceship inertialess, or "free," permitted her to move at whatever velocity her ravening jets could achieve against the meager resistance of the almost perfect vacuum of interstellar space. Unfortunately, the Bergenholm, while it could completely neutralize *inertial* mass, never quite knew what to do with *gravitational* mass, which seems to come and go as the circumstances require.

As the *Dentless* bored on through the awesome void toward her goal, Ginnison and Chief Firing Officer Flatworthy checked and rechecked her mighty armament. Hot and tight were her ravening primary beams, against which no material object, inert or free, can offer any resistance whatever. When struck by the irresistable torrents of energy from a primary, any form of matter, however hard, however resistant, however refractory, becomes, in a minute fraction of a second, an unimaginably hot cloud of totally ionized gases.

Equally tight, but not so hot, were the ultrapowerful secondaries, whose beams could liquify or gassify tungsten or even the ultraresistant neocarballoy in the blink of an eye.

The inspection over, Ginnison lit a cigarette with a tertiary and Lensed a thought to an entity in another part of the ship. "Woozle, old snake, I hate to disturb your contemplations, but could you come to my cabin? We have things to discuss."

"Immediately, Ginnison," that worthy replied, and shortly thereafter Ginnison's door opened and there entered a leather-winged, crocodile-headed, thirty-foot-long, crooked-armed, pythonish, reptilian nightmare. He draped himself across a couple of parallel bars, tied himself into a tasteful bow-knot, and extended a few weirdly-stalked eyes. "Well?"

Ginnison looked affectionately at the horribly monstrous Lensman. "Concerning *l'affaire* Cadilax," he began.

"I know nothing about it, fortunately," Woozle interrupted. "That gives you a chance to explain everything."

"Very well, then. As you well know, I have spent a long time searching for clues that will lead me to the top echelon of Boskonia—Boskonia, that frightful, inimical, soul-destroying, intergalactic organization which is so ineradicably opposed to all the moral values which we of Civilization hold so dear."

Woozle closed a few eyes. "Yes. Continue."

"On Leanonabar," Ginnison continued, "I got a line through Banjo Freeko, the planetary dictator, but only after I blew up the mining industry on his planet and killed a few thousand innocent people—regretfully, of course. But I do that all the time. It revolts me, but I do it."

"What boots it?" Woozle asked. "You got your line, didn't you? You humans are so squeamish."

"To continue," said Ginnison. "This is the line I traced."

And in Woozle's mind there appeared a three-dimensional representation of intergalactic space. Two galaxies floated there in the awesome awfulness of the unimaginable vastness of the intergalactic void.

From Leanonabar, in the First, or Tellurian, Galaxy, a thin, hard red line ran straight through and past the Second Galaxy, out into the vast reaches of the intergalactic space beyond.

"Isn't that rather overdoing it?" came Woozle's thought. "You think this line may extend beyond—?"

Ginnison shook his head. "Not really. There's nothing along that line for half a billion parsecs, and that's a Seyfert Galaxy."

"Tough about them," Woozle opinioned. "Let's get back to Cadilax."

"Oh, yes. Well, Cadilax is clear across the Galaxy from Leanonabar, so that would give us a good baseline for our second triangulation."

"I trust," Woozle thought, "that you have a better reason than that for picking Cadilax."

"Certainly." Rising from his seat, Ginnison paced across the deck of his cabin, turned, and paced back. "In the past several months, all hell has broken loose on Cadilax. The drug trade has gone up three hundred percent. Thionite, heroin, hashish, nitro-labe, cocaine, bentlam, and caffeine—all of them have increased tremendously, and Narcotics can't find the source. The adolescents have gone wild; the boys are wearing their hair long, and the girls have given up perms. Illicit sex is rampant. They live in unstructured social groups." He took a deep breath, and said, in a hushed voice: "There have even been demonstrations against the way the Patrol is running the Boskonian War!"

"Madness, indeed," Woozle agreed, "but are you certain that your information is up-to-date?"

"Reasonably certain," Ginnison pondered. "The latest information we have—"

At that point, a sharp, cold, Lensed thought intruded.

"Lensman Ginnison, greeting. I humbly request communication with you."

Ginnison recognized that thought. It was that of Shadrack, a poison-blooded, frigid-breathing Lensman he had known of yore.

"Sure, little chum; what is it?"

"I do not interrupt?" Shadrack quavered.

"Not at all. Go ahead."

"I trust I do not intrude upon matters of far greater importance than that of my own meager and faulty information?"

"Certainly not," Ginnison reassured.

"As is well known," continued the soft thought, "I am a yellow-bellied, chicken-livered, jelly-gutted coward — a racial characteristic which I cannot and do not deny. Therefore, I most humbly apologize for this unwarranted intrusion upon your thoughts."

"No need to overdo it, little chum," said Ginnison. "A simple grovel will be enough."

"Thank you, Ginnison," Shadrack snivelled gravely. "Then may I inquire, in my own small way, if you are aware of the existence of an entity known as Banlon of Downlo? He is, like myself, a creature accustomed to temperatures scarcely above zero absolute, but of far greater courage and bravery than any of my race possess."

"BANLON!" Ginnison's Lensed thought fairly shrieked. "Klono, yes, I know of him!" Then, more calmly: "He's been out after my hide since we destroyed Downlo."

"That, I fear, is true," Shadrack commented. "Even now, he has, according to the information which my poor powers have allowed me to glean, englobed the *Dentless* with a fleet of twelve ships which are prepared to blast you out of the ether."

"*Klono's curving carballoy claws and gilded gadolinium gizzard!*" Ginnison roared mentally. "Why didn't you say so in the first place?"

"I am devastated," Shadrack replied. "It is, again, a racial characteristic which I cannot avoid. It took me too long to apologize." A pause, then: "I fear, even now, that I may have been too late," Shadrack apologized. "Clear ether, Ginnison."

"Clear ether, little chum."

The Lensed connection cut off, and Ginnison flashed a thought to the control room, only to discover that, indeed, the *Dentless* was surrounded.

In a black, indetectable, refrigerated speedster, many parsecs from the soon-to-be scene of battle, that entity known as Banlon of Downlo gloated over his instruments as he watched the englobement of the *Dentless* take form.

Like the Meich, and like Shadrack, he was of a race whose normal temperature was near that of boiling helium, and thus required extra-dimensional extensions in order to gather enough energy to survive. Superficially, that sounds glib enough, but, unfortunately, your historian knows less about dimensional a-nalysis than you do, so let's drop it right there.

To return to our narrative, Banlon, a safe distance away from the impending conflict, observed minutely the behavior of the Boskonian squadron which had englobed the *Dentless*. Each captain of the twelve Boskonian warships had done his job to perfection.

"Very well," Banlon radiated harshly to his minions, "en-globement is now complete. Tractors and pressors on! Cut your Bergenholms and go inert! Blast that ship out of the ether!"

Inertialess as she was, the mighty *Dentless*, caught in a web of tractor and pressor beams, could not continue at speed against the resistance of an inert combined mass twelve times that of her own. Relative to the Boskonian squadron, she came to a dead halt in space, easy prey for the Boskonians.

At Banlon's order, all twelve Boskonian ships fired at once toward the center of their englobement, where the apparently helpless Patrol ship floated.

Beams, rods, cones, stilettoes, icepicks, corkscrews, knives, forks, and spoons of energy raved against the screens of the *Dentless*. Quasi-solid bolts of horrendous power chewed, gnawed, flared, snarled, and growled against the energy screens of the Patrol ship, seeking eagerly to blast through them to the hull metal. All of circumambient space was filled with the fright-ful discharge of those tremendous bolts of power.

The screens of the *Dentless* flared red, orange, yellow, green, blue, and into the violet. From there, they went into the ultraviolet and x-ray spectrum. But still they held.

Gimble Ginnison, teeth clenched and jaw muscles knotted, stared with unblinking gaze of gray eyes at the plate before him, listening to the reports from the officers commanding the various functions of the ship. But only one of those reports was really important.

"Screens holding, Lensman!"

"Fire secondaries!" the Lensman ordered crisply.

The prodigious might of the Patrol ship's secondaries flared out toward the twelve Boskonian ships. Those screens, too, blazed up the spectrum toward the ultraviolet, then toward blackness.

"Primaries one through twelve! Ready?"

"Ready, sir!"

"At my order, then." Ginnison watched his plate closely.

"Five seconds! Four...Three...Two...One...FIRE!"

Twelve primary batteries flamed forth as one, each ravening beam smashing into, through, and past the already weakened shields of the Boskonian battleships. Like tissue paper in the flame of an oxyhydrogen torch, the dozen ships dissolved into whitehot gas.

As far as his detectors could scan, Ginnison could see that there was not a single threat in the ether about the *Dentless.*

"Navigator," he ordered crisply, "continue toward Cadilax."

From his coign of vantage, so many parsecs away, Banlon stared in unbelief at his instruments, knowing to the full what they had reported. But after that first momentary shock, the ultrahard logic of his ultracold brain reasserted itself.

"Shit," he thought. And, flipping his speedster end-for-end, he turned around and ran.

Came, betimes, to Cadilax, a bum.

He showed up, unobtrusively, in the streets of Ardis, the capital of that disturbed planet. He was, apparently, a man approaching sixty—graying, flabby, rheumy-eyed, alcoholic, and not too bright. He was so typical of his kind that no one noticed him; he was merely one of ten thousand such who wandered about the streets of the various cities of Cadilax. He hung around the bars and bistros of the spaceport, cadging drinks, begging for small change, leering innocuously at the hookers, and telling stories of the days of his youth, when he was "somebody." He claimed to have been a doctor, a lawyer, a pimp, a confidence man, a bartender, a judge, a police officer, a religious minister, and other such members of highly respected occupations, but he could never produce any proof that he had ever been any one of them.

And no one expected him to, for that was the *sine qua non* of the spaceport bum. He was what he was, and no one expected more of him. He called himself Goniff, and, because of his vaguely erudite manner of speech, soon became known as "Professor" Goniff.

He was never completely sober, and never completely drunk.

The student of this history has, of course, already surmised that beneath this guise lay the keen mind and brain of Gimble Ginnison, Gray Lensman, and he is right.

Throughout this time, Ginnison was searching out and finding a wight bedight Gauntluth.

It had taken time. The Gray Lensman's mind had probed into the depths of degradation, the valleys of vileness, the caverns of corruption, in the dregs of the noxious minds of the foulest folk of a planet before finding that name and that individual. He might have found him earlier, had he not been enjoying himself so much.

At first, only vaguely had he been able to construct from the clues available a picture of the all-powerful drug baron and pirate who ruthlessly ruled the underworld of Cadilax. Then, as time went on and more and more data came in, his visualization of Gauntluth became complete.

Gauntluth was tall, lean, and tough, with the all-pervading cadaverous blue of a Kalonian. His headquarters were in the Queen Ardis Hotel, the biggest luxury hotel on the planet, which catered only to the top fringe of the upper crust of the ultra-ultra.

There, in his superbly screened and shielded suite of offices, Gauntluth controlled, through an intricate webwork of communications, and by a highly efficiently organized army of minions, the drug traffic of half a dozen solar systems.

For long Ginninson pondered, and came to the obvious conclusion that "Professor" Goniff could in no wise gain admission to the elite society of the Queen Ardis Hotel. Therefore Goniff the bum vanished.

Instead, it was Lester Q. Twodyce, cosmopolitan, and wealthy playboy, who checked into the Queen Ardis with an entourage of flunkies and yes-men, not one of whom could easily be detected as an officer of the Galactic Patrol. As was de rigeur on Cadilax, every one of Twodyce's men wore a thought-screen.

Carefully, step by step, Ginnison laid his trap. Through the highest ranks of Gauntluth's organization, it became known that Lester Q. Twodyce had something valuable that he was eager to sell. It became clear, even to Gauntluth, that whatever it was Twodyce had, it was certainly worth investigating.

Thus it came about that one evening, when the impeccably dressed Mr. Twodyce was seated at a table in the grand dining room of the hotel with two of his hard-faced gunmen, he was approached by two equally well-dressed men who bowed politely and smiled pleasantly.

One of them said: "Good evening, Mr. Twodyce. I trust we do not interrupt your repast?"

Twodyce looked up. "Not at all," he said. "Will you be seated?"

Then, almost as an afterthought: "May I order you drinks? Such distinguished men as yourselves deserve only the best, of course."

"You know, then, who we are?" asked the spokesman.

"Certainly, Mr. Thord," replied the Lensman suavely, "you and Mr. Thield are hardly anonymous." Drinks were brought.

"These—" he gestured toward the men on either side of him. "—are my associates, Mr. Kokomo and Mr. De Katur."

After several minutes of preliminary conversation, the ape-faced Thord finally broached the subject which they had all been anticipating.

"I hear, Mr. Twodyce," he said, "you are here to do business."

"Not primarily," said the Lensman nonchalantly. "I am here to enjoy myself. Business is not a primary concern of mine."

"I understand," said Thord, "for such a man as yourself..."

"Nevertheless," continued Ginnison, "I do have a small trifle which I am willing to dispose of for a proper price."

The lizard-like Mr. Thield spoke. "And that is?"

Twodyce said off-handedly, "Fifty grams of clear-quill thionite."

There was a stunned silence from Thord and Thield.

Thionite! Thionite, that dreadful and dreadfully expensive drug which, in microgram doses, induces in the user clear, three-dimensional, stereosonic visions in which he indulges in his every desire to the point of ecstasy. *Every* desire, base or noble, mental or physical, conscious or subconscious. Whatever pleasurable experience he wishes for himself, he experiences. It is addictive to the nth degree. It is the ultimate high, but the slightest overdose is deadly.

It is also purple.

One milligram of that dire drug was enough for a thousand doses, and the insouciant Mr. Twodyce was offering fifty thousand times that amount!

"Gad!" murmured Mr. Thield.

"Indeed?" said Thord. "If that is true, we are prepared to offer..."

"You will offer nothing," Ginnison said calmly. "I do not deal with underlings."

Thord's face darkened. "Underlings? *Underlings?* To whom do you think you are speaking, *Mister* Twodyce?"

"To underlings," said the unruffled Twodyce. "And you may tell Gauntluth I said so."

There was a momentary silence from Thord and Thield as their eyes darted from Ginnison's face to those of the bodyguards. Each bodyguard was fingering his necktie, his right hand only inches away from the DeLameter that was undoubtedly in a shoulder holster concealed by the loose-fitting dress jacket that each man wore.

Thord and Thield rose, superficially regaining their composure. "We will speak to you later, Mr. Twodyce," said Thord.

"You will not," said Ginnison in a low, deadly voice. "I have no desire to see either of you again. Gauntluth may contact me if he so wishes. Tell Gauntluth that I caution him to think of a hamburger."

"A...a hamburger?" gasped Thord.

"Precisely. A hamburger."

"—But—"

"You may not be able to figure it out," Ginnison said coldly, "but your boss will. Now go."

Without another word, the two underlings turned and went.

That night, in his own suite, Lester Q. Twodyce was Lensing a thought to Lieutenant-Admiral Partisipple, the Lensman in charge of the Patrol base on Cadilax.

"Partisipple?"

"Yes, Ginnison, what is it?" came the Lensman-Admiral's thought,

"This thing's about to bust wide open," Ginnison declared, "and I'll need some help."

"Anything you want, Gray Lensman."

"Good. Can you get me about fifty logons?"

"Logons?" Lensed the base commander in astonishment. "LOGONS!"

There was reason for his astonishment, for the logon, or Cadiligian rateagle, is one of the nastiest, most vicious, and intractable beasts in the galaxy. Its warped mind is capable of containing but one emotion: HATRED! The Cadiligian rateagle hates anything and everything living, the only desire in the small compass of its mind being to reduce that life to something edible.

EICH AND

MEICH, THEY

The logon resembles the Tellurian rat at its worst, but it is the size of a Tellurian terrier and has the wings and claws of an eagle. Logons do not make nice pets.

"Yes, logons," Ginnison replied. "I can control them."

"With your superior mental equipment," the base commander thought humbly, "I am sure you can. How do you want them packaged?"

"Put them in a 'copter. Have the pilot ready to release them on my order, within one kilometer of the roof of the Queen Ardis Hotel."

"Certainly. Clear ether, Gray Lensman."

"Clear ether, Partisipple."

Then, another Lensed thought to Woozle, in the *Dentless*, hovering invisibly in orbit high above the surface of Cadilax. "Woozle, old serpent, here's the story so far." And in flashing thoughts he told the reptilian Lensman his plans. "So have Lieutenant Hess von Baschenvolks and his company of Dutch Valerians down here and ready to go."

"Will do, Ginnison. Clear ether."

"Clear ether."

In the office on the top floor of the Queen Ardis Hotel, the inscrutable face of Gauntluth stared thoughtfully at the banks of screens, meters, switches, dials, indicators, knobs, buttons, and flickering lights on the panels and control boards which surrounded him.

Finally, after long pondering, he touched a button on one of his control panels. "Give me suite 3305," he said.

Ginnison was waiting for the call when it came. The cadaverous blue face of the gaunt Gauntluth appeared on his visiscreen. "Yes?" he said calmly.

"I am told," came Gauntluth's rasping voice, "that you are in a position to deal with me concerning a certain—ah—article."

"As long as the deal is on the up-and-up, I am," replied Ginnison. "Of course, the usual precautions must be taken on both sides."

"Of course, my dear fellow," Gauntluth said agreeably. "Shall we, then, make arrangements that are agreeable to both sides?"

"Let us do so," said Ginnison.

On cold and distant Jugavine, the planet of the Meich, the

First of the frightful Council, Meichfrite, radiated harshly to the others: "You have all scanned the tapes containing the report of our agent, Banlon of Downlo. Somehow, by what means we know not, the Lensman, Ginnison, escaped the trap Banlon set for him. Twelve of our ships have vanished utterly, and Banlon's report is neither complete nor conclusive. I would now like to hear your comments. Meichrobe."

"It seems to me," that worthy radiated, "that the strawberries are—"

"*Forget the goddam strawberries!*" Meichfrite riposted. "*What about Ginnison?*"

"Well, then," Meichrobe thought raspingly, "our computers have calculated that with a probability of point oh oh four, Gimble Ginnison has either gone to Cadilax or somewhere else."

"Indeed," Meichfrite thought thoughtfully. "Meichrodot, Fifth of the Meich, give us your thoughts on this subject."

"Our reports from Cadilax," informed Meichrodot, "indicate that all is going smoothly. There is no trace of the Lensman on or near the planet. However, Banlon's agent Gauntluth has reported through Banlon that he is running short of thionite. He wants to make a buy."

Meichfrite turned his attention to the Sixth of the Meich. "Meichroft, this is your department."

"Banlon," Meichroft emitted, "must go to Trenco."

Trenco! That planet was, and is, unique. Its atmosphere and its liquid are its two outstanding peculiarities. Half of the atmosphere and almost all of the liquid of the planet is a compound with an extremely low heat of vaporization. It has a boiling point such that during the day it is a vapor and it condenses to a liquid at night. The days are intensely hot, the nights intensely cold.

The planet rotates on its axis in a little less than twenty-six hours; during the night it rains exactly forty-seven feet, five inches—no more and no less, every night of every year.

The winds are of more than hurricane velocity, rising to some eight hundred miles per hour, accompanied by blinding, almost continuous lightning discharges.

What makes the planet unique, however, is that, with compounds of such low latent heat, the energy transfer is almost nil. Theoretically, the hot days should evaporate that liquid as quietly and gently as a ghost evaporates in a spotlight, and during the night it should condense as softly as dew from heaven falling upon the place beneath. Thermodynamically speaking, the planet Trenco should be about as turbulent as a goldfish bowl. Nobody can figure out where those winds or the lightning come from.

Be that as it may, Trenco was, and is, the only planet where the plant known as Trenconian broadleaf grows, and that plant is the only source of thionite in any of several galaxies.

In addition, Trenco has a strong Galactic Patrol base, manned by Rigellian Patrolmen whose sole job it is to kill anyone who comes to Trenco. One can well understand why thionite was, and is, so expensive.

"Ah, a cogent thought indeed!" radiated Meichfrite. "Very well, then, relay to Banlon that he is to proceed at speed to Trenco and pick up a cargo of broadleaf, to bring here for processing. Meantime he is to order his underling Gauntluth to report directly to us."

In his office atop the Queen Ardis, Gauntluth the Kalonian watched with hard, steel-blue eyes as a figure on his spy-ray plate moved toward his suite of offices.

Twodyce, with the exception of the DeLameter in his shoulder holster, was unarmed; he was carrying nothing else but the hermetically sealed container which bore within itself fifty grams of almost impalpable purple powder.

A smile twisted Gauntluth's face. "Fool!" he gritted harshly under his breath.

He continued to watch as Twodyce came to the outer door and activated the announcer. He activated the door-opener. "Come in, Mr. Twodyce," he spoke into a microphone. "Down the hall and first door to your left."

Gimble Ginnison, fully alert, strode down the corridor and opened the door. Alone behind his desk sat the unsuspecting Kalonian.

"I perceive," said the zwilnik,* "that you have brought the thionite with you."

---

*A zwilnik is anyone connected with the drug trade.

"I have," said the Lensman. "Have you the payment ready?"

"Certainly. Half in bar platinum, half in Patrol credits, as specified. But first, of course, I must test the thionite."

"First I test the platinum," said Twodyce impassively.

Gauntluth blinked. "We seem to be at an impasse," he murmured. "However, I think I see a way around it. Know, Twodyce, that you stand now in the focus of a complex of robotic devices which, with rays and beams of tremendous power, will reduce

46

you to a crisp unless you hand over that thionite container instantly."

"Since it is inevitable," Ginnison said calmly, "I might as well enjoy it." He carefully put the thionite container on Gauntluth's desk.

Gauntluth needed no further check. Directing his thought toward a lump of force in a nearby corner of the room, he sent a message to Jugavine.

This was the moment for which Ginnison had been waiting. In an instant, he effortlessly took over the zwilnik's* mind. He allowed Gauntluth to send the message, since it would only further confuse all those concerned. Gauntluth reported in full to Meichfrite that he had, indeed, obtained a goodly supply of thionite.

---

*A zwilnik is still a zwilnik.

"Excellent," the cold thought returned. "There will be more coming. End communication."

By main force and awkwardness, Ginnison held Gauntluth's mind in thrall. He now had his second line to the Boskonian base, but Gauntluth, although taken by surprise at first, was now fighting Ginnison's mental control with every mega-erg of his hard Kalonian mind.

"Think you can succeed, even now?" sneered the still-rigid Kalonian mentally. And, with a tremendous effort of will, he moved a pinkie a fraction of a millimeter to cover a photocell. Every alarm in the building went off.

Ginnison's mind clamped down instantly to paralyze the hapless zwilnik.* With a mirthless smile on his face, Ginnison said: "I permitted that as a gesture of futility. You did not, as I suggested, contemplate a hamburger."

---

*See above.

"Bah!" came Gauntluth's thought. "That childishness?"

"Not childishness," said the Lensman coldly. "A hamburger is so constructed that most of the meat is hidden by the bun. My resources are far greater than those which appear around the edge."

Then Ginnison invaded Gauntluth's mind and took every iota of relevant information therein, following which, he hurled a bolt of mental energy calculated to slay any living thing. Perforce, Gauntluth ceased to be a living thing.

Meanwhile, from a hidden and shielded barracks in a sub-basement of the Queen Ardis came a full squadron of armed and armored space-thugs, swarming up stairways and elevators to reach the late Gauntluth's suite. Closer, and, at this point in space and time, far more dangerous, were the DeLameter-armed, thought-screened executives and plug-uglies who were even now battering down the doors of the suite.

Calmly and with deliberation, Ginnison flashed a thought to Woozle: "HE-E-E-ELP!"

"At speed, Ginnison," came the reply.

Ginnison went into action. Snatching the hermetically sealed thionite container from the desk at which lay the cooling corpse of Gauntluth, he broke the seal and emptied the contents into the intake vent of the air conditioner. He had, of course, taken the precaution of putting anti-thionite plugs in his nostrils; all he had to do was to keep his mouth shut and he would be perfectly safe.

The impalpable purple powder permeated the atmosphere of the hotel. There was enough of the active principle of that deadly drug to turn on fifty million people; since the slightest overdose could kill, every person in the hotel not wearing anti-thionite plugs or space armor died in blissful ecstasy. Most of Gauntluth's thugs were wearing one or the other, but at least the Galactic Patrol need no longer worry about interference from innocent bystanders.

With lightning speed, Ginnison grabbed a heavy-caliber, water-cooled machine rifle that just happened to be standing near Gauntluth's desk, swiveled it to face the doors of the office, and waited.

At the same moment, a borazon-hard, bronze-beryllium-steel-prowed landing craft smashed into the side of the Hotel Queen Ardis at the fifteenth floor. Steel girders, ferroconcrete walls, and brick facing alike splattered aside as that hard-driven, specially-designed space boat, hitting its reverse jets at the last second to bring it to a dead halt, crashed into and through the bridal suite. The port slammed open and from it leaped, strode, jumped and strutted a company of Dutch Valerians in full space armor, swinging their mighty thirty-pound space axes.

No bifurcate race, wherever situate, will voluntarily face a

Valerian in battle. Those mighty warriors, bred in a gravitational field three times that of Tellus, have no ruth for any of Civilization's foes. The smallest Valerian can, in full armor, do a standing high jump of nearly fifteen feet in a field of one Tellurian gravity; he can feint, parry, lunge, swing, and duck with a speed utterly impossible for any of the lesser breeds of man. Like all jocks, they are not too bright.

Led by Lieutenant Hess von Baschenvolks, they charged in to block off the armed and armored space-thugs who were heading toward the top floor. As they charged in, the Lieutenant shouted their battle-cry.

"Kill! Bash! Smash! Cut! Hack! Destroy! Bleed, you bastards! Bleed and die!" And, of course, they did.

A thirty-pound space axe driven by the muscles of a Valerian can cut its way through any armor. Heads fell; arms were lopped off; gallons of gore flowed over the expensive carpetry. Leaving behind them dozens of corpses, the Valerians charged upward, toward the suite of offices where the Gray Lensman awaited the assault of Gauntluth's men, fingers poised, ready to press the hair triggers of the heavy machine rifle.

The news of the attack, however, reached those winsome wights long before the Valerians did. They knew that, unarmored as they were, they stood no chance against those Patrolmen. They headed for the roof, where powerful 'copters awaited them for their getaway.

It was not until they were all on the roof that the logons, released from the special 'copter less than a kilometer away, and individually controlled by the mighty mind of Gimble Ginnison, launched their attack. The zwilnik* executives and plug-uglies had no chance. Only a few managed to draw and fire their ray guns, and even those few missed their targets. Within a space of seconds, the entire group had been slashed, cut, scratched, bitten, killed, and half-eaten by the winged horrors that had been released upon them.

---

*Forget it.

In Gauntluth's office, Ginnison waited behind the machine rifle, his fingers still poised on the hair-triggers. The door smashed and fell. But Ginnison recognized the bulky space-armored eight-foot figure that loomed before him. His hands came away from the triggers as he said: "Hi, Hess!"

"Duuuhh...Hi, Boss," said Lieutenant Hess von Baschen-volks.

In a totally black, intrinsically undetectable, ultrapowered speedster, towing three negaspheres of planetary antimass, Gimble Ginnison cautiously approached the hollow sphere of light-obliterating dust which surrounded the dread planet Jugavine of the Meich.

With his second line of communication, it had been a simple job to locate exactly and precisely the planet which had been the source of the disruption which had hit the planet Cadilax.

Further, that mental communication had given Ginnison all the information he needed to wipe out this pernicious pesthole of pediculous parasites on the body politic of Civilization.

The negashperes were an integral part of the plan.

The negasphere was, and is, a complete negation of matter. To it, a push is, or becomes, a pull, and vice versa. No radiation of whatever kind can escape from or be reflected by its utterly black surface. It is dense beyond imagining; even a negasphere of planetary antimass is less than a kilometer in diameter. When a negasphere strikes ordinary matter, the two cancel out, bringing into being vast quantities of ultrahard and very deadly radiation. A negasphere is, by its very nature, inherently indetectable by any form of radar or spy-ray beam. Even extra-sensory perception reels dizzyingly away from that vast infinitude of absolute negation.

Like the Bergenholm, the negasphere can never really make up its mind about gravity; gravity is, was, and always has been a pull, and it *should* act as a *push* against a negasphere; since it does not do so, we must conclude that there is something peculiar about the mathematics of the negasphere.

It is to Ginnison's credit that he had perceived this subtle, but inalterable, anomaly.

Into the hollow cloud of black interstellar dust that surrounded frigid Jugavine, there was but one entrance, and into that entrance the Gray Lensman's speedster, towing with tractors and pressors those three deadly negaspheres, wended its intricate way.

In his office, the Starboard Admiral glowered. "I don't like it. Ginnison should have taken the full fleet with him."

The personage he was addressing was Sir Houston Carbarn, the most brilliant mathematical physicist in the known universe.

He was one of a handful of living entities who could actually think in the abstruse and abstract language of pure mathematics.

"I don't like his going in there alone," the Starboard Admiral continued. "If that hollow sphere of dust is as black and bleak as he says it is, he will have nothing to guide him but his sense of perception."

"DIV $\vec{B}$ = O; CURL $\vec{B}$ = j_e + $\frac{\partial E}{\partial \tau}$; DIV $\vec{E}$ = P_e; CURL $\vec{E}$ = O - $\frac{\partial B}{\partial \tau}$." said Sir Houston Carbarn thoughtfully.

"True," agreed the Starboard Admiral, "but I can see no way for him to illuminate such a vast amount of space with the means at his command. That hollow globe is two parsecs across, and contains within it only a single solid body—the planet Jugavine. How can he possibly get enough illumination to find the planet?"

"$x^2 + y^2 + z^2 = r^2$," murmured Sir Houston, "$E = Mc^2$."

"Yes, yes, obviously!" snapped the Starboard Admiral, "but in order to illumine the interior of that hollow globe, he will have to find Jugavine first, and to do that he needs illumination. It seems to me this involves a paradox."

"$pq \neq qp$," Sir Houston snapped forcefully.

"Ah, I see what you mean," said the Starboard Admiral. "But what about Banlon of Downlo? According to Ginnison's report, Banlon is returning to Jugavine with a cargo of Trenconian broadleaf which he somehow managed to steal from under the very noses of Trigonemetree, the Rigellian Lensman in charge of our base on Trenco. If Ginnison destroys Jugavine, Banlon's sense of perception will immediately tell him that the planet no longer exists, and he will not fall into Ginnison's trap. How is he going to get around that?"

"?" mused Sir Houston abstractedly.

Gimble Ginnison, Gray Lensman, had no need of slow, electromagnetic radiation to locate the planet of the Meich. His tremendous sense of perception had pinpointed that doomed planet exactly. Calculating carefully the intrinsic velocity of his first negasphere in relation to that of the planet of the Meich, he released that black, enigmatic ball of negation toward its hapless target.

The negasphere struck. Or perhaps not. Is it possible for nothing to strike anything? Let us say, then, that the negasphere began to occupy the same space as that of Jugavine. At the hyperdimensional surface of contact, the matter and antimatter mutually vanished. Where the negasphere struck, a huge hole appeared in that theretofore frigid planet. The planet collapsed in on itself, its very substance eaten away by the all-devouring negasphere. The radiation of that mutual annihilation wrought heated havoc upon the doomed planet. Helium boiled; hydrogen melted; nitrogen fizzed; and all fell collapsingly into the rapidly diminishing negasphere.

When the awful and awesome process had completed itself, there was nothing left. Thus perished the Meich.

When the process was completed, the Gray Lensman hurled his two remaining negaspheres toward the exact same spot in space.

Then he sat and waited for Banlon of Downlo.

Time passed. Ginnison, ever on the alert with his acute sense of perception, at last detected Banlon's speedster entering the globe of dust. Banlon could not detect, at that distance, the flare of radiation which had resulted from the destruction of Jugavine. That radiation, struggling along at the speed of light, would require years to reach the interior surface of the globe.

Ginnison, waiting like a cat at a mouse hole, pounced at the instant that Banlon entered the globe. One flash of a primary beam, and Banlon of Downlo was forced into the next plane of existence. He ceased to be, save as white-hot gas, spreading and dissipating its energy through a relatively small volume of space.

Immediately, Ginnison Lensed his report back to Prime Base, then made his way out of the hollow globe and back to the *Dentless*.

The Starboard Admiral frowned and looked up at Sir Houston Carbarn. "I'm afraid I still don't understand. After Jugavine was destroyed, Banlon, with his sense of perception, which is instantaneous and is not hampered by the velocity of light, should have detected the fact that the planet no longer existed. Why did he continue on in toward a non-existent planet?"

Sir Houston Carbarn smiled. "$(-1)(-1) = +1$," he informed.

The Starboard Admiral slammed his palm on the desk. "Of course! The principle of the double negative! Two negaspheres made a posisphere! Banlon thought it was Jugavine! Our Gray Lensman has genius, Sir Houston!"

"!" agreed Sir Houston.

When Gimble Ginnison strode into his quarters aboard the *Dentless*, Woozle was waiting for him. "What now?" queried that sapient serpent.

"Now for a decent meal, Woozle." He activated a communicator. "Galley? Send up a two-inch-thick steak, rare. Mashed potatoes and thick brown gravy. And a quart of black coffee."

"Yes, sir," came the reply. "And what about dessert, sir?"

Ginnison sat down in his chair with a triumphant sigh of relief. "Now, at last," he said, "I can enjoy that for which I have waited so long."

"The strawberries, sir?"

"Exactly. The strawberries."

THE BEST POLICY
By Randall Garrett

Much to my chagrin, I never met the late Eric Frank Russell. I have admired his writing over the years, and wanted to meet him, but the opportunity never presented itself.

But if this story sounds like his work, it is because of my appreciation of his style.

Thagobar Larnimisculus Verf, Borgax of Fenigwisnok, had a long name and an important title, and he was proud of both. The title was roughly translatable as "High-Sheriff-Admiral of Fenigwisnok," and Fenigwisnok was a rich and important planet in the Dal Empire. Title and name looked very impressive together on documents, of which there were a great many to be signed.

Thagobar himself was a prime example of his race, a race of power and pride. Like the terrestrial turtles, he had both an exo- and an endoskeleton, although that was his closest resemblance to the *chelonia*. He was humanoid in general shape, looking something like a cross between a medieval knight in full armor and a husky football player clad for the gridiron. His overall color was similar to that of a well-boiled lobster, fading to a darker purple at the joints of his exoskeleton. His clothing was sparse, consisting only of an abbreviated kilt embroidered with fanciful designs and emblazoned with a swirl of glittering gems. The emblem of his rank was engraved in gold on his plastron and again on his carapace, so that he would be recognizable both coming and going.

All in all, he made quite an impressive figure, in spite of his five feet two inch height.

As commander of his own spaceship, the *Verf*, it was his duty to search out and explore planets which could be colonized by his race, the Dal. This he had done diligently for many years, following exactly his General Orders as a good commander should.

And it had paid off. He had found some nice planets in his time, and this one was the juiciest of the lot.

Gazing at the magniscreen, he rubbed his palms together in satisfaction. His ship was swinging smoothly in an orbit high above a newly-discovered planet, and the magniscreen was focused on the landscape below. No Dal ship had ever been in this part of the galaxy before, and it was comforting to have discovered a colonizable planet so quickly.

"A magnificent planet!" he said. "A wonderful planet! Look at that green! And the blue of those seas!" He turned to Lieutenant Pelquesh. "What do you think? Isn't it fine?"

"It certainly is, Your Splendor," said Pelquesh. "You should receive another citation for this one."

Thagobar started to say something, then suddenly cut it short. His hands flew out to the controls and slapped at switch plates; the ship's engines squealed with power as they brought the ship to a dead stop in relation to the planet below. In the magniscreen, the landscape became stationary.

He twisted the screen's magnification control up, and the scene beneath the ship ballooned outward, spilling off the edges as the surface came closer.

"There!" he said. "Pelquesh, what is that?"

It was a purely rhetorical question. The wavering currents of two hundred odd miles of atmosphere caused the image to shimmer uncertainly, but there was no doubt that it was a city of some kind. Lieutenant Pelquesh said as much.

"Plague take it!" Thagobar snarled. "An occupied planet! Only intelligent beings build cities."

"That's so," agreed Pelquesh.

Neither of them knew what to do. Only a few times in the long history of the Dal had other races been found—and under the rule of the Empire, they had all slowly become extinct. Besides, none of them had been very intelligent, anyway.

"We'll have to ask General Orders," Thagobar said at last. He went over to another screen, turned it on, and began dialing code numbers into it.

Deep in the bowels of the huge ship, the General Orders robot came sluggishly to life. In its vast memory lay ten thousand years of accumulated and ordered facts, ten thousand years of the experiences of the Empire, ten thousand years of the final decisions on every subject ever considered by Thagobar's race. It was

more than an encyclopedia—it was a way of life.

In a highly logical way, the robot sorted through its memory until it came to the information requested by Thagobar; then it relayed the data to the screen.

"Hm-m-m," said Thagobar. "Yes. General Order 333,953,216-A-j, Chapter MMCMXLIX, Paragraph 402. 'First discovery of an intelligent or semi-intelligent species shall be followed by the taking of a specimen selected at random. No contact shall be made until the specimen has been examined according to Psychology Directive 659-B, Section 888,077-q, at the direction of the Chief Psychologist. The data will be correlated by General Orders. If contact has already been made inadvertently, refer to GO 472,678-R-s, Ch. MMMCCX, Par. 553. Specimens shall be taken according to...' "

He finished reading off the General Order and then turned to the lieutenant. "Pelquesh, you get a spaceboat ready to pick up a specimen. I'll notify psychologist Zandoplith to be ready for it."

Ed Magruder took a deep breath of spring air and closed his eyes. It was beautiful; it was filled with spicy aromas and tangy scents that, though alien, were somehow homelike—more homelike than Earth.

He was a tall, lanky man, all elbows and knees, with nondescript brown hair and bright hazel eyes that tended to crinkle with suppressed laughter.

He exhaled the breath and opened his eyes. The city was still awake, but darkness was coming fast. He liked his evening stroll, but it wasn't safe to be out after dark on New Hawaii, even yet. There were little night things that fluttered softly in the air, giving little warning of their poisonous bite, and there were still some of the larger predators in the neighborhood. He started walking back toward New Hilo, the little city that marked man's first foothold on the new planet.

Magruder was a biologist. In the past ten years, he had prowled over half a dozen planets, collecting specimens, dissecting them with precision, and entering the results in his notebooks. Slowly, bit by bit, he was putting together a pattern—a pattern of life itself. His predecessors stretched in a long line, clear back to Karl von Linné, but none of them had realized what was missing in their work. They had had only one type of life to deal with—terrestrial life. And all terrestrial life is, after all, homogenous.

But, of all the planets he'd seen, he liked New Hawaii best. It was the only planet besides Earth where a man could walk around without a protective suit of some kind—at least, it was the only one discovered so far.

He heard a faint swishing in the air over his head and glanced up quickly. The night things shouldn't be out this early!

And then he saw that it wasn't a night thing; it was a metallic-looking globe of some kind, and—

There was a faint greenish glow that suddenly flashed from a spot on the side of the globe, and all went black for Ed Magruder.

Thagobar Verf watched dispassionately as Lieutenant Pelquesh brought the unconscious specimen into the biological testing section. It was a queer-looking specimen; a soft-skinned, sluglike parody of a being, with a pale, pinkish-tan complexion and a repulsive, fungoidal growth on its head and various other areas.

The biologists took the specimen and started to work on it. They took nips of skin and samples of blood and various electrical readings from the muscles and nerves.

Zandoplith, the Chief Psychologist, stood by the commander, watching the various operations.

It was Standard Procedure for the biologists; they went about it as they would with any other specimen that had been picked up. But Zandoplith was going to have to do a job he had never done before. He was going to have to work with the mind of an intelligent being.

He wasn't worried, of course; it was all down in the Handbook, every bit of Proper Procedure. There was nothing at all to worry about.

As with all other specimens, it was Zandoplith's job to discover the Basic Reaction Pattern. Any given organism could react only in a certain very large, but finite number of ways, and these ways could be reduced to a Basic Pattern. All that was necessary to destroy a race of creatures was to get their Basic Pattern and then give them a problem that couldn't be solved by using that pattern. It was all very simple, and it was all down in the Handbook.

Thagobar turned his head from the operating table to look at Zandoplith. "Do you think it really will be possible to teach it our language?"

"The rudiments, Your Splendor," said the psychologist. "Ours is, after all, a very complex language. We'll give him all of it, of course, but it is doubtful whether he can assimilate more than a small portion of it. Our language is built upon logic, just as thought is built upon logic. Some of the lower animals are capable of the rudiments of logic, but most are unable to grasp it."

"Very well; we'll do the best we can. I, myself, will question it."

Zandoplith looked a little startled. "But, Your Splendor! The questions are all detailed in the Handbook!"

Thagobar Verf scowled. "I can read as well as you, Zandoplith. Since this is the first semi-intelligent life discovered in the past thousand years or so, I think the commander should be the one to do the questioning."

"As you say, Your Splendor," the psychologist agreed.

Ed Magruder was placed in the Language Tank when the biologists got through with him. Projectors of light were fastened over his eyes so that they focused directly on his retinas; sound units were inserted into his ears; various electrodes were fastened here and there; a tiny network of wires was attached to his skull. Then a special serum which the biologists had produced was injected into his bloodstream. It was all very efficient and very smoothly done. Then the Tank was closed, and a switch was thrown.

Magruder felt himself swim dizzily up out of the blackness. He saw odd-looking, lobster-colored things moving around while noises whispered and gurgled into his ears.

Gradually, he began to orient himself. He was being taught to associate sounds with actions and things.

Ed Magruder sat in a little four-by-six room, naked as a jaybird, looking through a transparent wall at a sextette of the aliens he had seen so much of lately.

Of course, it wasn't these particular bogeys he'd been watching, but they looked so familiar that it was hard to believe they were here in the flesh. He had no idea how long he'd been learning the language; with no exterior references, he was lost.

Well, he thought, I've picked up a good many specimens, and here I am, a specimen myself. He thought of the treatment he'd given his own specimens and shuddered a little.

Oh, well. Here he was; might as well put on a good show—stiff upper lip, chin up, and all that sort.

One of the creatures walked up to an array of buttons and pressed one. Immediately, Magruder could hear sounds from the room on the other side of the transparent wall.

Thagobar Verf looked at the specimen and then at the question sheet in his hand. "Our psychologists have taught you our language, have they not?" he asked coldly.

The specimen bobbled his head up and down. "Yup. And that's what I call real force-feeding, too."

"Very well; I have some questions to ask; you will answer them truthfully."

"Why, sure," Magruder said agreeably. "Fire away."

"We can tell if you are lying," Thagobar continued. "It will do you no good to tell us untruths. Now—what is your name?"

"Theophilus Q. Hassenpfeffer," Magruder said blandly.

Zandoplith looked at a quivering needle and then shook his head slowly as he looked up at Thagobar.

"That is a lie," said Thagobar.

The specimen nodded. "It sure is. That's quite a machine you've got there."

"It is good that you appreciate the superiority of our instruments," Thagobar said grimly. "Now—your name."

"Edwin Peter St. John Magruder."

Psychologist Zandoplith watched the needle and nodded.

"Excellent," said Thagobar. "Now, Edwin—"

"Ed is good enough," said Magruder.

Thagobar blinked. "Good enough for what?"

"For calling me."

Thagobar turned to the psychologist and mumbled something. Zandoplith mumbled back. Thagobar spoke to the specimen.

"Is your name Ed?"

"Strictly speaking, no," said Magruder.

"Then why should I call you that?"

"Why not? Everyone else does," Magruder informed him.

Thagobar consulted further with Zandoplith and finally said: "We will come back to that point later. Now...uh...Ed, what do you call your home planet?"

"Earth."

"Good. And what does your race call itself?"

"*Homo sapiens.*"

"And the significance of that, if any?"

Magruder considered. "It's just a name," he said, after a moment.

The needle waggled.

"Another lie," said Thagobar.

Magruder grinned. "Just testing. That really *is* a whizzer of a machine."

Thagobar's throat and face darkened a little as his copper-bearing blue blood surged to the surface in suppressed anger. "You said that once," he reminded blackly.

"I know. Well, if you really want to know, *Homo sapiens* means 'wise man.' "

Actually, he hadn't said "wise man"; the language of the Dal didn't quite have that exact concept, so Magruder had to do the best he could. Translated back into English, it would have come out something like "beings with vast powers of mind."

When Thagobar heard this, his eyes opened a little wider, and he turned his head to look at Zandoplith. The psychologist spread his horny hands; the needle hadn't moved.

"You seem to have high opinions of yourselves," said Thagobar, looking back at Magruder.

"That's possible," agreed the Earthman.

Thagobar shrugged, looked back at his list, and the questioning went on. Some of the questions didn't make too much sense to Magruder; others were obviously psychological testing.

But one thing was quite clear; the lie detector was indeed quite a whizzer. If Magruder told the exact truth, it didn't indicate. But if he lied just the least tiny bit, the needle on the machine hit the ceiling—and, eventually, so did Thagobar.

Magruder had gotten away with his first few lies—they were unimportant, anyway—but finally, Thagobar said: "You have lied enough, Ed."

He pressed a button, and a nerve-shattering wave of pain swept over the Earthman. When it finally faded, Magruder found his belly muscles tied in knots, his fists and teeth clenched, and tears running down his cheeks. Then nausea overtook him, and he lost the contents of his stomach.

Thagobar Verf turned distastefully away. "Put him back in his cell and clean up the interrogation chamber. Is he badly hurt?"

Zandoplith had already checked his instruments. "I think not, Your Splendor; it is probably only slight shock and nothing more. However, we will have to retest him in the next session anyhow. We'll know then."

Magruder sat on the edge of a shelflike thing that doubled as a low table and a high bed. It wasn't the most comfortable seat in the world, but it was all he had in the room; the floor was even harder.

It had been several hours since he had been brought here, and he still didn't feel good. That stinking machine had *hurt!* He clenched his fists; he could still feel the knot in his stomach and—

And then he realized that the knot in his stomach hadn't been caused by the machine; he had thrown that off a long time back.

The knot was caused by a towering, thundering-great, ice-cold rage.

He thought about it for a minute and then broke out laughing. Here he was, like a stupid fool, so angry that he was making himself sick! And that wasn't going to do him or the colony any good.

It was obvious that the aliens were up to no good, to say the least. The colony at New Hilo numbered six thousand souls—the only humans on New Hawaii, except for a couple of bush expeditions. If this ship tried to take over the planet, there wouldn't be a devil of a lot the colonists could do about it. And what if the aliens found Earth itself? He had no idea what kind of armament this spaceship carried nor how big it was—but it seemed to have plenty of room inside it.

He knew it was up to him. He was going to have to do something, somehow. What? Could he get out of his cell and try to smash the ship?

Nope. A naked man inside a bare cell was about as helpless as a human being can get. What, then?

Magruder lay on his back and thought about it for a long time.

Presently, a panel opened in the door and a red-violet face appeared on the other side of a transparent square in the door.

"You are doubtless hungry," it said solemnly. "An analysis of your bodily processes had indicated what you need in the way of sustenance. Here."

The quart-size mug that slid out of a niche in the wall had an odd aroma drifting up from it. Magruder picked it up and looked inside. It was a grayish-tan, semitranslucent liquid about the consistency of thin gravy. He touched the surface with his finger and then touched the finger with his tongue. Its palate appeal was definitely on the negative side of zero.

He could guess what it contained: a score, more or less, of various amino acids, a dozen vitamins, a handful of carbohydrates, and a few percent of other necessities. A sort of pseudo-protoplasmic soup; an overbalanced meal.

He wondered whether it contained anything that would do him harm, decided it probably didn't. If the aliens wanted to dope him, they didn't need to resort to subterfuge, and besides, this was probably the gunk they had fed him while he was learning the language.

Pretending to himself that it was beef stew, he drank it down. Maybe he could think better on a full stomach. And, as it turned out, he was right.

Less than an hour later, he was back in the interrogation chamber. This time, he was resolved to keep Thagobar's finger off that little button.

After all, he reasoned to himself, I might want to lie to someone, when and if I get out of this. There's no point in getting a conditioned reflex against it.

And the way the machine had hurt him, there was a strong possibility that he just might get conditioned if he took very many jolts like that.

He had a plan. It was highly nebulous—little more than a principle, really, and it was highly flexible. He would simply have to take what came, depend on luck, and hope for the best.

He sat down in the chair and waited for the wall to become

transparent again. He had thought there might be a way to get out as he was led from his cell to the interrogation chamber, but he didn't feel like tackling six heavily armored aliens all at once. He wasn't even sure he could do much with just one of them. Where do you slug a guy whose nervous system you know nothing about, and whose body is plated like a boiler?

The wall became transparent, and the alien was standing on the other side of it. Magruder wondered whether it was the same being who had questioned him before, and after looking at the design on the plastron, decided that it was.

He leaned back in his chair, folded his arms, and waited for the first question.

Thagobar Verf was a very troubled Dal. He had very carefully checked the psychological data with General Orders after the psychologists had correlated it according to the Handbook. He definitely did not like the looks of his results.

General Orders merely said: "No race of this type has ever been found in the galaxy before. In this case, the commander will act according to GO 234,511,006-R-g, Ch. MMCDX, Par. 666."

After looking up the reference, he had consulted with Zandoplith. "What do you think of it?" he asked. "And why doesn't your science have any answers?"

"Science, Your Splendor," said Zandoplith, "is a process of obtaining and correlating data. We haven't enough data yet, true, but we'll get it. We absolutely must not panic at this point; we must be objective, purely objective." He handed Thagobar another printed sheet. "These are the next questions to be asked, according to the Handbook of Psychology."

Thagobar felt a sense of relief. General Orders had said that in a case like this, the authority of action was all dependent on his own decision; it was nice to know that the scientist knew what he was doing, and had authority to back it.

He cut off the wall polarizer and faced the specimen on the other side.

"You will answer the next several questions in the negative," Thagobar said. "It doesn't matter what the real and truthful answer may be, you will say No; is that perfectly clear?"

"No," said Magruder.

Thagobar frowned. The instructions seemed perfectly lucid to him; what was the matter with the specimen? Was he possibly more stupid than they had at first believed?

"He's lying," said Zandoplith.

It took Thagobar the better part of half a minute to realize what had happened, and when he did, his face became unpleasantly dark. But there was nothing else he could do; the specimen had obeyed orders.

His Splendor took a deep breath, held it for a moment, eased it out, and began reading the questions in a mild voice.

"Is your name Edwin?"

"No."

"Do you live on the planet beneath us?"

"No."

"Do you have six eyes?"

"No."

After five minutes of that sort of thing, Zandoplith said: "That's enough, Your Splendor; it checks out; his nervous system wasn't affected by the pain. You may proceed to the next list."

"From now on, you will answer truthfully," Thagobar said. "Otherwise, you will be punished again. Is *that* clear?"

"Perfectly clear," said Magruder.

Although his voice sounded perfectly calm, Magruder, on the other side of the transparent wall, felt just a trifle shaky. He would have to think quickly and carefully from now on. He didn't believe he'd care to take too much time in answering, either.

"How many *Homo sapiens* are there?"

"Several billions." There were actually about four billions, but the Dal equivalent of "several" was vaguely representative of numbers larger than five, although not necessarily so.

"Don't you know the actual number?"

"No," said Magruder. *Not right down to the man, I don't.*

The needle didn't quiver. Naturally not—he was telling the truth, wasn't he?

"All of your people surely aren't on Earth, then?" Thagobar asked, deviating slightly from the script. "In only one city?"

With a sudden flash of pure joy, Magruder saw the beautifully monstrous mistake the alien had made. He had not suspected until now that Earthmen had developed space travel. Therefore, when he had asked the name of Magruder's home planet, the answer he'd gotten was "Earth." But the alien had been thinking of New Hawaii! *Wheeee!*

"Oh, no," said Magruder truthfully. "We have only a few thousand down there." Meaning, of course, New Hawaii, which was "down there."

"Then most of your people have deserted Earth?"

"Deserted Earth?" Magruder sounded scandalized. "Heavens

68

to Betsy, no! We have merely colonized; we're all under one central government."

"How many are there in each colony?" Thagobar had completely abandoned the script now.

"I don't know exactly," Magruder told him, "but not one of our colonized planets has any more occupants on it than Earth."

Thagobar looked flabbergasted and flicked off the sound transmission to the prisoner with a swift movement of his finger.

Zandoplith looked pained. "You are not reading the questions from the Handbook," he complained.

"I know, I know. But did you hear what he said?"

"I heard it." Zandoplith's voice sounded morose.

"It wasn't true, was it?"

Zandoplith drew himself up to his full five feet one. "Your Splendor, you have taken it upon yourself to deviate from the Handbook, but I will not permit you to question the operation of the Reality Detector. Reality is truth, and therefore truth is reality; the Detector hasn't erred since—since *ever!*"

"I know," Thagobar said hastily. "But do you realize the implications of what he said? There are a few thousand people on the home planet; all the colonies have less. And yet, there are *several billion* of his race! That means they have occupied around ten million planets!"

"I realize it sounds queer," admitted Zandoplith, "but the Detector never lies!" Then he realized whom he was addressing and added, "Your Splendor."

But Thagobar hadn't noticed the breach of etiquette. "That's perfectly true. But, as you said, there's something queer here. We must investigate further."

Magruder had already realized that his mathematics was off kilter; he was thinking at high speed.

Thagobar's voice said: "According to our estimates, there are not that many habitable planets in the galaxy. How do you account, then, for your statement?"

With a quick shift of viewpoint, Magruder thought of Mars, so many light-years away. There had been a scientific outpost on Mars for a long time, but it was a devil of a long way from being a habitable planet.

"My people," he said judiciously, "are capable of living on planets with surface conditions which vary widely from those of Earth."

Before Thagobar could ask anything else, another thought occurred to the Earthman. The thousand-inch telescope on Luna had discovered, spectroscopically, the existence of large planets in the Andromeda Nebula. "In addition," he continued blandly, "we have found planets in other galaxies than this."

There! *That* ought to confuse them!

Again the sound was cut off, and Magruder could see the two aliens in hot discussion. When the sound came back again, Thagobar had shifted to another tack.

"How many spaceships do you have?"

Magruder thought that one over for a long second. There were about a dozen interstellar ships in the Earth fleet—not nearly enough to colonize ten million planets. He was in a jam!

No! Wait! A supply ship came to New Hawaii every six months. But there were no ships on New Hawaii.

"Spaceships?" Magruder looked innocent. "Why, we have no spaceships."

Thagobar Verf shut off the sound again, and this time, he made the wall opaque, too. "No spaceships? *No spaceships?* He lied...I hope?"

Zandoplith shook his head dolefully. "Absolute truth."

"But—but—but—"

"Remember what he said his race called themselves?" the psychologist asked softly.

Thagobar blinked very slowly. When he spoke, his voice was a hoarse whisper. *"Beings with minds of vast power."*

"Exactly," said Zandoplith.

Magruder sat in the interrogation chamber for a long time without hearing or seeing a thing. Had they made sense out of his statements? Were they beginning to realize what he was doing? He wanted to chew his nails, bite his lip, and tear his hair; instead, he forced himself to outward calm. There was a long way to go yet.

When the wall suddenly became transparent once more, he managed to keep from jumping.

"Is it true," asked Thagobar, "that your race has the ability to move through space by means of mental power alone?"

For a moment, Magruder was stunned. It was beyond his wildest expectations. But he rallied quickly.

How does a man walk? he thought.

"It is true that by using mental forces to control physical energy," he said carefully, "we are able to move from place to place without the aid of spaceships or other such machines."

Immediately, the wall blanked again.

Thagobar turned around slowly and looked at Zandoplith.

Zandoplith's face looked a dirty crimson; the healthy violet had faded.

"I guess you'd best call in the officers," he said slowly; "we've got a monster on our hands."

It took three minutes for the twenty officers of the huge *Verf* to assemble in the Psychology Room. When they arrived, Thagobar asked them to relax and then outlined the situation.

"Now," he said, "are there any suggestions?"

They were definitely not relaxed now. They looked as tense as bowstrings.

Lieutenant Pelquesh was the first to speak. "What are the General Orders, Your Splendor?"

"The General Orders," Thagobar said, "are that we are to protect our ship and our race, if necessary. The methods for doing so are left up to the commander's discretion."

There was a rather awkward silence. Then a light seemed to come over Lieutenant Pelquesh's face. "Your Splendor, we could simply drop an annihilation bomb on the planet."

Thagobar shook his head. "I've already thought of that. If they can move themselves through space by means of thought alone, they would escape, and their race would surely take vengeance for the vaporization of one of their planets."

Gloom descended.

"Wait a minute," said Pelquesh. "If he can do that, *why hasn't he escaped from us?*"

Magruder watched the wall become transparent. The room was filled with aliens now. The big cheese, Thagobar, was at the pickup.

"We are curious," he said, "to know why, if you can go anywhere at will, you have stayed here. Why don't you escape?"

More fast thinking. "It is not polite," Magruder said, "for a guest to leave his host until the business at hand is finished."

"Even after we...ah...disciplined you?"

"Small discomforts can be overlooked, especially when the host is acting in abysmal ignorance."

There was a whispered question from one of Thagobar's underlings and a smattering of discussion, and then:

"Are we to presume, then, that you bear us no ill will?"

"Some," admitted Magruder candidly. "It is only because of your presumptuous behavior toward me, however, that I personally am piqued. I can assure you that my race as a whole bears no ill will whatever toward your race as a whole or any member

71

of it."

Play it up big, Magruder, he told himself. *You've got 'em rocking—I hope.*

More discussion on the other side of the wall.

"You say," said Thagobar, "that your race holds no ill will toward us; how do you know?"

"I can say this," Magruder told him; "I know—beyond any shadow of a doubt—exactly what every person of my race thinks of you at this very moment.

"In addition, let me point out that I have not been harmed as yet, they would have no reason to be angry. After all, you haven't been destroyed yet."

Off went the sound. More heated discussion. On went the sound.

"It has been suggested," said Thagobar, "that, in spite of appearances, it was intended that we pick you, and you alone, as a specimen. It is suggested that you were sent to meet us."

Oh, brother! This one would have to be handled with very plush gloves.

"I am but a very humble member of my race," Magruder said as a prelude—mostly to gain time. But wait! He was an extraterrestrial biologist, wasn't he? "However," he continued with dignity, "my profession is that of meeting alien beings. I was, I must admit, appointed to the job."

Thagobar seemed to grow tenser. "That, in turn, suggests that you knew we were coming."

Magruder thought for a second. It had been predicted for centuries that mankind would eventually meet an intelligent alien race.

"We have known you were coming for a long time," he said quite calmly.

Thagobar was visibly agitated now. "In that case, you must know where our race is located in the galaxy; you must know where our home base is."

Another tough one. Magruder looked through the wall at Thagobar and his men standing nervously on the other side of it. "I know where you are," he said, "and I know exactly where every one of your fellows is."

There was sudden consternation on the other side of the wall, but Thagobar held his ground.

"What is our location then?"

For a second, Magruder thought they'd pulled the rug out

from under him at last. And then he saw that there was a perfect explanation. He'd been thinking of dodging so long that he almost hadn't seen the honest answer.

He looked at Thagobar pityingly. "Communication by voice is so inadequate. Our coordinate system would be completely unintelligible to you, and you did not teach me yours if you will recall." Which was perfectly true; the Dal would have been foolish to teach their coordinate system to a specimen—the clues might have led to their home base. Besides, General Orders forbade it.

More conversation on the other side.

Thagobar again: "If you are in telepathic communication with your fellows, can you read *our* minds?"

Magruder looked at him superciliously. "I have principles, as does my race; we do not enter any mind uninvited."

"Do the rest of your people know the location of our bases, then?" Thagobar asked plaintively.

Magruder's voice was placid. "I assure you, Thagobar Verf, that every one of my people, on every planet belonging to our race, knows as much about your home base and its location as I do."

Magruder was beginning to get tired of the on-and-off sound system, but he resigned himself to wait while the aliens argued among themselves.

"It has been pointed out," Thagobar said, after a few minutes, "that it is very odd that your race has never contacted us before. Ours is a very old and powerful race, and we have taken planets throughout a full half of the galaxy, and yet, your race has never been seen nor heard of before."

"We have a policy," said Magruder, "of not disclosing our presence to another race until it is to our advantage to do so. Besides, we have no quarrel with your race, and we have never had any desire to take your homes away from you. Only if a race becomes foolishly and insanely belligerent do we trouble ourselves to show them our power."

It was a long speech—maybe too long. Had he stuck strictly to the truth? A glance at Zandoplith told him; the chief psychologist had kept his beady black eyes on the needle all through the long proceedings, and kept looking more and more worried as the instrument indicated a steady flow of truth.

Thagobar looked positively apprehensive. As Magruder had become accustomed to the aliens, it had become more and more automatic to read their expressions. After all, he held one great advantage: they had made the mistake of teaching him their language. He knew them, and they didn't know him.

Thagobar said: "Other races, then, have been...uh...punished by yours?"

"Not in my lifetime," Magruder told him. He thought of *Homo neanderthalensis* and said: "There was a race, before my time, which defied us. It no longer exists."

"Not in your lifetime? How old are you?"

"Look into your magniscreen at the planet below," said the Earthman in a solemn tone. "When I was born, not a single one of the plants you see existed on Earth. The continents of Earth were nothing like that; the seas were entirely different.

"The Earth on which I was born had extensive ice caps; look below you, and you will see none. And yet, we have done nothing to change the planet you see; any changes that have taken place have come by the long process of geologic evolution."

Gleek!" It was a queer sound that came from Thagobar's throat just before a switch cut off the wall and the sound again.

Just like watching a movie on an old film, Magruder thought. *No sound half the time, and it breaks every so often.*

The wall never became transparent again. Instead, after about half an hour, it slid up silently to disclose the entire officer's corp of the *Verf* standing at rigid attention.

Only Thagobar Larnimisculus Verf, Borgax of Fenigwisnok, stood at ease, and even so, his face seemed less purple than usual.

"Edwin Peter St. John Magruder," he intoned, "as commander of this vessel, Noble of the Grand Empire, and representative of the Emperor himself, we wish to extend to you our most cordial hospitality.

"Laboring under the delusion that you represented a lower form of life, we have treated you ignominiously, and for that we offer our deepest apologies."

"Think nothing of it," said Magruder coolly. "The only thing that remains is for you to land your ship on our planet so that your race and mine can arrange things to our mutual happiness." He looked at all of them. "You may relax," he added imperiously. "And bring me my clothes."

The human race wasn't out of the hole yet; Magruder was perfectly well aware of that. Just what should be done with the ship and the aliens when they landed, he wasn't quite sure; it would have to be left up to the decision of the President of New Hawaii and the Government of Earth. But he didn't foresee any great difficulties.

As the *Verf* dropped toward the surface of New Hawaii, its commander sidled over to Magruder and said, in a troubled voice:

"Do you think your people will like us?"

Magruder glanced at the lie detector. It was off.

"*Like* you? Why, they'll *love* you," he said.

He was sick and tired of being honest.

THE COSMIC BEAT

This one is not a takeoff on any particular author; it is a takeoff on the so-called "beat generation" of the late Fifties—a generation which was soon to be replaced by the "hippies," who are now as defunct as the "beatniks."

(Ever wonder where the word "beatnik" came from? It was a takeoff on the word "sputnik"—the Earth's first orbital satellite, sent up by the Russians. The word "sputnik" means "fellow traveler." Work that one out in your home computer.)

By Randall Garrett

"That's very odd," said Lady Curvert.

The sound that accompanied her voice was that of her egg spoon taking the top off her egg in its cup, so it is not remarkable that Lord Curvert, without lowering his copy of the *Times*, merely inquired: "Something wrong with the egg, my dear?"

"What? Egg? No, silly; it's this night club in New York."

Lord Curvert, well aware that his wife never remarked on anything of that sort without good reason, reluctantly lowered his newspaper and looked at her. She was absently spooning up egg with her right hand while her left held the tabloid upon which her gaze was fastened.

"What is it, Evelyn?" his lordship asked. "Something?"

"I'm not certain," she said. "Listen to this: 'The Village's newest and farthest-out *espressoteria*, the *Venus Club*, is the latest subject of a quiet investigation by the Musician's Union, according to the B'way scuttlebutt. Seems that the weirdly-dressed musicos who are pulling in the jazz-lovers by the horde are too good to be believed. The management claims they're unpaid amateurs and don't need a union card, but the big-name pros who've heard them don't believe any amateur group could be that good. The "Venusian" get-ups they wear, which make them look as though the instruments they play are part of their bodies, make the players unrecognizable, and Union officials can't find out who they are. Since a combo as good as the "Venusians" could get hi-pay spots easily, according to Union officials, it doesn't make sense for them to keep on at the *Venus Club* unless they actually are getting something under the counter. If they are, the Union wants its cut.'" Lady Curvert looked up at her husband through glorious deep blue eyes. "Isn't that odd?"

His lordship blinked thoughtfully. "Odd, yes," he said after a moment, "but hardly world-shattering. I scarcely see how it concerns us."

Lady Curvert tapped the paper. "Venusians."

Lord Curvert elevated an eyebrow a fraction of a millimeter. "My dear old girl," he said in a voice tinged with sarcasm, "the last time I was on Venus, back in 1948, nothing on that vast over-heated Turkish bath had evolved any higher than the sponges. I hardly think that the succeeding fifteen years could have produced the intelligence required to beat out a hot rhythm on a set of bongo drums in a beatnik coffee house—though that is admittedly not such a tremendous leap in intelligence."

"I'm quite aware of that, Charles," his wife said coolly. "It's merely that this article has apparently started an intuitive chain-web in my mind. Something will come of it, I'm sure."

"Ah, I see." Lord Curvert was well aware of his wife's mental abilities. "Very well, my dear; when you've formed a full intuition, let me know. Meantime, I'll have some more kippers."

Lord Curvert finished the kippers, the *Times*, and the coffee, excused himself, and headed toward the library, leaving his wife to continue her reading. She had already finished the American papers and had begun on *Pravda*. Within an hour, she would have all the salient points of the day's news filed away in her capacious and accurate memory, where her subconscious could get at them in its ceaseless work of forming the "hunches" that made Evelyn Curvert so useful in her position as Assistant to the Galactic Observer.

Fesswick, the butler—tall, broadshouldered, a pluperfectly correct expression on his very human-looking face—was waiting for his lordship in the library.

"Good morning, Fesswick. Anything interesting this morning?"

"Very little, my lord," said Fesswick in his precise voice. "The instrument readings are normal. The Russians attempted to launch another of their new rockets at 0517 this morning. It exploded at 0521."

"They won't publish this failure, either," said Lord Curvert.

"Very likely not, my lord," said Fesswick. "According to the neutrino emission detectors, the new reactor at Tel-Aviv suffered a slight misfunction at 1143 last night. Nothing serious, but it was damped at 1144 and has remained so."

"Down for repairs, eh?" his lordship commented.

"Precisely so, my lord. Solar emission," Fesswick continued, "remains normal. The..."

Fesswick took nearly seven minutes more to deliver his report of the happenings of the past twenty-four hours as they had been recorded on the special instruments concealed within the depths of Castle Curvert. They had been reporting their data precisely since they had been built into the castle, six hundred years before, and they would go on doing so until they were shut off—or destroyed.

All in all, everything was quite normal.

Lord Curvert sat down behind his desk and sighed gently. "Rather dull, isn't it, Fesswick? I mean, we haven't had any real excitement since that squadron of Mizarian ships got off course and tried to land, back in '47." He gazed reminiscently at the ceiling. "Had the devil's own time with them for a while, there."

"A masterful piece of work on your part, if I may say so."

"Thank you," his lordship said absently. "Fesswick, has it occurred to you that our work may soon be completed on this planet?"

"The thought has crossed my mind, my lord."

"They've come up fast, Fesswick. In another half century, they may be ready to go to the stars, and a hidden Observer will no longer be necessary. Still, it's been interesting, hasn't it?"

"Very interesting, my lord."

There was a note in Fesswick's voice that made Lord Curvert look curiously at his butler. He had always regarded Fesswick as—well, as part of the machinery. He was simply *there*. He had *always* been there. To imagine Castle Curvert without Fesswick was to imagine Egypt without the pyramids. And yet—

"You've been with the family for a long time, haven't you, Fesswick?"

Instead of answering immediately, Fesswick turned to look at the shield on the wall, upon which was emblazoned the Curvert arms—*Vert, on a pale or, a heart of the field.*

There was pride in Fesswick's voice when he spoke. "In a sense, my lord, I have only been with the family four generations. I was sent in as a new model to replace my predecessor in the year 1155, shortly after your great-grandfather was created the first Baron du Coeur Vert by Henry II for his services following the overthrow of the unhappy usurper, Stephen. Those were exciting times, my lord." He turned to face his master again.

"In another sense, my lord," he went on, "I have been with the family much longer. Since all the pertinent memories were transferred from the brain of my predecessor to my own, I have a sense of continuity that goes back to the establishment of the Observership, more than eight thousand years ago."

Lord Curvert, who had scarcely entered his twelfth decade, felt suddenly humble before the majesty of eighty centuries of time.

There was a rap at the door. "Charles!" The door opened before either Fesswick or Lord Curvert could answer, and Lady Curvert swept in. "Ah, there you are. Good morning, Fesswick. Charles, I have arrived at a full intuition. The Thregonnese. We should investigate at once."

"The metamorphs of Thregonn? Good heavens, you don't say so!" Lord Curvert stood up from his chair. "But how could they have come here?"

Lady Curvert shook her head. "I can't tell you that."

His lordship looked at Fesswick. "How about that, Fesswick, old man? Could a spaceship have landed recently without registering on the detectors?"

"Highly unlikely, my lord."

Lord Curvert looked back at his wife. "Fesswick says it's highly unlikely, my dear."

"My intuition is never wrong, Charles," Lady Curvert replied with dignity.

"That's true, eh, Fesswick?"

"Quite true, my lord. Her ladyship has never been known to err in matters of intuition."

"Very well, then; given the datum that there are Thregonnese on the planet, the question is: how did they get here? That seems to me to be logically deducible, which puts it in your department."

"I shall endeavor to give satisfaction, my lord." His high speed robotic brain was capable of working such problems in minute fractions of a second, so he continued without a pause: "It is obvious, my lord, that, in order to get from Thregonn, the metamorphs must have come by interstellar vessel. The only way such a vessel could have entered the Solar System without registering on the detectors would be to utilize a screen that would prevent the telltale wake from the drive energies from reaching us."

"But there is no such screen, Fesswick," Lady Curvert objected.

"With all due apologies, my lady," said Fesswick, "there *is* such a screen. The Sun itself. Interstellar drive energies cannot penetrate through the core of a star without absorption."

"Then their ship must have entered the Solar System by coming in from the opposite side of the Sun from Earth?" Lady Curvert said.

"Precisely so, my lady."

"But look here, Fesswick," said his lordship, "that's all very well for getting them into the Solar System, but it doesn't answer at all for getting them to Earth itself. So far, you've gotten them a hundred million miles from Earth, with the Sun between us. The question is: How did they get *here?*"

"The *Viper*, my lord," said Fesswick imperturbably.

"The *Viper?*"

"Exactly, my lord. The Venus Interplanetary Probe Electro-Rocket. It was, if you will recall, an unmanned automatic probe rocket designed to make an orbit close to Venus, take photographs, and return to Earth—an orbit which necessitated its being, for a time, on the opposite side of the Sun from Earth."

"Oh, yes. I remember seeing the photographs in the *Times.* Quite good ones they were, too," Lord Curvert said musingly. "Then, while the *Viper* was on the other side of the Sun, the Thregonnese simply attached a capsule to the side of it and rode it back to Earth."

"Exactly, my lord. It could have been done in no other way."

"The timing is exactly right, too," said Lord Curvert thoughtfully. "Naturally, we had no reason to suspect anything at the time; it was simply another American rocket returning home. It landed in the Pacific, as I recall, and the American Navy didn't find it for nearly an hour—plenty of time for the Thregonnese to detach their capsule and be on their way. Probably used a distorter to foul up the Navy's radar a bit, so that it would take more time to find the *Viper*."

"Without doubt, my lord," Fesswick agreed.

"Very ingenious of them," said his lordship. "Very. But you

see what this implies, don't you? They have been on Earth for nearly a year—for what purpose we have, as yet, no notion. And now, suddenly, they advertise their presence almost blatantly.

"Their very method of entry shows that they are aware of the presence of a Galactic Observer on this planet, so one would think that they would do their best to remain in concealment."

"Do you fear a trap, Charles?" Lady Curvert asked calmly.

"Let us say that, at the very least, they are attempting to draw the attention of the Galactic Observer, and that they have succeeded. Why? They want to find out who the Galactic Observer is; they want to be able to put their finger on me, as it were.

"On the other hand, this is almost too blatant to be a trap. They not only advertise their presence, but practically tell me how they got here. It's almost as if they wanted me to recognize it as a trap. Still, that seems a little too much, doesn't it? We don't have all the data as yet, and, as a chap I used to know once remarked, 'It is a capital mistake to theorize before you have all the evidence. It biases the judgement.' "

"Shall I begin preparations, my lord?" asked Fesswick.

"Immediately. That's where they've baited their hook very nicely, you see; we have no choice but to investigate. However, we shall take every precaution." He frowned suddenly. "By the by, Fesswick, I am scheduled to address the House of Lords tomorrow. We'll have to send a proxy. Fortunately, I've already written the speech."

"Shall I attend to it personally, my lord?"

"By no means! I want you here—at the controls."

"Certainly, my lord. I'll send Elsie, the upstairs maid; she should be able to carry out the deception competently."

"Quite. Now, let's get with it, Fesswick. The game, as my friend used to remark, is afoot."

During the reign of Queen Victoria, when the British Empire was at its peak, Lord Curvert had had the opportunity of chuckling inwardly—though deploring outwardly—when he was told of the horrible fate that might face an Englishman stationed in some far-off place. Accompanied by a sad shake of the head, the story usually went something like this: "Terrible thing about Lord Greystoke. Hadn't you heard? Greystoke's gone native. Africa, you know. Deplorable. Doesn't even dress for dinner any more, so I hear."

What caused Lord Curvert's inward mirth was, of course, that the first thing a Galactic Observer did when stationed on a planet was to "go native." One not only had to blend in, one had to change with the times. One had to age one's appearance slowly and bring up "children"—parts played by one or more of the robots—and then, at the right time, one became one's own son while a robot played the older man and finally "died." Such things required a chameleonlike ability to adapt, to change one's personality as one might change one's hat.

Thus it is not to be considered remarkable that Ben and Cordelia Holler, who stepped out of a dark alley near Fisherman's Wharf in San Francisco, bore no resemblance whatever to Lord and Lady Curvert, either in appearance or manner.

"Do we make the scene here for a bit," Cordelia asked, "or do we cut out for New York soonest?"

"We cut out for N.Y., chick," Ben said. "Those squares might have pegged us if we'd used a teleporter into the Village, but they won't dig the G.O. making it on a jet plane. Let's get this wild gig going, chicky."

They walked out into the fog-filled light that spilled from the street lamps.

Ben chuckled. "Let's grab a cab. I mean, like we got bread to blow, so let's blow it."

She grinned up at him. "Crazy, man! I mean, *real* crazy!"

A few hours later, they were in Manhattan.

The roundabout method of arrival had been absolutely necessary. If Fesswick, at the controls of the teleportation projector, had put them directly in New York, there was a slight chance that the Thregonnese detectors might have registered the activity of the materialization field. On the other hand, it was necessary to get into the United States without going through the formality of passing through Immigration and Customs.

"First thing, baby," Ben said as they came out of the subway exit at Waverly Place, "is to tag us a pad. Dig? Then we make the scene at the Kettle and a couple of the other cool spots for kicks."

Ben and Cordelia made the scene in the Village for seven days before they went anywhere near the Venus Club. They didn't want to seem anxious, so they played it cool. They strolled into the Venus Club late one Friday evening, and the joint was really swinging. The kookiest-looking quartet this side of an H-kick nightmare were blowing out a beat crazy enough to make any cat flip his gasket.

Ben and Cordelia sat down, ordered a couple espressos, and kept playing it cool, just digging the whole bit.

The four musicians were hot; there was no question of that. And cool at the same time. But both Ben and Cordelia could tell at a glance that they were not—definitely not—human beings dressed up in fancy suits. They varied in color from pale pink to deep purple—a drummer, a trumpeter, a clarinetist, and a bass viol player. The lips of the trumpeter and the clarinetist formed the instruments they played. The bass player's belly formed the sounding box of his instrument, with the strings running from his nose to a point below where his navel should have been. The drummer's belly ballooned out like a kettledrum, with a flat drumhead just below his sternum.

It was easy to see why they had been able to pass themselves off as dressed-up humans; the "costumes" looked too outré, too artificial to be real. But the dead giveaway was the drummer.

He had four arms.

Try *that* with a costume sometime!

"Frantically cool," said Cordelia.

Ben scratched thoughtfully at his beard. "I'm hip," he agreed.

They were Thregonnese, all right. There was no other race in the known Galaxy that could change the shape of their bodies that way.

The bass player stepped out from the others and began chanting in time to the music. At first, it seemed to be nothing but nonsense syllables of the *rooty-ooty-yeek-yeek-boo-da-da* type, then both Ben and Cordelia recognized that he was chanting in a jazzed-up version of Basic Galactic, the *lingua franca* of space.

"*Hey, Observer, give us a buzz!*
We're in trouble like never was!
Every night we sing this bit,
Hoping you'll be digging it.
Listen, G.O., to our moan;
Kindly call us on the phone!
Listen to our wailing yelp;
What we mean is: Man, like—help!"

There was a long wailing note on the trumpet and a little flurry of sobs from the coronet, and the piece ended with a teeth-rattling roll from the drum.

"Cool," said Cordelia, crushing out her cigarette.

"Frantically cool," agreed Ben. He looked at his wristwatch. "Time to cut out now, but we will definitely have to make this scene tomorrow."

They finished their coffee and strolled out. By then, the musicians had left the bandstand and were nowhere to be seen.

Cordelia waited until they were a full block away before she spoke. "Do we give them a buzz? What kind of crazy hassle do you figure they're hung up in?"

"You got no hunch?"

"Man, like I dig them the least. Can it hurt to phone?"

"Don't know, chick. Maybe we ought to—"

He thought it over for a minute. Which would be best—to sneak up on them quietly, without letting them know he was anywhere around, and hit all four of them fast—or to take them at their word and call them on the phone?

The trouble was that it was impossible to trust a Thregonnese any farther than you could throw a bonfire by the smoke. The metamorphs of Thregonn weren't vicious, but they were characterized by a low sense of humor and a way of thinking that was definitely weird by human standards.

He decided he'd chance it. He said, "Come on, chick," and went into a drug store on the next corner. He got the number of the Venus Club and dialed it.

"Venus Club," said a voice.

"You are under arrest," said the Observer in clipped Galactic.

"Are you the Observer?" asked the voice in the same language.

"That's right. And you know you're not supposed to be on this planet. It's still under quarantine."

"Believe me," said the other, "I wouldn't be here at all if I could get away. None of us would. For a while, there, we were afraid maybe you'd never notice us."

"So far," said the Observer, "you haven't attracted the attention of the local authorities, but if you do, I'll slap a charge against you that will—"

"Hey, now!" the Thregonnese interrupted. "We know the law! This was only a misdemeanor. Landing for refueling without authorization, is all."

"*I'll* tell *you* what the law is," the Observer said. "Now, what's all this fuss about, anyhow?"

"Well, first of all, it started out as a joke. You know?"

"Sure. I know all about it," the Observer said sarcastically. "That's why I'm spending my time asking you questions. What the hell happened?"

"Well, there was this bet, see. Lubix, Forbin, Alisnokine, and I had bet some friends of ours that we could come in here, land, pick up a —uh—a souvenir, and come back without your catching us. Without even knowing we'd been here. See?"

"So far, yes," said the Observer in a very cold voice.

"Well, the guys we were betting against must've got cute," the Thregonnese went on. "They bollixed up our space capsule, and we couldn't take off again. And now that the U.S. Navy has the capsule, we can't do anything about it at all."

"The U.S. Navy? Now wait a minute; you can't..."

Then he heard sudden loud noises from the phone, a voice in English said, "Chiggers! The cops!" and the line went dead.

Cordelia, who had been standing near the doorway of the drugstore, where she could watch the door of the Venus Club, walked over to the phone booth and said, in a low voice, "Like, some cops just went in. Wonder what they're bugged about?"

"I hope," Ben said fervently, "that those cats don't goof now. Otherwise, we'll all be in the soup!"

Lord Curvert glared at his copy of the New York *Daily News* in a medium dudgeon. There, looking out from the front page with idiotic grins, were four of the most disreputable-looking men his lordship had ever had the misfortune to gaze upon.

"At least," he said grudgingly, "they managed to metamorphose into reasonably human shape before they were arrested. I hate to think what might have happened if the police had arrested them while they were still in the outlandish shapes they were wearing when we saw them last."

Lady Curvert sipped at her tea and looked at the headlines.

VENUS CLUB OWNERS NABBED IN
NARCOTICS RAID

$10,000 Heroin Cache Found in Coffee House

"It's ridiculous," said her ladyship rather peevishly. "It makes no sense at all! Why should four Thregonnese want to do anything so silly as use or sell heroin? They couldn't have become addicted to it, could they, Charles?"

"I think not. Incompatible metabolism, eh, Fesswick?"

Fesswick placed more buttered toast on the small tray next to the marmalade pot. "Quite incompatible, my lord. Heroin would kill a Thregonnese within three minutes if injected into the bloodstream. Sniffing it, as I believe is often done by addicts, would cause unconsciousness very rapidly."

"Then why should they do anything so silly?" her ladyship

85

repeated.

"I confess, my lady, that I am thus far unable to deduce the machinations lying behind these highly peculiar circumstances," Fesswick admitted.

Lord Curvert poured himself another cup of tea. "All the data we have thus far aren't worth a ha'penny for the lot. The story they gave me over the telephone was that they had come to Earth on a bet, to pick up a souvenir of some kind, that one of the Thregonnese betting against them had done something to their space capsule, and that somehow—Heaven only knows how!—the United States Navy has gained possession of the capsule. All of which could be a tissue of lies from one end to the other, damn it." He looked searchingly at his butler. "What's your opinion, Fesswick?"

"The story as it stands, my lord, is not consistent with the facts as we know them, but that is merely to say that we have no conclusive evidence of any kind."

Lord Curvert snorted at that and looked at his wife. "And how is your intuition this morning, my dear?"

"Well, Charles," she said, smiling rather timidly, "I have a feeling you ought to do *something*—but I'm not at all sure what."

"Well, damn it all, we *have* to do something! The family has held the Observership perfectly for eight thousand years—guarded Earthmen from interference, so that they could develop their own civilization. I'm not going to have that record spoilt by four Thregonnese clowns!"

"Couldn't we just help them to escape with the teleporter?" Lady Curvert asked helpfully. "Then you could put the collars on them and ship them off."

"Don't be an idiot," his lordship growled, staring into his teacup.

Lady Curvert looked hurt.

"It can't be done, my lady," Fesswick said quietly. "We used to be able to do such things easily, but, in these days, when the cells of a modern gaol are made of steel, we find ourselves hampered by the fact that a teleporter field is badly distorted if one attempts to project it into a metal-enclosed space."

"Dear me," said Lady Curvert. She looked at her husband, saw that he was far too deep in thought to be disturbed, and turned back to Fesswick. "Is there anything at all I can do?"

"Not, I'm afraid, at the moment, my lady," said the robot with dignity. "When both Logic and Intuition have failed, we must resort to Action and Ingenuity, and those are in his lordship's department." He poured Lady Curvert another cup ot tea. "I am quite sanguine, my lady, over the prospect of his lordship's solving the problem very shortly. He always has."

The police chemist who took the small package of heroin from the safe to analyze it was very careful with the stuff. His job was to run it through an analysis so that he could testify in court that it really was heroin. He didn't let the package out of his sight for more than thirty seconds.

Which was plenty long enough.

He was setting up his testing apparatus, so he didn't see a long-fingered, aristocratic hand appear out of nowhere, take the package, and replace it with an exactly similar one.

When the contents of the package turned out to be sugar, the chemist was surprised. The District Attorney was more than surprised; he was furious.

But there was nothing that either of them could do.

There was even more surprise in Castle Curvert when Fesswick reported his own analysis of the powder to his master.

"The substance, my lord," he said in his precise voice, "is not heroin."

"Not heroin?" said his lordship.

"No, my lord. It is Varesh powder."

"Ah-hah!" his lordship expostulated. "And they brought plenty of it, didn't they?"

"Yes, my lord. Enough, shall we say, to hypnotize every government official on Earth, if that became necessary. It only needs to be activated."

"Things are beginning to fall into place, Fesswick."

"Yes, my lord."

"Lost their equipment, didn't they, Fesswick?" he said, grinning.

"It would appear so, my lord," said Fesswick, returning the grin.

"The next step, Fesswick, is to appear to fall in with their nefarious plan."

"Yes, my lord. I shall begin preparation immediately."

Omboser, Lubix, Forbin, and Alsnokine stepped out of the court building and walked down the imposing-looking steps toward the sidewalk.

"It's about time they let us out," Omboser snarled in Thregonnese. "I knew that as soon as they analyzed the Varesh powder they would realize that it was not one of their local drugs—but I didn't know it would take the primitive fools that long to analyze it."

Lubix patted the pocket of the suit he was wearing. "Well, we got it back, and that's what's important."

"You idiots!" Forbin hissed, "cease your chatter! The Galactic Observer could be anywhere around."

They all glanced around apprehensively. Alsnokine whispered, "Do you think he can speak or understand Thregonnese?"

"Probably not," said Forbin, "but there's no need of talking loud enough for everyone to hear."

"What I want to know," Lubix said as they headed toward the subway entrance, "is, who's the creep who called the cops on us?"

"That character from the Musician's Union, obviously," said Omboser. "If Alsnokine hadn't acted so guilty when he came into the office, nothing would have happened."

"What was I supposed to do? Leave it out there for him to look at?" Alsnokine asked defensively. "How could I know he wasn't the Observer himself?"

"Quit arguing, you two!" Forbin snapped. "We haven't lost anything but a little time. Let's get back to the club and hope that the Observer will contact us again."

"If Omboser hadn't been such a blockhead," Alsnokine began, "we wouldn't..."

"Ahh, shut up!" said Forbin.

When they reached the Venus Club, a little more than a mile north of the station at Centre Street, Omboser produced his key, unlocked the front door, and went in, followed by his three co-conspirators. They stopped suddenly at the sight of a tall, rather handsome, impeccably dressed gentleman who was seated at a table in the middle of the room, sipping at a small cup of espresso.

"Good afternoon, gentlemen," he said with utter aplomb. "That machine of yours makes quite excellent coffee." He was speaking very cultivated Galactic.

"The Observer," the four Thregonnese said in a ragged chorus.

"Exactly," said Lord Curvert. "You may refer to me as Mr. Smith. Not as original an alias, perhaps, as, say, 'Sebastian Tombs,' but it will suffice. Now, to which of you was I speaking when the local constabulary so precipitately interrupted?"

"That was me," said Omboser.

"Then pray sit down, make yourselves comfortable, and tell

me all about your troubles. Consider me your Father Confessor, and tell all."

They sat down slowly, all four pairs of eyes focused steadily on the intruder.

Finally, Omboser smiled. "Well, sir, as I was saying," he began, "we had this little bet, you see. We knew it was illegal, but it was just a harmless prank. We were to come here, and then go back, that's all. Nobody would be hurt, nobody would be the wiser, and we would win our bet. See?"

"I understand so far," Lord Curvert said agreeably. "Then what happened?"

"Well..." Omboser began very hesitantly.

"This idiot," said Forbin, pointing a thumb at Omboser, "was supposed to stay behind with our capsule. Instead, he went swimming."

"It gets pretty boring, doing nothing," said Omboser pettishly.

"He went swimming," Forbin repeated. "We had the capsule underwater, in a little bay at Lukiuni Atoll, out in the Pacific."

"There was nobody on the atoll at all," Omboser said. "It looked perfectly all right to go swimming."

"Nevertheless," Forbin continued, "while Omboser was out cavorting—he'd changed himself into a porpoise for the purpose —a United States Navy patrol plane spotted the capsule from the air."

"I told you we should have sunk it in deeper water," Omboser said.

Forbin ignored him. "By the time Omboser got back from his spree, the U.S. Navy was in charge—with a light cruiser. Since we'd left most of our equipment in the capsule, we didn't even have the instruments we needed to sneak in and get the capsule back."

"The Navy thinks the capsule is a Russian job," Lubix supplied helpfully. "They haven't opened it yet, because they're afraid there might be a thermonuclear bomb inside it. But they've sure got it surrounded while they try to figure out what to do."

"So," Forbin finished, "we figured we'd better get in touch with you and tell you what happened. We rented this place and put on a show that we thought would attract your attention without revealing ourselves to the natives. It took us a long time to get the hang of how things are done on this planet, though. Otherwise, we'd've done this sooner."

Then all four of them sat there in silence, watching the Observer, waiting for his decision.

Lord Curvert thought the matter over carefully, then came to a decision. "Very well, my fumble-fingered friends, we'll see what can be done. He looked up into the air a foot or so above his head. "Rally round, Mr. Jones," he said, "there's work to be done."

The calm voice of Fesswick came out of the air. "Anytime you're ready, Mr. Smith."

Sergeant Thaddeus McClusky, USMC, shrugged his shoulder a little to adjust the weight of the heavy machine rifle that was slung there. So did Corporal Quinn. Both of them looked with respectful eyes at Lieutenant (jg) Fordham, USN, and listened silently as he spoke.

"Remember, men; that may be an atomic bomb down there, so keep on your toes. Absolutely no one is allowed to pass inside this perimeter after dark. Understand?"

"Yes, sir," said Sargeant McClusky.

"Yes, sir," said Corporal Quinn.

"Very well. Carry on."

Salutes were exchanged, and the two Marines waited silently while the Naval officer went on down the line to the next post. As soon as he was out of earshot, McClusky muttered a dirty word. "...deckape shavetail," he added.

"That's the way the goddam Navy operates," said Quinn philosophically. "We been here six months watching that gizmo while the Navy sits on its duff and wonders what to do about it. And what do they do? Why, they send us a fresh jaygee from Stateside who tells us to do exactly what we been doin' all along. That takes real brains, that does."

Sergeant McClusky nodded his agreement. "'Remember, that may be an atomic bomb, down here, so keep on your toes,'" he mimicked. "Well, you can just bet your stripey little shoulder boards we will, sir. Yes, sir. We'll watch very closely, sir, and if that thing goes off, we'll call you right up on the telephone, sir. Won't we, Corporal Quinn?"

"Just as fast as ever we can," agreed Corporal Quinn. "We will be moving very rapidly, Sergeant McClusky."

They turned to look at the little, shallow lagoon which held the unknown thing. There were no lights illuminating it; the Navy didn't want to attract the attention of any high-flying Russian planes that might be looking the area over. But the light of a tropical full moon cast its silvery radiance over the glittering waters of the lagoon.

The thing itself had been surrounded with a steel net to keep large fish from approaching it and—possibly—setting it off. Underwater sonar constantly probed the depths to make sure that Russian frogmen didn't try to sneak in. The Navy didn't think the Russians knew where their toy was, but they were taking no chances.

"You know," said McClusky, "when I was a kid, I used to love those movies of the South Seas. Remember? They had scenes in 'em just like this."

"Yeah," Quinn agreed softly. "Tropical moon—sea breezes—palm trees gently waving—waves rolling softly against the warm sands."

"That's very poetic," McClusky said in mild astonishment.

"I remember it from an old movie ad," Quinn said.

"All we need is some guitar music," McClusky said.

"Yeah. And Dorothy Lamour in a sarong."

"Will I do?" asked a soft, throaty contralto voice from behind them.

Both men spun around, unslinging their rifles with the easy grace of long practice.

Then they froze, as if someone had doused them with a few gallons of liquid air. Their eyes glazed, and their mouths hung agape.

It was not Dorothy Lamour, they decided, because she was not wearing a sarong. She was not even wearing a grass skirt.

Sergeant McClusky recovered his voice. "You ain't supposed to be here, dressed like that, ma'am," he said to the vision of loveliness.

"Undressed like that," Corporal Quinn corrected automatically.

"Even if you was dressed," said McClusky, "you hadn't ought to be here. Women aren't allowed on this island." He was still trying to figure out what to do when a voice bellowed out from the next post down the shore.

"Corporal of the guard! Post Number Five! I got a woman on my post—a *nekkid* woman! Whadda I do now?"

Before Corporal Quinn could answer, two more posts called out that they had the same trouble.

"Why all the fuss?" asked the girl, wide-eyed. "We just want to go swimming in your pretty lagoon."

"No, you don't," said McClusky, recovering his wits at last. "You're under arrest, lady." He reached out to grab her with one brawny fist, but his hand closed on empty air. The girl was deceptively fast. She backed away, still smiling, and McClusky made another lunge for her.

He missed and lost his balance as she danced back out of the way. As he fell forward, he heard Quinn yell: "Halt! Halt or I fire!"

He broke his fall with the butt of his rifle, and twisted to an upright sitting position. The girl, he noticed, was running away from the lagoon, toward the sea, with Quinn after her in hot pursuit, still calling for her to halt.

All around, there were similar cries. Sergeant McClusky wondered how many unclad females there were running around on Lukiuni Atoll—where there couldn't possibly be any women.

Not a man there noticed what was going on out in the lagoon itself. The figure of a man suddenly materialized from nowhere a few inches above the surface of the water. Then he dropped in with scarcely a splash.

Since Fesswick did not breathe, there was no necessity for him to wear any of the usual diving equipment. All he had to do was swim to the steel net, cut through it, and head for the little Thregonnese space capsule. He wasn't the least bit worried about the Navy's probing sonar beams; the nullifiers operated by Lord Curvert would take care of them. As far as the sonar operators could tell, there was nothing at all unusual in the lagoon.

Fesswick got busy opening the airlock of the little capsule.

Up on shore, Sergeant McClusky yelled at Corporal Quinn, who was several yards away, at the sea's edge, staring into the waves. Lights were coming on all over the tiny atoll. Pounding footsteps could be heard from every quarter as confused men ran every which way.

"She just dived into the sea and never came up," Corporal Quinn was saying wonderingly.

"Why didn't you shoot?" bellowed McClusky.

"Who the hell do you think I am?" Quinn bellowed back. "Mike Hammer?"

So far, nobody else had fired a shot, either, and by that time, all four of the Thregonnese had dived into the sea, changed into porpoises, and were swimming rapidly away from the atoll.

The final surpise came when, with a great geyser of erupting water, the Thregonnese space capsule shot up out of the lagoon and vanished rapidly into the moonlit sky.

There would be a lot of explaining to do that night and for many nights to come, in Navy circles.

But there would never be any explanation.

"And now," said Lord Curvert gently, "the question arises as to what to do with you gentlemen."

They were sitting in the Venus Club again. The space capsule, indetectable to any Earth science, was sitting on the roof of the building.

"Why, just make your report and let us go," Forbin said politely. "It was only a misdemeanor. We haven't done anything felonious. We didn't expose anything to the natives or interfere in any way. Just let us go, and we'll pay the fine according to the law."

Lord Curvert was nodding slowly, and there was an oddly sleepy look in his eyes. "Yes," he said. "Certainly. Just let you go."

The Thregonnese looked at each other with delight, and then looked back at the Observer.

"Or, better yet," said Forbin insidiously, "just let us stay for a while. How about that?"

"Yes. Yes," his lordship said rather glassily. "I could just let you stay for a while."

"As a matter of fact," Forbin went on in the same tone, "we have a few favors we'd like you to do for us."

"Favors," said Lord Curvert. "Certainly. What favors?"

"Well, for instance, why don't you stand on your head?"

"Certainly."

"And click your heels together," added Omboser, ignoring the scowls that Forbin and the others shot him.

"Certainly," agreed his lordship. Placing hands and head on the floor, Lord Curvert solemnly upended himself, balanced carefully, and clapped his heels together.

"We've done it!" Forbin said gleefully. "We're in!"

"You sure that assistant of his—that Mr. Jones can't reach us here?" Alsnokine asked, a trifle apprehensively. "Or see us?"

"Not a chance," Forbin said. "I turned on the nullifiers in our ship myself."

"We've done it," Lubix gloated. "In spite of all the setbacks, we have our ship, and we have the Observer. Now we can start having a little fun."

"Are you gentlemen just going to leave me like this?" Lord Curvert asked politely.

They all turned to look at him.

He did a neat handspring-and-flip, and landed on his feet. "A confession of intent," he said mildly, "is bad enough. When combined with an actual attempt, it becomes very bad indeed."

None of them said anything.

"Oh, no," his lordship went on, "I'm not hypnotized. In the

first place, the substance you have been thinking is Varesh powder is nothing but powdered sugar. I saw you put it in the activator in your capsule, and I saw you put a pinch of it into the air. But I'm afraid sugar just doesn't have the proper effect.

"In the second place, even if it had been Varesh powder, nothing would have happened, because I am wearing filter plugs in my nostrils, just as you are. The one difference is that my plugs function, while yours don't.

"I'm afraid that while my assistant, Mr. Jones, was in your capsule, he put a few rather clever little gimmicks into your controls. In addition, he sprayed a little genuine Varesh powder through the teleporter just a few seconds ago. And it's having its effect, isn't it?"

It was. Robbed of their conscious volition, the human body shapes which the Thregonnese had assumed were beginning to look oddly lumpy as they tended to return to their normal shapes.

"I am sending you back to Thregonn for punishment," he said. "I'll tell you what the conspiracy was, and you correct me if I'm wrong, so that everything will be nice and legal.

"You intended to use this Venus Club set-up to trap me first. Then, after I had been hypnotized, you intended to take over the various governments of Earth. Now, there, I'm a little hazy—just what was your reason for wanting to take over? Were you going to set yourselves up as supreme dictators, so that you could push everybody around?" He looked at Forbin as he spoke.

"For a while," admitted the thoroughly hypnotized Forbin. "Then, if we got bored, we thought it might be fun to start an atomic war among these primitive people."

"Worse than I thought," said Lord Curvert distastefully. "I hope they straighten you out thoroughly on Thregonn."

By this time, the four Thregonnese had returned to their "normal" shape. They looked like four fat, pink kewpie dolls.

"All right," said Lord Curvert, "let's go. You'll get in your ship and go straight to Thregonn, understand?"

"Yes, sir," they chorused. "Straight to Thregonn."

"And just to make sure you do, you'll give yourselves another dose of Varesh powder every twenty-four hours. Understand?"

"Yes, sir," they chorused.

"Fine. Let's go."

They went up to the roof, and the four fat kewpies climbed into the vessel. The airlock closed, and a few seconds later the little spaceship fired skywards.

"Take me home, Fesswick," said Lord Curvert.

"That's very odd," said Lady Curvert.

Lord Curvert looked up apprehensively from his *Times*. "Not another one, I hope."

"Oh, no, Charles. Not another case. I was just thinking that it was very odd that the paper should come out with an editorial on the Teddy boys today. The editor says that juvenile delinquency is getting worse and something must be done to stop it."

"I'll write a letter to the *Times*, my dear," said Lord Curvert.

Fesswick shimmered in through the doorway. "I beg to report, my lord, that Thregonn acknowledges the landing of the capsule. The four have been placed in arrest by the authorities. Their parents have been notified."

"Good," said Lord Curvert. "People here on Earth complain about juvenile delinquency, Fesswick. Just wait until they find out what it's like on a Galactic scale."

DESPOILERS OF THE GOLDEN EMPIRE

This is an odd one. It needs an Afterword instead of a Foreword.

By Randall Garrett

I

In the seven centuries that had elapsed since the Second Empire had been founded on the shattered remnants of the First, the nobles of the Imperium had come slowly to realize that the empire was not to be judged by the examples of its predecessor. The First Empire had conquered most of the known universe by political intrigue and sheer military strength; it had fallen because that same propensity for political intrigue had gained over every other strength of the Empire, and the various branches and sectors of the First Empire had begun to use it against one another.

The Second Empire was politically unlike the First; it tried to balance a centralized government against the autonomic governments of the various sectors, and had almost succeeded in doing so.

But, no matter how governed, there are certain essentials which are needed by any governmental organization.

Without power, neither Civilization nor the Empire could hold itself together, and His Universal Majesty, the Emperor Carl, well knew it. And power was linked solidly to one element, one metal, without which Civilization would collapse as surely as if it had been blasted out of existence. Without the power metal, no ship could move or even be built; without it, industry would come to a standstill.

In ancient times, even as far back as the early Greek and Roman civilizations, the metal had been known, but it had been used, for the most part, as decoration and in the manufacture of jewelry. Later, it had been coined as money.

It had always been relatively rare, but now, weight for weight, atom for atom, it was the most valuable element on Earth. Indeed, the most valuable in the known universe.

The metal was Element Number Seventy-nine—gold.

To the collective mind of the Empire, gold was the prime object in any kind of mining exploration. The idea of drilling for petroleum, even if it had been readily available, or of mining coal or uranium would have been dismissed as impracticable and even worse than useless.

Throughout the Empire, research laboratories worked tirelessly at the problem of transmuting commoner elements into Gold-197, but thus far none of the processes was commercially feasible. There was still, after thousands of years, only one way to get the power metal: extract it from the ground.

So it was that, across the great gulf between the worlds, ship after ship moved in search of the metal that would hold the far-flung colonies of the Empire together. Every adventurer who could manage to get aboard was glad to be cooped up on a ship during the long months it took to cross the empty expanses, was glad to endure the hardships on alien terrain, on the chance that his efforts might pay off a thousand or ten thousand fold.

Of these men, a mere handful were successful, and of these one or two stand well above the rest. And for sheer determination, drive, and courage, for the will to push on toward his goal, no matter what the odds, a certain Commander Frank had them all beat.

II

Before you can get a picture of the commander—that is, as far as his personality goes—you have to get a picture of the man physically.

He was enough taller than the average man to make him stand out in a crowd, and he had broad shoulders and a narrow waist to match. He wasn't heavy; his was the hard, tough, wirelike strength of a steel cable. The planes of his tanned face showed that he feared neither exposure to the elements nor exposure to violence; it was seamed with fine wrinkles and the thin white lines that betray scar tissue. His mouth was heavy-lipped, but firm, and the lines around it showed that it was unused to smiling. The commander could laugh, and often did—a sort of roaring explosion that burst forth suddenly whenever something struck him as particularly uproarious. But he seldom just smiled; Commander Frank rarely went halfway in anything.

His eyes, like his hair, were a deep brown—almost black, and they were set well back beneath heavy brows that tended to frown most of the time.

Primarily, he was a military man. He had no particular flair for science, and, although he had a firm and deep-seated grasp of the essential philosophy of the Universal Assembly, he had no inclination towards the kind of life necessarily led by those who would become higher officers of the Assembly. It was enough that the Assembly was behind him; it was enough to know that he was a member of the only race in the known universe which had a working knowledge of the essential, basic Truth of the Cosmos. With a weapon like that, even an ordinary soldier had little to fear, and Commander Frank was far from being an ordinary soldier.

He had spent nearly forty of his sixty years of life as an explorer-soldier for the Emperor, and during that time he'd kept his eyes open for opportunity. Every time his ship had landed, he'd watched and listened and collected data. And now he knew.

If his data were correct—and he was certain that they were—he had found his strike. All he needed was the men to take it.

III

The expedition had been poorly outfitted and undermanned from the beginning. The commander had been short of money at the outset, having spent almost all he could raise on his own, plus nearly everything he could beg or borrow, on his first two probing expeditions, neither of which had shown any real profit.

But they *had* shown promise; the alien population of the target which the commander had selected as his personal claim wore gold as ornaments, but didn't seem to think it was much above copper in value, and hadn't even progressed to the point of using it as coinage. From the second probing expedition, he had brought back two of the odd-looking aliens and enough gold to show that there must be more where that came from.

The old, hopeful statement, "There's gold in them thar hills," should have brought the commander more backing than he got, considering the Empire's need of it and the commander's evidence that it was available; but people are always more ready to bet on a sure thing than to indulge in speculation. Ten years before, a strike had been made in a sector quite distant from the commander's own find, and most of the richer nobles of the Empire preferred to back an established source of the metal than to sink money into what might turn out to be the pursuit of a wild goose.

Commander Frank, therefore, could only recruit men who were willing to take a chance, who were willing to risk anything, even their lives, against tremendously long odds.

And, even if they succeeded, the Imperial Government would take twenty per cent of the gross without so much as a by-your-leave. There was no other market for the metal except back home, so the tax could not be avoided; gold was no good whatsoever in the uncharted wilds of an alien world.

Because of his lack of funds, the commander's expedition was not only dangerously undermanned, but illegally so. It was only by means of out-and-out trickery that he managed to evade the official inspection and leave port with too few men and too little equipment.

There wasn't a scientist worthy of the name in the whole outfit, unless you call the navigator, Captain Bartholomew, an astronomer, which is certainly begging the question. There was no anthropologist aboard to study the semibarbaric civilization of the natives; there was no biologist to study the alien flora and fauna. The closest thing the commander had to physicists were engineers who could take care of the ship itself—specialist technicians, nothing more.

There was no need for armament specialists; each and every man was a soldier, and, as far as his own weapons went, an ordnance expert. As far as Commander Frank was concerned, that was enough. It had to be.

Mining equipment? He took nothing but the simplest testing apparatus. How, then, did he intend to get the metal that the Empire was screaming for?

The commander had an answer for that, too, and it was as simple as it was economical. The natives would get it for him.

They used gold for ornaments; therefore, they knew where the gold could be found. And, therefore, they would bloody well dig it out for Commander Frank.

IV

Due to atmospheric disturbances, the ship's landing was several hundred miles from the point the commander had originally picked for the debarkation of his troops. That meant a long, forced march along the coast and then inland, but there was no help for it; the ship simply wasn't built for atmospheric navigation.

That didn't deter the commander any. The orders rang through the ship: "All troops and carriers prepare for landing!"

Half an hour later, they were assembled outside the ship, fully armed and armored, and with full field gear. The sun, a yellow G-O star, hung hotly just above the towering mountains to the east. The alien air smelled odd in the men's nostrils, and the weird foliage seemed to rustle menacingly. In the distance, the shrieks of alien fauna occasionally echoed through the air.

A hundred and eighty-odd men and some thirty carriers stood under the tropic blaze for forty-five minutes while the commander checked over their equipment with minute precision. Nothing faulty or sloppy was going into that jungle with him if he could prevent it.

When his hard eyes had inspected every bit of equipment, when he had either passed or ordered changes in the manner of its carrying or its condition, when he was fully satisfied that every weapon was in order—then, and only then, did he turn his attention to the men themselves.

He climbed atop a little hillock and surveyed them carefully, letting his penetrating gaze pass over each man in turn. He stood there, his fists on his hips, with the sunlight gleaming from his burnished armor, for nearly a full minute before he spoke.

Then his powerful voice rang out over the assembled adventurers.

"My comrades-at-arms! We have before us a world that is ours for the taking! It contains more riches than any man on Earth ever dreamed existed, and those riches, too, are ours for the taking. It isn't going to be a picnic, and we all knew that when we came. There are dangers on every side—from the natives, from the animals and plants, and from the climate.

"But there is not one of these that cannot be overcome by the onslaught of brave, courageous, and determined men!

"Ahead of us, we will find the Four Horsemen of the Apocalypse arrayed against our coming—Famine, Pestilence, War, and Death. Each and all of these we must meet and conquer as brave men should, for at their end we will find wealth and glory!"

A cheer filled the air, startling the animals in the forest into momentary silence.

The commander stilled it instantly with a raised hand.

"Some of you know this country from our previous expeditions together. Most of you will find it utterly strange. And not one of you knows it as well as I do.

"In order to survive, you must—and *will*—follow my orders to the letter—and beyond.

"First, as to your weapons. We don't have an unlimited supply of charges for them, so there will be no firing of any power weapon unless absolutely necessary. You have your swords and your pikes—use them."

Several of the men unconsciously gripped the hafts of the long steel blades at their sides as he spoke the words, but their eyes never left the commanding figure on the hummock.

"As for food," he continued, "we'll live off the land. You'll find that most of the animals are edible, but stay away from the plants unless I give the O.K.

"We have a long way to go, but, by Heaven, I'm going to get us there alive! Are you with me?"

A hearty cheer rang from the throats of the men. They shouted the commander's name with enthusiasm.

"All right!" he bellowed. "There is one more thing! Anyone who wants to stay with the ship can do so; anyone who feels too ill to make it should consider it his duty to stay behind, because sick men will simply hold us up and weaken us more than if they'd been left behind. Remember, we're not going to turn back as a body, and an individual would never make it alone." He paused.

"Well?"

Not a man moved. The commander grinned—not with humor, but with satisfaction. "All right, then: let's move out."

V

Of them all, only a handful, including the commander, had any real knowledge of what lay ahead of them, and that knowledge only pertained to the periphery of the area the intrepid band of adventurers were entering. They knew that the aliens possessed a rudimentary civilization—they did not, at that time, realize they were entering the outposts of a powerful barbaric empire—an empire almost as well-organized and well-armed as that of First Century Rome, and, if anything, even more savage and ruthless.

It was an empire ruled by a single family who called themselves the Great Nobles; at their head was the Greatest Noble—the Child of the Sun Himself. It has since been conjectured that the Great Nobles were mutants in the true sense of the word; a race apart from their subjects. It is impossible to be absolutely sure at this late date, and the commander's expedition, lacking any qualified geneticists or genetic engineers, had no way of determining—and, indeed, no real *interest* in determining—whether this was or was not true. None the less, historical evidence seems to indicate the validity of the hypothesis.

Never before—not even in ancient Egypt—had the historians ever seen a culture like it. It was an absolute monarchy that would have made any Medieval king except the most saintly look upon it in awe and envy. The Russians and the Germans never even approached it. The Japanese tried to approximate it at one time in their history, but they failed.

Secure in the knowledge that theirs was the only civilizing force on the face of the planet, the race of the Great Nobles spread over the length of a great continent, conquering the lesser races as they went.

Physically, The Great Nobles and their lesser subjects were quite similar. They were, like the commander and his men, human in every sense of the word. That this argues some ancient, prehistoric migration across the empty gulfs that separate the worlds cannot be denied, but when and how that migration took place are data lost in the mists of time. However it may have happened, the fact remains that these people *were* human. As someone observed in one of the reports written up by one of the officers: "They could pass for Indians, except their skins are of a decidedly redder hue."

The race of the Great Nobles held their conquered subjects in check by the exercise of two powerful forces: religion and physical power of arms. Like the feudal organizations of Medieval Europe, the Nobles had the power of life and death over their subjects, and to a much greater extent than the European nobles had. Each family lived on an allotted parcel of land and did a given job. Travel was restricted to a radius of a few miles. There was no money; there was no necessity for it, since the government of the Great Nobles took all produce and portioned it out again according to need. It was communism on a vast and—incomprehensible as it may seem to the modern mind—*workable*— scale. Their minds were as different from ours as their bodies were similar; the concept "freedom" would have been totally incomprehensible to them.

They were sun-worshipers, and the Greatest Noble was the Child of the Sun, a godling subordinate only to the Sun Himself. Directly under him were the lesser Great Nobles, also Children of the Sun, but to a lesser extent. They exercised absolute power over the conquered peoples, but even they had no concept of freedom, since they were as tied to the people as the people were tied to them. It was a benevolent dictatorship of a kind never seen before or since.

At the periphery of the Empire of the Sun-Child lived still unconquered savage tribes, which the Imperial forces were in the process of slowly taking over. During the centuries, tribe after tribe had fallen before the brilliant leadership of the Great Nobles and the territory of the Empire had slowly expanded until, at the time the invading Earthmen came, it covered almost as much territory as had the Roman Empire at its peak.

The Imperial Army, consisting of upwards of fifty thousand troops, was extremely mobile in spite of the handicap of having no form of transportation except their own legs. They had no cavalry; the only beasts of burden known to them—the flame-beasts—were too small to carry more than a hundred pounds, in spite of their endurance. But the wide, smooth roads that ran the length and breadth of the Empire enabled a marching army to make good time, and messages carried by runners in relays could traverse the Empire in a matter of days, not weeks.

And into this tight-knit, well-organized, powerful barbaric world marched Commander Frank with less than two hundred men and thirty carriers.

VI

It didn't take long for the men to begin to chafe under the constant strain of moving through treacherous and unfamiliar territory. And the first signs of chafing made themselves apparent beneath their armor.

Even the best designed armor cannot be built to be worn for an unlimited length of time, and, at first, the men could see no reason for the order. They soon found out.

One evening, after camp had been made, one young officer decided that he had spent his last night sleeping in full armor. It was bad enough to have to march in it, but sleeping in it was too much. He took it off and stretched, enjoying the freedom from the heavy steel. His tent was a long way from the center of camp, where a small fire flickered, and the soft light from the planet's single moon filtered only dimly through the jungle foliage overhead. He didn't think anyone would see him from the commander's tent.

The commander's orders had been direct and to the point: "You will wear your armor at all times; you will march in it, you will eat in it, you will sleep in it. During such times as it is necessary to remove a part of it, the man doing so will make sure that he is surrounded by at least two of his companions in full armor. There will be no exceptions to this rule!"

The lieutenant had decided to make himself an exception.

He turned to step into his tent when a voice came out of the nearby darkness.

"Hadn't you better get your steel plates back on before the commander sees you?"

The young officer turned quickly to see who had spoken. It was another of the junior officers.

"Mind your own business," snapped the lieutenant.

The other grinned sardonically. "And if I don't?"

There had been bad blood between these two for a long time; it was an enmity that went back to a time even before the expedition had begun. The two men stood there for a long moment, the light from the distant fire flickering uncertainly against their bodies.

The young officer who had removed his armor had not been foolish enough to remove his weapons too; no sane man did that in hostile territory. His hand went to the haft of the blade at his side.

"If you say a single word—"

Instinctively, the other dropped his hand to his own sword.

"Stop! Both of you!"

And stop they did; no one could mistake the crackling authority in that voice. The commander, unseen in the moving, dim light, had been circling the periphery of the camp, to make sure that all was well. He strode toward the two younger men, who stood silently, shocked into immobility. The commander's sword was already in his hand.

"I'll split the first man that draws a blade," he snapped.

His keen eyes took in the situation at a glance.

"Lieutenant, what are you doing out of armor?"

"It was hot, sir, and I—"

"Shut up!" The commander's eyes were dangerous. "An asinine statement like that isn't even worth listening to! Get that armor back on! *Move!*"

He was standing approximately between the two men, who had been four or five yards apart. When the cowed young officer took a step or two back toward his tent, the commander turned toward the other officer. "And as for you, if—"

He was cut off by the yell of the unarmored man, followed by the sound of his blade singing from its sheath.

The commander leaped backwards and spun, his own sword

at the ready, his body settling into a swordsman's crouch.

But the young officer was not drawing against his superior. He was hacking at something ropy and writhing that squirmed on the ground as the lieutenant's blade bit into it. Within seconds, the serpentine thing gave a convulsive shudder and died.

The lieutenant stepped back clumsily, his eyes glazing in the flickering light. "Dropped from th' tree," he said thickly. "Bit me."

His hand moved to a dark spot on his chest, but it never reached its goal. The lieutenant collapsed, crumpling to the ground.

The commander walked over, slammed the heel of his heavy boot hard down on the head of the snaky thing, crushing it. Then he returned his blade to its sheath, knelt down by the young man, and turned him over on his face.

The commander's own face was grim.

By this time, some of the nearby men, attracted by the yell, had come running. They came to a stop as they saw the tableau before them.

The commander, kneeling beside the corpse, looked up at them. With one hand, he gestured at the body. "Let this be a lesson to all of you," he said in a tight voice. "This man died because he took off his armor. That"—he pointed at the butchered reptile—"thing is full of as deadly a poison as you'll ever see, and it can move like lightning. *But it can't bite through steel!*

"Look well at this man and tell the others what you saw. I don't want to lose another man in this idiotic fashion."

He stood up and gestured.

"Bury him."

VII

They found, as they penetrated deeper into the savage-infested hinterlands of the Empire of the Great Nobles, that the armor fended off more than just snakes. Hardly a day passed but one or more of the men would hear the sharp *spang!* of a blowgun-driven dart as it slammed ineffectually against his armored back or chest. At first, some of the men wanted to charge into the surrounding forest, whence the darts came, and punish the sniping aliens, but the commander would have none of it.

"Stick together," he ordered. "They'll do worse to us if we're split up in this jungle. Those blowgun darts aren't going to hurt you as long as they're hitting steel. Ignore them and keep moving."

They kept moving.

Around them, the jungle chattered and muttered, and, occasionally, screamed. Clouds of insects, great and small, hummed and buzzed through the air. They subsided only when the drizzling rains came, and then lifted again from their resting places when the sun came out to raise steamy vapors from the moist ground.

It was not an easy march. Before many days had passed, the men's feet were cracked and blistered from the effects of fungus, dampness, and constant marching. The compact military marching order which had characterized the first few days of march had long since deteriorated into a straggling column, where the weaker were supported by the stronger.

Three more men died. One simply dropped in his tracks. He was dead before anyone could touch him. Insect bite? Disease? No one knew.

Another had been even less fortunate. A lionlike carnivore had leaped on him during the night and clawed him badly before one of his companions blasted the thing with a power weapon. Three days later, the wounded man was begging to be killed; one arm and one leg were gangrenous. But he died while begging, thus sparing any would-be executioner from an unpleasant duty.

The third man simply failed to show up for roll call one morning. He was never seen again.

But the rest of the column, with dauntless courage, followed the lead of their commander.

It was hard to read their expressions, those reddened eyes that peered at him from swollen, bearded faces. But he knew his own face looked no different.

"We all knew this wasn't going to be a fancy-dress ball when we came," he said. "Nobody said this was going to be the easiest way in the world to get rich."

The commander was sitting on one of the carriers, his eyes watching the men, who were lined up in front of him. His voice was purposely held low, but it carried well.

"The marching has been difficult, but now we're really going to see what we're made of.

"We all need a rest, and we all deserve one. But when I lie down to rest, I'm going to do it in a halfway decent bed, with some good, solid food in my belly.

"Here's the way the picture looks: An hour's march from here, there's a good-sized village." He swung partially away from them and pointed south. "I think we have earned that town and everything in it."

He swung back, facing them. There was a wolfish grin on his face. "There's gold there, too. Not much, really, compared with what we'll get later on, but enough to whet our appetites."

The men's faces were beginning to change now, in spite of the swelling.

"I don't think we need worry too much about the savages that are living there now. With God on our side, I hardly see how we can fail."

He went on, telling them how they would attack the town, the disposition of men, the use of the carriers, and so forth. By the time he was through, every man there was as eager as he to move in. When he finished speaking, they set up a cheer:

"For the Emperor and the Universal Assembly!"

The natives of the small village had heard that some sort of terrible beings were approaching through the jungle. Word had come from the people of the forest that the strange monsters were impervious to darts, and that they had huge dragons with them which were terrifying even to look at. They were clad in metal and made queer noises as they moved.

The village chieftain called his advisers together to ponder the situation. What should they do with these strange things? What were the invaders' intentions?

Obviously, the things must be hostile. Therefore, there were only two courses open—fight or flee. The chieftain and his men decided to fight. It would have been a good thing if there had only been some Imperial troops in the vicinity, but all the troops were farther south, where a civil war was raging over the right of succession of the Greatest Noble.

Nevertheless, there were two thousand fighting men in the village—well, two thousand men at any rate, and they would certainly all fight, although some were rather young and a few were too old for any really hard fighting. On the other hand, it would probably not come to that, since the strangers were outnumbered by at least three to one.

The chieftain gave his orders for the defense of the village.

The invading Earthmen approached the small town cautiously from the west. The commander had his men spread out a little, but not so much that they could be separated. He saw the aliens grouped around the square, boxlike buildings, watching and waiting for trouble.

"We'll give them trouble," the commander whispered softly. He waited until his troops were properly deployed, then he gave the signal for the charge.

The carriers went in first, thundering directly into the massed alien warriors. Each carrier-man fired a single shot from his power weapon, and then went to work with his carrier, running down the terrified aliens, and swinging a sword with one hand while he guided with the other. The commander went in with that first charge, aiming his own carrier toward the center of the fray. He had some raw, untrained men with him, and he believed in teaching by example.

The aliens recoiled at the onslaught of what they took to be horrible living monsters that were unlike anything ever seen before.

Then the commander's infantry charged in. The shock effect of the carriers had been enough to disorganize the aliens, but the battle was not over yet by a long shot.

There were yells from other parts of the village as some of the other defenders, hearing the sounds of battle, came running to reinforce the home guard. Better than fifteen hundred men were converging on the spot.

The invading Earthmen moved in rapidly against the armed natives, beating them back by the sheer ferocity of their attack. Weapons of steel clashed against weapons of bronze and wood.

The power weapons were used only sparingly; only when the necessity to save a life was greater than the necessity to conserve weapon charges was a shot fired.

The commander, from the center of the fray, took a glance around the area. One glance was enough.

"They're dropping back!" he bellowed, his voice carrying well above the din of the battle. "Keep 'em moving!" He singled out one of his officers at a distance, and yelled: "Hernan! Get a couple of men to cover that street!" He waved toward one of the narrow streets that ran off to one side. The others were already being attended to.

The commander jerked around swiftly as one of the natives grabbed hold of the carrier and tried to hack at the commander with a bronze sword. The commander spitted him neatly on his blade and withdrew it just in time to parry another attack from the other side.

By this time, the reinforcements from the other parts of the village were beginning to come in from the side streets, but they were a little late. The warriors in the square—what was left of them—had panicked. In an effort to get away from the terrible monsters with their deadly blades and their fire-spitting weapons, they were leaving by the same channels that the reinforcements were coming in by, and the resultant jam-up was disastrous. The panic communicated itself like wildfire, but no one could move fast enough to get away from the sweeping, stabbing, glittering blades of the invading Earthmen.

"All right," the commander yelled, "we've got 'em on the run now! Break up into squads of three and clear those streets! Clear 'em out! Keep 'em moving!"

After that, it was the work of minutes to clear the town.

The commander brought his carrier to a dead stop, reached out with his sword, and snagged a bit of cloth from one of the fallen native warriors. He began to wipe the blade of his weapon as Lieutenant Commander Hernan pulled up beside him.

"Casualties?" the commander asked Hernan without looking up from his work.

"Six wounded, no dead," said Hernan. "Or did you want me to count the aliens, too?"

The commander shook his head. "No. Get a detail to clear out the carrion, and then tell Frater Vincent I want to talk to him. We'll have to start teaching these people the Truth."

VIII

"Have you anything to say in your defense?" the commander asked coldly.

For a moment, the accused looked nothing but hatred at the commander, but there was fear behind that hatred. At last he found his voice. "It was mine. You promised us all a share."

Lieutenant Commander Hernan picked up a leather bag that lay on the table behind which he and the commander were sitting. With a sudden gesture, he upended it, dumping its contents on the flat, wooden surface of the table.

"No," said the accused soldier. "Why should I? It's mine. Rightfully mine. I fought for it. I found it. I kept it. It's mine." He glanced to either side, towards the two guards who flanked him, then looked back at the commander.

The commander ran an idle finger through the pound or so of golden trinkets that Hernan had spilled from the bag. He knew what the trooper was thinking. A man had a right to what he had earned, didn't he?

The commander picked up one of the heavier bits of primitive jewelry and tossed it in his hand. Then he stood up and looked around the town square.

The company had occupied the town for several weeks. The stored grains in the community warehouse, plus the relaxation the men had had, plus the relative security of the town, had put most of the men back into condition. One had died from a skin infection, and another from wounds sustained in the assault on the town, but the remainder were in good health.

And all of them, with the exception of the sentries guarding the town's perimeter, were standing in the square, watching the court-martial. Their eyes didn't seem to blink, and their breathing was soft and measured. They were waiting for the commander's decision.

The commander, still tossing the crude golden earring, stood tall and straight, estimating the feeling of the men surrounding him.

"Gold," he said finally. "Gold. That's what we came here for, and that's what we're going to get. Five hundred pounds of the stuff would make any one of you wealthy for the rest of his life. Do you think I blame any one of you for wanting it? Do you think I blame this man here? Of course not." He laughed—a short, hard bark. "Do I blame myself?"

He tossed the bauble again, caught it. "But wanting it is one thing; getting it, holding it, and taking care of it wisely are something else again.

"I gave orders. I have expected—and still expect—that they will be obeyed. But I didn't give them just to hear myself give orders. There was a reason, and a good one.

"Suppose we let each man take what gold he could find. What would happen? The lucky ones would be wealthy, and the unlucky would still be poor. And then some of the lucky ones would wake up some morning without the gold they'd taken because someone else had relieved them of it while they slept.

"And others wouldn't wake up at all, because they'd be found with their throats cut.

"I told you to bring every bit of the metal to me. When this thing is over, every one of you will get his share. If a man dies, his share will be split among the rest, instead of being stolen by someone else or lost because it was hidden too well."

He looked at the earring in his hand; then, with a convulsive sweep of his arm, he tossed it out into the middle of the square.

"There! Seven ounces of gold! Which of you wants it?"

Some of the men eyed the circle of metal that gleamed brightly on the sunlit ground, but none of them made any motion to pick it up.

"So." The commander's voice was almost gentle. He turned

his eyes back toward the accused. "You know the orders. You knew them when you hid this." He gestured negligently toward the small heap of native-wrought metal. "Suppose you'd gotten away with it. You'd have ended up with your own share, *plus* this, thereby cheating the others out of—" He glanced at the pile. "Hm-m-m—say, twenty-five each. And that's only a little compared with what we'll get from now on."

He looked back at the others. "Unless the shares are taken care of *my* way, the largest shares will go to the dishonest, the most powerful, and the luckiest. Unless the division is made as we originally agreed, we'll end up trying to cut each other's heart out."

There was hardness in his voice when he spoke to the accused, but there was compassion there, too.

"First: You have forfeited your share in this expedition. All that you have now, and all that you might have expected will be divided among the others according to our original agreement.

"Second: I do not expect any man to work for nothing. Since you will not receive anything from this expedition, there is no point in your assisting the rest of us or working with us in any way whatsoever.

"Third: We can't have anyone with us who does not carry his own weight."

He glanced at the guards. "Hang him." He paused. "Now."

As he was led away, the commander watched the other men. There was approval in their eyes, but there was something else there, too—a wariness, a concealed fear.

The condemned man turned suddenly and began shouting at the commander, but before he could utter more than three syllables, a fist smashed him down. The guards dragged him off.

"All right, men," said the commander carefully, "let's search the village. There might be more gold about; I have a hunch that this isn't all he hid. Let's see if we can find the rest of it." He sensed the relief of tension as he spoke.

The commander was right. It was amazing how much gold one man had been able to stash away.

IX

They couldn't stay long in any one village; they didn't have the time to sit and relax any more than was necessary. Once they had reached the northern marches of the native empire, it was to the commander's advantage to keep his men moving. He didn't know for sure how good or how rapid communications were among the various native provinces, but he had to assume that they were top-notch, allowing for the limitations of a barbaric society.

The worst trouble they ran into on their way was not caused by the native warriors, but by disease.

The route to the south was spotted by great strips of sandy barrenness, torn by winds that swept the grains of sand into the troopers' eyes and crept into the chinks of their armor. Underfoot, the sand made a treacherous pathway; carriers and men alike found it heavy going.

The heat from the sun was intense; the brilliant beams from the primary seemed to penetrate through the men's armor and through the insulation underneath, and made the marching even harder.

Even so, in spite of the discomfort, the men were making good time until the disease struck. And that stopped them in their tracks.

What the disease was or how it was spread is unknown and unknowable at this late date. Virus or bacterium, amoeba or fungus—whatever it was, it struck.

Symptoms: Lassitude, weariness, sickness, and pain.

Signs: Great, ulcerous, wartlike, blood-filled blisters that grew rapidly over the body.

A man might go to sleep at night feeling reasonably tired, but not ill, and wake up in the morning to find himself unable to rise, his muscles too weak to lift him from his bed.

If the blisters broke, or were lanced, it was almost impossible to stop the bleeding, and many died, not from the toxic effect of the disease itself, but from simple loss of blood.

But, like many epidemics, the thing had a fairly short life span. After two weeks, it had burned itself out. Most of those who got it recovered, and a few were evidently immune.

Eighteen men remained behind in shallow graves.

The rest went on.

X

No man is perfect. Even with four decades of training behind him, Commander Frank couldn't call the turn every time. After the first few villages, there were no further battles. The natives, having seen what the invaders could do, simply showed up missing when the commander and his men arrived. The villages were empty by the time the column reached the outskirts.

Frater Vincent, the agent of the Universal Assembly, complained in no uncertain terms about this state of affairs.

"As you know, commander," he said frowningly one morning, "it's no use trying to indoctrinate a people we can't contact. And you can't subject a people by force of arms alone; the power of the Truth—"

"I know, Frater," the commander interposed quickly. "But we can't deal with these savages in the hinterlands. When we get a little farther into this barbarian empire, we can take the necessary steps to—"

"The Truth," Frater Vincent interrupted somewhat testily, "is for all men. It works, regardless of the state of civilization of the society."

The commander looked out of the unglazed window of the native hut in which he had established his temporary headquarters, in one of the many villages he had taken—or, rather, walked into without a fight because it was empty. "But you'll admit, Frater, that it takes longer with savages."

"True," said Frater Vincent.

"We simply haven't the time. We've got to keep on the move. And, besides, we haven't even been able to contact any of the natives for quite a while; they get out of our way. And we have taken a few prisoners—" His voice was apologetic, but there was a trace of irritation in it. He didn't want to offend Frater Vincent, of course, but dammit, the Assemblyman didn't understand military tactics at all. Or, he corrected himself hastily, at least only slightly.

"Yes," admitted Frater Vincent, "and I've had considerable success with the prisoners. But, remember—we're not here just to indoctrinate a few occasional prisoners, but to change the entire moral and philosophical viewpoint of an entire race."

"I realize that, Frater," the commander admitted. He turned from the window and faced the Assemblyman. "We're getting close to the Great Bay now. That's where our ship landed on the second probing expedition. I expect we'll be more welcome there than we have been, out here in the countryside. We'll take it easy, and I think you'll have a chance to work with the natives on a mass basis."

The Frater smiled. "Excellent, commander. I...uh...want you to understand that I'm not trying to tell you your business; you run this campaign as you see fit. But don't lose sight of the ultimate goal of life."

"I won't. How could I? It's just that my methods are not, perhaps, as refined as yours."

Frater Vincent nodded, still smiling. "True. You are a great deal more direct. And—in your own way—just as effective. After all, the Assembly could not function without the military, but there were armies long before the Universal Assembly came into being."

The commander smiled back. "Not any armies like this, Frater."

Frater Vincent nodded. The understanding between the two men—at least on that point—was tacit and mutual. He traced a symbol in the air and left the commander to his thoughts.

Mentally, the commander went through the symbol-patterns that he had learned as a child—the symbol-patterns that brought him into direct contact with the Ultimate Power, the Power that controlled not only the spinning of atoms and the whirling of electrons in their orbits, but the workings of probability itself.

Once indoctrinated into the teachings of the Universal Assembly, any man could tap that Power to a greater or lesser degree, depending on his mental control and ethical attitude. At the top level, a first-class adept could utilize that Power for telepathy, psychokinesis, levitation, teleportation, and other powers that the commander only vaguely understood.

He, himself, had no such depth of mind, such iron control over his will, and he knew he'd never have it. But he could and did tap that Power to the extent that his physical body was under near-perfect control at all times, and not even the fear of death could shake his determination to win, or his great courage.

He turned again to the window and looked at the alien sky. There was a great deal yet to be done.

The commander needed information—needed it badly. He had to know what the government of the alien empire was doing. Had they been warned of his arrival? Surely they must have, and yet they had taken no steps to impede his progress.

For this purpose, he decided to set up headquarters on an island just offshore in the Great Bay. It was a protected position, easily defended from assault, and the natives, he knew from his previous visit, were friendly.

They even helped him to get his men and equipment and the carriers across on huge rafts.

From that point, he began collecting the information he needed to invade the central domains of the Greatest Noble himself. It seemed an ideal spot—not only protection-wise, but because this was the spot he had originally picked for the landing of the ship. The vessel, which had returned to the base for reinforcements and extra supplies, would be aiming for the Great Bay area when she came back. And there was little likelihood that atmospheric disturbances would throw her off course again; Captain Bartholomew was too good a man to be fooled twice.

But landing on that island was the first—and only—mistake the commander made during the campaign. The rumors of internal bickerings among the Great Nobles of the barbarian empire were not the only rumors he heard. News of more local treachery came to his ears through the agency of natives, now loyal to the commander, who had been indoctrinated into the philosophy of the Assembly.

A group of native chieftains had decided that the invading Earthmen were too dangerous to be allowed to remain on their island, in spite of the fact that the invaders had done them no harm. There were, after all, whisperings from the north, whence the invaders had come, that the armored beings with the terrible weapons had used their power more than once during their march to the south. The chieftains were determined to rid their island of the potential menace.

As soon as the matter was brought to the commander's attention, he acted. He sent out a patrol to the place where the ringleaders were meeting, arrested them, and sentenced them to death. He didn't realize what effect that action would have on the rest of the islanders.

He almost found out too late.

XI

"There must be three thousand of them out there," said Lieutenant Commander Hernan tightly, "and every one of them's crazy."

"Rot!" The commander spat on the ground and then sighted again along the barrel of his weapon. "I'm the one who's crazy. I'm a lousy politician; that's my trouble."

The lieutenant commander shrugged lightly. "Anyone can make a mistake. Just chalk it up to experience."

"I will, when we get out of this mess." He watched the gathering natives through hard, slitted eyes.

The invading Earthmen were in a village at the southern end of the eight-mile-long island, waiting inside the mud-brick huts, while the natives who had surrounded the village worked themselves into a frenzy for an attack. The commander knew there was no sense in charging into them at that point; they would simply scatter and reassemble. The only thing to do was wait until they attacked—and then smash the attack.

"Hernan," he said, his eyes still watching the outside, "you and the others get out there with the carriers after the first volley. Cut them down. They're twenty-to-one against us, so make every blow count. Move."

Hernan nodded wordlessly and slipped away.

The natives were building up their courage with some sort of war dance, whooping and screaming and making threatening gestures toward the embattled invaders. Then the pattern of the dance changed; the islanders whirled to face the mud-brick buildings which housed the invading Earthmen. Suddenly, the dance broke, and the warriors ran in a screaming charge, straight for the trapped soldiers.

The commander waited. His own shot would be the signal, and he didn't want the men to fire too quickly. If the islanders were hit too soon, they might fall back into the woods and set up a siege, which the little company couldn't stand. Better to mop up the natives now, if possible.

Closer. Closer—

Now!

The commander's first shot picked off one of the leaders in the front ranks of the native warriors, and was followed by a raking volley from the other power weapons, firing from the windows of the mud-brick buildings. The warriors in the front rank dropped, and those in the second rank had to move adroitly to keep from stumbling over the bodies of their fallen fellows. The firing from the huts became ragged, but its raking effect was still deadly. A cloud of heavy, stinking smoke rolled across the clearing between the edge of the jungle and the village, as the bright, hard lances of heat leaped from the muzzles of the power weapons toward the bodies of the charging warriors.

The charge was gone from the commander's weapon, and he didn't bother to replace it. As Hernan and his men charged into the melee with their carriers, the commander went with them.

At the same time, the armored infantrymen came pouring out of the mud-brick houses, swinging their swords, straight into the mass of confused native warriors. A picked group of sharp-shooters remained behind in the concealment of the huts to pick off the warriors at the edge of the battle with their sporadic fire.

The commander's lips were moving a little as he formed the symbol-patterns of power almost unconsciously; a lifetime of habit had burned them into his brain so deeply that he could form them automatically while turning the thinking part of his mind to the business at hand.

116

He soon found himself entirely surrounded by the alien warriors. Their bronze weapons glittered in the sunlight as they tried to fight off the onslaught of the invaders. And those same bronze weapons were sheared, nicked, blunted, bent, and broken as they met the harder steel of the commander's sword.

Then the unexpected happened. One of the warriors, braver than the rest, made a grab for the commander's sword arm. At almost the same moment, a warrior on the other side of the carrier aimed a spear thrust at his side.

Either by itself would have been ineffectual. The spear clanged harmlessly from the commander's armor, and the warrior who had attempted to pull him from the carrier died before he could give much of a tug. But the combination, plus the fact that the heavy armor was a little unwieldy, overbalanced him. He toppled to the ground with a clash of steel as he and the carrier parted company.

Without a human hand at its controls, the carrier automatically moved away from the mass of struggling fighters and came to a halt well away from the battle.

The commander rolled as he hit and leaped to his feet, his sword moving in flickering arcs around him. The natives had no knowledge of effective swordplay. Like any barbarians, they conceived of a sword as a cutting instrument rather than a thrusting one. They chopped with them, using small shields to protect their bodies as they tried to hack the commander to bits.

But the commander had no desire to become mincemeat just yet. Five of the barbarians were coming at him, their swords raised for a downward slash. The commander lunged forward with a straight stop-thrust aimed at the groin of the nearest one. It came as a complete surprise to the warrior, who doubled up in pain.

The commander had already withdrawn his blade and was attacking the second as the first fell. He made another feint to the groin and then changed the aim of his point as the warrior tried to cover with his shield. A buckler is fine protection against a man who is trying to hack you to death with a chopper, because a heavy cutting sword and a shield have about the same inertia, and thus the same maneuverability. But the shield isn't worth anything against a light stabbing weapon. The warrior's shield started downward and he was unable to stop it and reverse its direction before the commander's sword pierced his throat.

Two down, three to go. No, four. Another warrior had decided to join the little battle against the leader of the invading Earthmen.

The commander changed his tactics just slightly with the third man. He slashed with the tip of his blade against the descending sword-arm of his opponent—a short, quick flick of his wrist that sheared through the inside of the wrist, severing tendons, muscles, veins and arteries as it cut to the bone. The sword clanged harmlessly off the commander's shoulder. A quick thrust, and the third man died.

The other three slowed their attack and began circling warily, trying to get behind the commander. Instead of waiting, he charged forward, again cutting at the sword arm of his adversary, severing fingers this time. As the warrior turned, the commander's sword pierced his side.

How long it went on, he had no idea. He kept his legs and his sword-arm moving, and his eyes ever alert for new foes as man after man dropped beneath that snake-tonguing blade. Inside his armor, perspiration poured in rivulets down his skin, and his arms and legs began to ache, but not for one second did he let up. He could not see what was going on, could not tell the direction of the battle nor even allow his mind to wonder what was going on more than ten paces from him.

And then, quite suddenly, it seemed, it was all over. Lieutenant commander Hernan and five other men pulled up with their carriers, as if from nowhere, their weapons dealing death, clearing a space around their commander.

"You hurt?" bawled Hernan.

The commander paused to catch his breath. He knew there was a sword-slash across his face, and his right leg felt as though there was a cut on it, but otherwise—

"I'm all right," he said. "How's it going?"

"They're breaking," Hernan told him. "We'll have them scattered within minutes."

Even as he spoke, the surge of battle moved away from them, toward the forest. The charge of the carriers, wreaking havoc on every side, had broken up the battle formation the aliens had had; the flaming death from the horrible weapons of the invaders, the fearless courage of the foot soldiers, and the steel-clad monsters that were running amuck among them shattered the little discipline they had. Panicky, they lost their anger, which had taken them several hours to build up. They scattered, heading for the forest.

Shortly, the village was silent. Not an alien warrior was to be seen save for the hundreds of mute corpses that testified to the carnage that had been wrought.

Several of the commander's men had been wounded, and three had died. Lieutenant Commander Hernan had been severely wounded in the leg by a native javelin, but the injury was a long way from being fatal.

Hernan gritted his teeth while his leg was being bandaged. "The angels were with us on that one," he said between winces.

The commander nodded. "I hope they stick with us. We'll need 'em to get off this island."

XII

For a while, it looked as though they were trapped on the island. The natives didn't dare to attack again, but no hunting party was safe, and the food supply was dropping. They had gotten on the island only by the help of the natives, who had ferried them over on rafts. But getting off was another thing, now that the natives were hostile. Cutting down trees to build rafts might possibly be managed, but during the loading the little company would be too vulnerable to attack.

The commander was seated bleakly in the hut he had taken as his headquarters, trying to devise a scheme for getting to the mainland, when the deadlock was finally broken.

There was a flurry of footsteps outside, a thump of heavy boots as one of the younger officers burst into the room.

"Commander!" he yelled. "Commander! Come outside!"

The commander leaped to his feet. "Another attack?"

"No, sir! Come look!"

The commander strode quickly to the door. His sight followed the line of the young officer's pointing finger.

There, outlined against the blue of the sky, was a ship!

The news from home was encouraging, but it was a long way from being what the commander wanted. Another hundred men and more carriers had been added to the original company of now hardened veterans, and the recruits, plus the protection of the ship's guns, were enough to enable the entire party to leave the island for the mainland.

By this time, the commander had gleaned enough information from the natives to be able to plan the next step in his campaign. The present Greatest Noble, having successfully usurped the throne from his predecessor, was still not in absolute control of the country. He had won a civil war, but his rule was still too shaky to allow him to split up his armies, which accounted for the fact that, thus far, no action had been taken by the Imperial troops against the invading Earthmen.

The commander set up a base on the mainland, near the coast, left a portion of his men there to defend it, and, with the remainder, marched inland to come to grips with the Greatest Noble himself.

As they moved in toward the heart of the barbarian empire, the men noticed a definite change in the degree of civilization of the natives—or, at least, in the degree of technological advancement. There were large towns, not small villages, to be dealt with, and there were highways and bridges that showed a knowledge of engineering equivalent to that of ancient Rome.

The engineers of the Empire of the Great Nobles were a long way above the primitive. They could have, had they had any reason to, erected a pyramid the equal of great Khufu's in size, and probably even more neatly constructed. Militarily speaking, the lack of knowledge of iron hampered them, but it must be kept in mind that a well-disciplined and reasonably large army, armed with bronze-tipped spears, bronze swords, axes, and maces, can make a formidable foe, even against a much better equipped group.

The Imperial armies were much better disciplined and much better armed than any of the natives the commander had thus far dealt with, and there were reputed to be more than ten thousand of them with the Greatest Noble in his mountain stronghold. Such considerations prompted the commander to plan his strategy carefully, but they did not deter him in the least. If he had been able to bring aircraft and perhaps a thermonuclear bomb or two for demonstration purposes, the attack might have been less risky, but neither had been available to a man of his limited means, so he had to work without them.

But now, he avoided fighting if at all possible. Working with Frater Vincent, the commander worked to convince the natives on the fertile farms and in the prosperous villages that he and his company were merely ambassadors of good will—missionaries and traders. He and his men had come in peace, and if they were received in peace, well and good. If not . . . well, they still had their weapons.

The commander was depending on the vagueness of the information that may have filtered down from the north. The news had already come that the invaders were fierce and powerful fighters, but the commander gave the impression that the only reason any battles had taken place was because the northern tribes had been truculent in the extreme. He succeeded fairly well; the natives he now met considered their brethren of the northern provinces to be little better than savages, and therefore to be expected to treat strangers inhospitably and bring about their own ruin. The southern citizens of the empire eyed the strangers with apprehension, but they offered very little resistance. The commander and his men were welcomed warily at each town, and, when they left, were bid farewell with great relief.

It took a little time for the commander to locate the exact spot where the Greatest Noble and his retinue were encamped. The real capital of the empire was located even farther south, but the Greatest Noble was staying, for the nonce, in a city nestled high in the mountains, well inland from the seacoast. The commander headed for the mountains.

The passage into the mountains wasn't easy. The passes were narrow and dangerous, and the weather was cold. The air became thinner at every step. At eight thousand feet, mountain climbing in heavy armor becomes more than just hard work, and at twelve thousand it becomes exhausting torture. But the little company went on, sparked, fueled, and driven by the personal force of their commander, who stayed in the vanguard, his eyes ever alert for treachery from the surrounding mountains.

When the surprise came, it was of an entirely different kind than he had expected. The commander's carrier came over a little rise, and he brought it to an abrupt halt as he saw the valley spread out beneath him. He left the carrier, walked over to a boulder near the edge of the cliff, and looked down at the valley.

It was an elongated oval of verdant green, fifteen miles long by four wide, looking like an emerald set in the rocky granite of the surrounding peaks that thrust upward toward the sky. The valley ran roughly north-and-south, and to his right, at the southern end, the commander could see a city, although it was impossible to see anyone moving in it at this distance.

To his left, he could see great clouds of billowing vapor that rolled across the grassy plain—evidently steam from the volcanic hot springs which he had been told were to be found in this valley.

But, for the moment, it was neither the springs nor the city that interested him most.

In the heart of the valley, spreading over acre after acre, were the tents and pavilions of a mighty army encampment. From the looks of it, the estimate of thirty thousand troops which had been given him by various officials along the way was, if anything, too small.

It was a moment that might have made an ordinary man stop to think, and, having thought, to turn and go. But the commander was no ordinary man, and the sheer remorseless courage that had brought him this far wouldn't allow him to turn back. So far, he had kept the Greatest Noble off balance with his advancing tactics; if he started to retreat, the Greatest Noble would realize that the invaders were not invincible, and would himself advance to crush the small band of strangers.

The Greatest Noble had known the commander and his men were coming; he was simply waiting to find out what they were up to, confident that he could dispose of them at his leisure. The commander knew that, and he knew he couldn't retreat now. There was no decision to be made, really—only planning to be done.

He turned back from the boulder to face the officers who had come to take a look at the valley.

"We'll go to the city first," he said.

XIII

The heavy tread of the invaders' boots as they entered the central plaza of the walled city awakened nothing but echoes from the stone walls that surrounded the plaza. Like the small villages they had entered farther north, the city seemed devoid of life.

There is nothing quite so depressing and threatening as a deserted city. The windows in the walls of the buildings seemed like blank, darkened eyes that watched—and waited. Nothing moved, nothing made a sound, except the troopers themselves.

The men kept close to the walls; there was no point in bunching up in the middle of the square to be cut down by arrows from the windows of the upper floors.

The commander ordered four squads of men to search the buildings and smoke out anyone who was there, but they turned up nothing. The entire city was empty. And there were no traps, no ambushes—nothing.

The commander, with Lieutenant Commander Hernan and another officer, climbed to the top of the central building of the town. In the distance, several miles away, they could see the encampment of the monarch's troops.

"The only thing we can do," the commander said, his face hard and determined, "is to call their bluff. You two take about three dozen men and go out there with the carriers and give them a show. Go right into camp, as if you owned the place. Throw a scare into them, but don't hurt anyone. Then, very politely, tell the Emperor, or whatever he calls himself, that I would like him to come here for dinner and a little talk."

The two officers looked at each other, then at the commander.

"Just like that?" asked Hernan.

"Just like that," said the commander.

The demonstration and exhibition went well—as far as it had gone. The native warriors had evidently been quite impressed by the onslaught of the terrifying monsters that had thundered across the plain toward them, right into the great camp, and come to a dead halt directly in front of the magnificent pavilion of the Greatest Noble himself.

The Greatest Noble put up a good face. He had obviously been expecting the visitors, because he and his lesser nobles were lined up before the pavilion, the Greatest Noble ensconced on a sort of portable throne. He managed to look perfectly calm and somewhat bored by the whole affair, and didn't seem to be particularly affected at all when Lieutenant Commander Hernan bowed low before him and requested his presence in the city.

And the Greatest Noble's answer was simple and to the point, although it was delivered by one of his courtiers.

"You may tell your commander," said the noble, "that His Effulgence must attend to certain religious duties tonight, since he is also High Priest of the Sun. However, His Effulgence will most graciously deign to speak to your commander tomorrow. In the meantime, you are requested to enjoy His Effulgence's gracious hospitality in the city, which has been emptied for your convenience. It is yours, for the nonce."

Which left nothing for the two officers and their men to do but go thundering back across the plain to the city.

The Greatest Noble did not bring his whole army with him, but the pageant of barbaric splendor that came tootling and drumming its way into the city the next evening was a magnificent sight. His Effulgence himself was dressed in a scarlet robe and a scarlet, turbanlike headcovering with scarlet fringes all around it. About his throat was a necklace of emerald-green gems, and his clothing was studded with more of them. Gold gleamed everywhere. He was borne on an ornate, gilded palanquin, carried high above the crowd on the shoulders of a dozen stalwart nobles, only slightly less gorgeously-dressed than the Greatest Noble. The nobility that followed was scarcely less showy in its finery.

When they came into the plaza, however, the members of the procession came to a halt. The singing and music died away.

The plaza was absolutely empty.

No one had come out to greet the Emperor.

There were six thousand natives in the plaza, and not a sign of the invaders.

The commander, hiding well back in the shadows in one of the rooms of the central building, watched through the window and noted the evident consternation of the royal entourage with satisfaction. Frater Vincent, standing beside him, whispered, "Well?"

"All right," the commander said softly, "they've had a taste of what we got when we came in. I suppose they've had enough. Let's go out and act like hosts."

The commander and a squad of ten men, along with Frater Vincent, strode majestically out of the door of the building and walked toward the Greatest Noble. They had all polished their armor until it shone, which was about all they could do in the way of finery, but they evidently looked quite impressive in the eyes of the natives.

"Greetings, Your Effulgence," said the commander, giving the Greatest Noble a bow that was hardly five degrees from the perpendicular. "I trust we find you well."

In the buildings surrounding the square, hardly daring to

move for fear the clank of metal on metal might give the whole plan away, the remaining members of the company watched the conversation between their commander and the Greatest Noble. They couldn't hear what was being said, but that didn't matter; they knew what to do as soon as the commander gave the signal. Every eye was riveted on the commander's right hand.

It seemed an eternity before the commander casually reached up to his helmet and brushed a hand across it—once—twice—three times.

Then all hell broke loose. The air was split by the sound of power weapons throwing their lances of flame into the massed ranks of the native warriors. The gunners, safe behind the walls of the buildings, poured a steady stream of accurately directed fire into the packed mob, while the rest of the men charged in with their blades, thrusting and slashing as they went.

The aliens, panic-stricken by the sudden, terrifying assault, tried to run, but there was nowhere to run to. Every exit had been cut off to bottle up the Imperial cortege. Within minutes, the entrances to the square were choked with the bodies of those who tried to flee.

As soon as the firing began, the commander and his men began to make their way toward the Greatest Noble. They had been forced to stand a good five yards away during the parlay, cut off from direct contact by the Imperial guards. The commander, sword in hand, began cutting his way through to the palanquin.

The palanquin bearers seemed frozen; they couldn't run, they couldn't fight, and they didn't dare drop their precious cargo.

The commander's voice bellowed out over the carnage. "Take him prisoner! I'll personally strangle the idiot who harms him!" And then he was too busy to yell.

Two members of the Greatest Noble's personal guard came for him, swords out, determined to give their lives, if necessary, to preserve the sacred life of their monarch. And give them they did.

The commander's blade lashed out once, sliding between the ribs of the first guard. He toppled and almost took the sword with him, but the commander wrenched it free in time to parry the downward slash of the second guard's bronze sword. It was a narrow thing, because the bronze sword, though of softer stuff than the commander's steel, was also heavier, and thus hard to deflect. As it sang past him, the commander swung a chop at the man's neck, cutting it halfway through. He stepped quickly to one side to avoid the falling body and thrust his blade through a third man, who was aiming a blow at the neck of one of the commander's officers. There were only a dozen feet separating the commander from his objective, the palanquin of the Greatest Noble, but he had to wade through blood to get there.

The palanquin itself was no longer steady. Three of the twelve nobles who had been holding it had already fallen, and there were two of the commander's men already close enough to touch the royal person, but they were too busy fighting to make any attempt to grab him. The Greatest Noble, unarmed, could only huddle in his seat, terrified, but it would take more than two men to snatch him from his bodyguard. The commander fought his way in closer.

Two more of the palanquin bearers went down, and the palanquin itself began to topple. The Greatest Noble screamed as he fell toward the commander.

One of the commander's men spun around as he heard the scream so close to him, and, thinking that the Greatest Noble was attacking his commander, lunged out with his blade.

It was almost a disaster. Moving quickly, the commander threw out his left arm to deflect the sword. He succeeded, but he got a bad slash across his hand for his trouble.

He yelled angrily at the surprised soldier, not caring what he said. Meanwhile, the others of the squad, seeing that the Greatest Noble had fallen, hurried to surround him. Two minutes later, the Greatest Noble was a prisoner, being half carried, half led into the central building by four of the men, while the remaining six fought a rear-guard action to hold off the native warriors who were trying to rescue the sacred person of the Child of the Sun.

Once inside, the Greatest Noble was held fast while the doors were swung shut.

Outside, the slaughter went on. All the resistance seemed to go out of the warriors when they saw their sacred monarch dragged away by the invading Earthmen. It was every man for himself and the Devil take the hindmost. And the Devil, in the form of the commander's troops, certainly did.

Within half an hour after it had begun, the butchery was over. More than three thousand of the natives had died, and an unknown number more had been badly wounded. Those who had managed to get out and get away from the city kept on going. They told the troops who had been left outside what had happened, and a mass exodus from the valley began.

Safely within the fortifications of the central building, the commander allowed himself one of his rare grins of satisfaction. Not a single one of his own men had been killed, and the only wound which had been sustained by anyone in the company was the cut on his own hand. Still smiling, he went into the room where the Greatest Noble, dazed and shaken, was being held by two of the commander's men. The commander bowed—this time, very low.

"I believe, Your Effulgence, that we have an appointment for dinner. Come, the banquet has been laid."

And, as though he were still playing the gracious host, the commander led the half-paralyzed Child of the Sun to the room where the banquet had been put on a table in perfect diplomatic array.

"Your Effulgence may sit at my right hand," said the commander pleasantly.

XIV

As MacDonald said of Robert Wilson, "This is not an account of how Boosterism came to Arcadia." It's a devil of a long way from it. And once the high point of a story has been reached and passed, it is pointless to prolong it too much. The capture of the Greatest Noble broke the power of the Empire of the Great Nobles forever. The loyal subjects were helpless without a leader, and the disloyal ones, near the periphery of the Empire, didn't care. The crack Imperial troops simply folded up and went home. The Greatest Noble went on issuing orders, and they were obeyed; the people were too used to taking orders from authority to care whether they were really the Greatest Noble's own idea or not.

In a matter of months, two hundred men had conquered an empire, with a loss of thirty-five or forty men. Eventually, they had to execute the old Greatest Noble and put his more tractable nephew on the throne, but that was a mere incident.

Gold? It flowed as though there were an endless supply. The commander shipped enough back on the first load to make them all wealthy.

The commander didn't go back home to spend his wealth amid the luxuries of the Imperial court, even though Emperor Carl appointed him to the nobility. That sort of thing wasn't the commander's meat. There, he would be a fourth-rate noble; here, he was the Imperial Viceroy, responsible only to the distant Emperor. There, he would be nothing; here, he was almost a king.

Two years after the capture of the Greatest Noble, he established a new capital on the coast and named it Kingston. And from Kingston he ruled with an iron hand.

As has been intimated, this was *not* Arcadia. A year after the founding of Kingston, the old capital was attacked, burned, and almost fell under siege, due to a sudden uprising of the natives under the new Greatest Noble, who had managed to escape. But the uprising collapsed because of the approach of the planting season; the warriors had to go back home and plant their crops or the whole of the agriculture-based country would starve—except the invading Earthmen.

Except in a few instances, the natives were never again any trouble.

But the commander—now the Viceroy—had not seen the end of his troubles.

He had known his limitations, and realized that the governing of a whole planet—or even one continent—was too much for one man when the population consists primarily of barbarians and savages. So he had delegated the rule of a vast area to the south to another—a Lieutenant Commander James, known as "One-Eye," a man who had helped finance the original expedition, and had arrived after the conquest.

One-Eye went south and made very small headway against the more barbaric tribes there. He did not become rich, and he did not achieve anywhere near the success that the Viceroy had. So he came back north with his army and decided to unseat the Viceroy and take his place. That was five years after the capture of the Greatest Noble.

One-Eye took Center City, the old capital, and started to work his way northward, toward Kingston. The Viceroy's forces met him at a place known as Salt Flats and thoroughly trounced him. He was captured, tried for high treason, and executed.

One would think that the execution ended the threat of Lieutenant Commander James, but not so. He had a son, and he had followers.

XV

Nine years. Nine years since the breaking of a vast empire. It really didn't seem like it. The Viceroy looked at his hands. They were veined and thin, and the callouses were gone. Was he getting soft, or just getting old? A little bit—no, *a great deal* of both.

He sat in his study, in the Viceregal Palace at Kingston, chewing over the events of the past weeks. Twice, rumors had come that he was to be assassinated. He and two of his councilors had been hanged in effigy in the public square not long back. He had been snubbed publicly by some of the lesser nobles.

Had he ruled harshly, or was it just jealousy? And was it,

really, as some said, caused by the Southerners and the followers of Young Jim?

He didn't know. And sometimes, it seemed as if it didn't matter.

Here he was, sitting alone in his study, when he should have gone to a public function. And he had stayed because of fear of assassination.

Was it—

There was a knock at the door.

"Come in."

A servant entered. "Sir Martin is here, my lord."

The Viceroy got to his feet. "Show him in, by all means."

Sir Martin, just behind the servant, stepped in, smiling, and the Viceroy returned his smile. "Well, everything went off well enough without you," said Sir Martin.

"Any sign of trouble?"

"None, my lord; none whatsoever. The—"

"Damn!" the Viceroy interrupted savagely. "I should have known! What have I done but display my cowardice? I'm getting yellow in my old age!"

Sir Martin shook his head. "Cowardice, my lord? Nothing of the sort. Prudence, I should call it. By the by, the judge and a few others are coming over." He chuckled softly. "We thought we might talk you out of a meal."

The Viceroy grinned widely. "Nothing easier. I suspected all you hangers-on would come around for your handouts. Come along, my friend; we'll have a drink before the others get here."

There were nearly twenty people at dinner, all, presumably, friends of the Viceroy. At least, it is certain that they were friends in so far as they had no part in the assassination plot. It was a gay party; the Viceroy's friends were doing their best to cheer him up, and were succeeding pretty well. One of the nobles, known for his wit, had just essayed a somewhat off-color jest, and the others were roaring with laughter at the punch line when a shout rang out.

There was a sudden silence around the table.

"What was that?" asked someone. "What did—"

"*Help!*" There was the sound of footsteps pounding up the stairway from the lower floor.

"*Help! The Southerners have come to kill the Viceroy!*"

From the sounds, there was no doubt in any of the minds of the people seated around the table that the shout was true. For a moment, there was shock. Then panic took over.

There were only a dozen or so men in the attacking party; if the "friends" of the Viceroy had stuck by him, they could have held off the assassins with ease.

But no one ran to lock the doors that stood between the Viceroy and his enemies, and only a few drew their weapons to defend him. The others fled. Getting out of a window from the second floor of a building isn't easy, but fear can lend wings, and, although none of them actually flew down, the retreat went fast enough.

Characteristically, the Viceroy headed, not for the window, but for his own room where his armor—long unused, except for state functions—hung waiting in the closet. With him went Sir Martin.

But there wasn't even an opportunity to get into the armor. The rebel band charged into the hallway that led to the bedroom, screaming: *"Death to the Tyrant! Long live the Emperor!"*

It was personal anger, then, not rebellion against the Empire which had appointed the ex-commander to his post as Viceroy.

"Where is the Viceroy? Death to the Tyrant!" The assassins moved in.

Swords in hand, and cloaks wrapped around their left arms, Sir Martin and the Viceroy moved to meet the oncoming attackers.

"Traitors!" bellowed the Viceroy. "Cowards! Have you come to kill me in my own house?"

Parry, thrust! Parry, thrust! Two of the attackers fell before the snake-tongue blade of the fighting viceroy. Sir Martin accounted for two more before he fell in a flood of his own blood.

The Viceroy was alone, now. His blade flickered as though inspired, and two more died under its tireless onslaught. Even more would have died if the head of the conspiracy, a supporter of Young Jim named Rada, hadn't pulled a trick that not even the Viceroy would have pulled.

Rada grabbed one of his own men and shoved him toward the Viceroy's sword, impaling the hapless man upon that deadly blade.

And, in the moment while the Viceroy's weapon was buried to the hilt in an enemy's body, the others leaped around the dying man and ran their blades through the Viceroy.

He dropped to the floor, blood gushing from half a dozen wounds.

Even so, his fighting heart still had seconds more to beat. As he propped himself up on one arm, the assassins stood back; even they recognized that they had killed something bigger and stronger than they. A better man than any of them lay dying at their feet.

He clawed with one hand at the river of red that flowed from his pierced throat and then fell forward across the stone floor. With his crimson hand, he traced the great symbol of his Faith on the stone—the Sign of the Cross. He bent his head to kiss it, and, with a final cry of "*Jesus!*" he died. At the age of seventy, it had taken a dozen men to kill him with treachery, something all the hell of nine years of conquest and rule had been unable to do.

And thus died Francisco Pizarro, the Conqueror of Peru.

Despoilers is, of course, a takeoff on history. It was actually the brainchild of John W. Campbell, Jr., the great editor who guided Astounding Science Fiction *from 1938, through its metamorphosis into* Analog *in 1962, until his untimely death in 1971.*

I was in his office one day, and he said: "There may be supermen in the future; have there ever been any in the past?"

Anyone who ever worked with John knows that that was a trick question. It, and others like it, were designed to make one think.

I hedged. (We all did.) "It's possible."

"Possible?" He sniffed. "Historical evidence shows that it was true."

I, of course, was thinking of "superman" in terms of Kimball Kinnison, Jommy Cross, or even Clark Kent. "You mean Biblical—"

"I mean historical. Four hundred years ago!" He paused. Then, in a low voice: "Do you realize that less than five hundred men conquered the Empire of Peru?"

Well—hell—with that to go on, what else could I do but write the story?

THE HORROR OUT OF TIME

H. P. Lovecraft was a master at writing creepy horror. Those who know him—among them Robert Bloch and Donald Wollheim —were aware of his horror of the sea and the things that lived in it.

This story is dedicated to H. P., Robert, and Don, to assure them that there are more horrid things beneath the sea than Chthulu.

It all depends on your viewpoint.

By Randall Garrett

It has been more than thirty years now since I saw that terrifying thing in the crypt-like temple, but I remember it as clearly, and with all the horror, as if I had seen it but an hour ago.

In those days, twenty years before the turn of the century, the sailing ship still held sway over most of the world's waters; now, the steam-driven vessels cover in days distances that took months. All that no longer matters to me; I have not been abroad since I returned from that South Sea voyage, still weak from fever and delirium, over thirty years ago.

I think that before the end of this new century, scientific researchers will have proven as fact things which I already know to be true. What facts lie behind the mysteries of certain megalithic ruined cities found buried beneath the shifting sands on three separate continents? Are they merely the constructs of our prehistoric ancestors? Or are they much older than we know, the products of some primal race, perhaps from this planet, perhaps from another, far distant in space? The latter sounds wild, phantastick, perhaps even...mad, but I believe it to be true, and mayhap this narrative will be of some service to those researchers who already suspect the truth. Long before our ancestors discovered the use of fire, even before they had evolved beyond animal form and intellect, there were beings of vast power and malignant intelligence who ruled supreme over this planet.

I have always been a person of leisure, spending my time in historical research, in reading books on philosophy, both natural and metaphysical, and in writing what I believe to be scholarly articles for various learned journals. When I was younger, I was more adventurous; I travelled a great deal, not only to read and research in the great universities of the world, but to do original research in hidden places of the earth, where few learned folk have gone. I was fearless then; neither the rotten foetidness of tropic jungles, nor the arid heat of harsh deserts, nor the freezing cold of polar regions daunted me.

Until the summer of my twenty-sixth year.

I was aboard the *White Moon*, sailing homeward through the South Seas, after having spent some months exploring the ancient ruins on one of the larger islands. (Their age can be measured in mere centuries; they have nothing to do with the present narrative.)

During the time I had been aboard, I had become quite friendly with Captain Bork, the commander of the three-masted vessel. He was a heavy-set, bluff, hearty fellow, an excellent ship's officer, and well-read in many subjects far divergent from mere nautical lore. Although self-educated, his behavior was that of one gently born, far above that of the common sailor of the day. He was perhaps a dozen years older than I, but we spent many an hour during that tedious journey discussing various subjects, and I dare say I learned as much from him as he learned from me. We became, I think, good friends.

One evening, I recall, we sat up rather late in his cabin, discoursing on daemonology.

"I'm not a superstitious chap, myself, sir," said he, "but I will tell you that there are things take place at sea that could never happen on land. Things I couldn't explain if I tried."

"And you attribute them to non-material spirits, Captain?" I asked. "Surely not."

In the dim light shed by the oil-lamp swinging gently overhead, his face took on a solemn expression. "Not spirits, perhaps, sir. No, not spirits exactly. Something...else."

I became interested. I knew the captain's sincerity, and I knew that, whatever he had to tell me, it would be told as he knew it to be.

"What, then, if not spirits?" I asked.

He looked broodingly out the porthole of his cabin. "I don't really know," he said slowly in his low, rumbling voice, staring out at the moonless sea-night. After a moment, he looked back at me, but there was no change in his expression. "I don't really know," he repeated. "It may be daemons or spirits or whatever, but it's not the feeling one gets in a graveyard, if you see what I mean. It's different, somehow. It's as if there were something down *there*—"

And he pointed straight downward, as though he were directing my attention down past the deck, past the hull, to the dreadful black sea-bottom so far beneath. I could say nothing.

"*Way* down there," he continued solemnly. "There is something *old* down there—something old, but living. It is far older than we can know. It goes far back beyond the dawn of time. But it is there and it...*waits*."

A feeling of revulsion came over me—not against the captain, but against the sea itself, and I realized that I, too, had felt that nameless fear without knowing it.

But of course I could not fall prey to that weird feeling.

"Come, Captain," said I, in what I hoped was a pleasant tone, "this is surely your imagination. What intelligence could live at the bottom of the sea?"

He looked at me for a long moment, then his countenance changed. There was a look of forced cheerfulness upon his broad face. "Aye, sir; you're right. A person gets broody at sea, that's all. I fear I've been at sea too long. Have to take a long rest ashore, I will. I've been planning a month in port, and it'll rid me of these silly notions. Will you have another drink, sir?"

I did, and by the time I was in my own cabin, I had almost forgotten the conversation. I lay down in my bunk and went fast asleep.

I was awakened by the howling of the wind through the rigging. The ship was heaving from side to side, and I realized that heavy seas had overtaken her. From above, I heard the shouts of the captain and the first mate. I do not remember what they were, for I am not fully conversant with nautical terms, but I could hear the various members of the crew shouting in reply.

It was still dark, and, as it was summertime in the southern hemisphere, that meant that it was still early. I hadn't the faintest notion of the time, but I knew I had not slept long.

I got out of my bunk and headed topside.

It is difficult, even now, for me to describe that storm. The sea was roiling like a thing alive, but the wind was almost mild. It shifted, now blowing one way, now another, but it came nowhere near heavy gale force. The *White Moon* swerved this way and that under its influence, as though we were caught in some monstrous whirlpool that changed its direction of swirl at varying intervals.

There were no clouds directly overhead. The stars shone as usual in every direction save to the west, where one huge black cloud seemed to blot the sky.

I heard the Captain shout: "Get below, sir! Get below! You're only a hindrance on deck! *Get below!*"

I was, after all, no sailor, and he was master of the ship, so I went back to my cabin to wait the storm out. I know not how long that dreadful storm lasted, for there was no dawn that day. The enveloping cloud from the west had spread like heavy smoke, almost blocking out the sun, and the sky was still a darkling grey when the sea subsided into gentle swells. Shortly after it had done so, there was a rap at my cabin door.

"The Captain would like to see you on deck, sir," said a sailor's rough voice from without.

I accompanied the sailor up the ladder to the weatherdeck, where Captain Bork was staring into the greyness abaft the starboard rail.

"What is it, Captain?" I inquired.

Without looking at me, he asked, "Do you smell that, sir?"

I had already perceived the stench which permeated the sea air about us. There was the nauseous aroma of rotting sea flesh combined with the acrid bitterness of burning sulphur. Before I could answer his question, the Captain continued. "I caught that smell once before many years ago." He turned to look at me. "Have you smelt it before, sir?"

"Once," I said. "Not exactly the same, Captain, but similar. It was near a volcano. But there was no smell of rotten fish."

Captain Bork nodded his massive head. "Aye, sir. That's the smell of it. Somewhere to the west—" He pointed toward the area where the black cloud was densest. "—there's been a volcanic explosion, the like of which we've not seen before. I knew it was no ordinary storm; this is not the season for typhoon."

"But what is that horrid miasma of decay?" I asked. "No volcano ever gave off a smell like that."

Before the Captain could answer, a call came from the top of the mizzenmast. "*Land Ho-o-o-o!*"

Captain Bork jerked his head around and squinted toward the north. He thrust an arm out, pointing. "Land it is, sir," he said to me, "and that's where your stench comes from. The seas are shallow in these parts, but there should be no islands about. Look."

In the dim, wan light I saw a low, bleak headland that loomed above the surging surface of the sea.

I knew then what had happened. The volcanic eruption, and the resulting seismic shock, had lifted a part of the sea bottom above the surface. There before us, in black basalt, was a portion of the seabed which had been inundated for untold millenia. It was from that newly-risen plateau that the revolting odour came, wafted by the gusting sea-breeze.

The captain began giving orders. There were certain repairs which had to be made, and he felt it would be better to have the ship at anchor for the work, so he directed that the ship be brought in close to the newly-risen island. Not too close, of course; if another volcanic quake stirred the sea, he wanted leeway between the White Moon and those forbidding rocks.

He found water shallow enough to set the anchors, and the crew went to work with a will. The stench from the island, while mephitic enough, was not really strong, and we soon grew accustomed to it.

I was of no use whatever aboard, and might well have gone to my cabin and stayed there while the crew worked, but there was something about that bleak, malodorous island that drew my attention powerfully. The ship was anchored roughly parallel to the beach, with the island to port, so I found a spot forward where I would be out of the way of the work and examined the island minutely with a spyglass I had borrowed from Captain Bork.

The island was tiny; one could have walked across it with no trouble at all, had it been level and even. But it would be much more difficult over that craggy, slippery black surface.

The close-up view through the spyglass only made the island look the more uninviting. Rivulets of sea water, still draining from the upper plateau, cut through sheets of ancient slime that oozed gelatinously down the precipitate slopes to the coral-crusted beach below. Pools of nauseous-looking liquid formed in pockets of dark rock and bubbled slowly and obscenely. As I watched, I became obsessed with the feeling that I had seen all this before in some hideous nightmare.

Then something at the top of the cliff caught my eye. It was something farther inland, and I had to readjust the focus of my instrument to see it clearly. For a moment, I held my breath. *It appeared to be the broken top of an embattled tower!*

It could not be, of course. I told myself that it was merely some chance formation of rock. But I had to get a better view of it.

I went in search of the Captain and requested his permission to climb a little way up the rigging, so that my point of view would be above the top of the cliff. Busy as he was, he granted my request almost offhandedly. Up I went, and used the spyglass once again.

The tower was plainly visible now. It appeared to be one of two, the second broken off much lower than the first. Both rose from one end of a rectangular block that might have been a partly buried building, as if some great fortress, aeons old, still stood there.

Or was my over-fervid imagination making too much of what, after all, was more likely to be a natural formation? I have often watched cloud formations take on weird and phantastick shapes as the wind shifts them across the sky; could not this be the same or a similar phenomenon? I forced my mind to be more objective, to look at the vista before me as it actually was, not as I might imagine it to be.

The spyglass showed clearly that the surface of that ugly, looming structure was composed of coral-like cells and small shellfish like those which cling to the bottoms of sea-going vessels when they have not been drydocked for too long a time. The edges of the building—if building it was—were rounded, and not angular. It could be merely a happenstance, a natural formation of rock which had been covered, over the millenia, by limeshell creatures which had given that natural structure a vague, blurred outline resembling an ancient fortress. Still, would not a genuine artifact of that size and shape have looked the same if it were covered with the same encrustations? I could not decide. Even after the most minute examination through the spyglass, I could not decide. There was but one thing to do, so I approached the Captain with my request.

"Go ashore?" Captain Bork said in astonishment. "No, sir; I could not allow that! In the first place, it is far too dangerous. Those rocks are slippery and afford too precarious a foothold. And look to the west; that volcano is still active; a second quake might submerge that island again as easily as the first raised it. In the second place, I cannot, at this time, spare the men to row you ashore in a longboat."

I had to make a firm stand. "Captain," said I, "surely you realise the tremendous scientific importance of this discovery. If that structure is, as I surmise, an artifact rather than a natural configuration of stone, the failure to investigate it would be an incalculable loss to science."

It required some little time to convince the Captain, but after I had persuaded him to climb the rigging and look for himself, he conceded to my request, albeit grudgingly.

"Very well, sir, since you insist. Two of my crew will row you ashore. Since we are within easy hailing distance, they will return and work until you call. I cannot do more. I feel it is risky—no, more than that; it is downright foolhardy. But you are not a cub, sir; you have the right to do as you wish, no matter how dangerous." Then his stern countenance changed. "To be honest, sir, I would come with you if I could. But my duty lies with my ship."

"I understand, Captain," said I. Actually, I had no desire for him to come ashore with me. At that time, I wanted to make any discovery that might be made by myself. If any glory were to be earned in that exploration, I wanted to earn it myself. How bitterly was I to repent that feeling later!

The "beach"—if such it could be called—was merely a slope of sharp coral permeated with stinking slime. I had had the good sense to dress properly in heavy boots and water-resistant clothing, but, close up, the nauseating odour was almost unbearable. Still, I had asked for it, and I must bear it.

The "beach" ended abruptly with a cliff nearly twice my own height, and I had to circle round to find a declivity I could negotiate.

Up I went, but it was hard going over those slippery, jagged rocks to the more level portion of the island.

I cannot, even now, describe the encroaching dread that came over me as I topped that rise and beheld the structure that squatted obscenely before me. Had I had less foolish courage, I might have turned, even then, and called back the longboat that was moving away, back toward the *White Moon*. But there was the matter of youthful pride. Having committed myself, I must go on, lest I be thought a coward by the Captain and crew of that gallant ship.

I made my way carefully across that broken field of coral-covered basalt but, try as I might, I could not avoid slipping now and then. More than once my feet slid into malodorous pools of ichthyc ooze. I would not care to take that walk today, for I am more brittle and my muscles are not as strong as they were then; even my younger, stronger self was fortunate that he did not break something.

Suddenly the going became easier. The area around that looming structure, some ten or twelve paces from the base of the wall, was quite level and covered with pebbles and fine sand rather than coral. But even up close those dripping, encrusted walls gave no clue as to whether they were natural or artificial. Slowly, carefully, I walked along the wall toward the east and, after thirty paces, turned the corner and continued north, along the shorter side of the structure. That eastern wall was as blank and unyielding of any evidence as the previous one had been. At the next corner I turned west and walked along the northern wall. It, too, looked exactly the same as the southern one. It was not until I came to the fourth side that I saw the opening.

I approached the breach in the wall with equal dread and fascination. Here, at last, I might find an avenue through which to reach the answers I sought. I paused at its edge, reluctant somehow to look inside. The way was difficult here, for a great stone slab lay flat on the sand, a mire-filled trench marking where it must have been resting upright for millenia, until the recent volcanic disturbance unbalanced and toppled it, unsealing the doorway before me.

There was no question remaining in my mind that it was indeed a doorway; a single fearful glance revealed a smooth, dry stone floor. Even in the wan grey light of the smoke-clouded day, an astounding fact was evident to me: that the mysterious structure was indeed an artifact constructed by intelligent beings, and that until a few hours ago the stone slab at my feet had covered the doorway which surrounded me, sealing out the corrosive sea water.

The vapours which wafted from within were malodorous enough, but the stench was musty and dry. In spite of the strong sense of foreboding that was tugging at my heart and bowels, I could no longer contain my scientific curiosity. I slipped from my back the supply pack provided me by the Captain, and drew out the most bulky object, one of the ship's lamps. Beside the great slab of stone, I struggled with flint and steel to light the oily wick.

I recall clearly how I felt at that moment. The White Moon seemed aeons away, unreachable. I told myself that the excitement which made my body tremble was the incredible fortune of my find. That I should be at this place and time to avail myself of this unprecedented opportunity seemed miraculous. A different angle of course, a slightly stronger wind, the Captain refusing flatly to have me escorted to these forbidding shores; any of these might have deprived me of the knowledge I was about to gain.

So I told myself then. But looking back I know that I searched my mind for some rational reason for the lump of fear that seemed to choke me. For I am sure, now, that in my heart I already knew that what I had found would change my life in ways far different from the fortune and acclaim I tried so hard to believe I would receive.

The lamp finally caught, and its cheerful yellow light was most welcome. Braced up by its dancing glow, shielded within it from the baleful grey of the day, I walked into that ancient, long-hidden temple.

How did I know, immediately, that the large, shadow-shrouded room I entered had been a place of worship? I have tried, many times, to understand what I sensed when I stepped through that doorway. I can describe it only as a many-particular presence, a malignant energy which swelled and eddied around me. And that energy was not random or undirected. It was focussed far across the floor, against the far wall. The area was completely hidden from the brave little light of my oil lamp—to inspect it I would have to cross the great room.

Gone, now, was the brief impulse of bravado inspired by the lighting of the lantern. I moved across that endless room in the grip of a terror so profound that my mind was virtually para-lyzed. I walked not through my own volition, but out of a reluctance to resist the pressure of that force which surrounded me, drawing me inexorably to the hidden area where I knew I would find an answer which I was becoming ever more certain *I did not want to find!*

The lamp swayed with my every step, casting inadequate illumination on the pillars that lined my path, and causing fearsome shadows to billow out into the blankness beyond them. I could see symbols on the pillars: unintelligible, weird carvings which were somehow utterly repulsive, and from which I looked quickly away. Now and then the nether regions of the room would catch a ray of light and reveal drifts of dust, all that remained of wooden furniture or fabric wall-hangings. A part of me still stubbornly mourned the loss and surmised that the originals had been perfectly preserved until the advent of fresh air had accelerated their long-delayed decomposition. But that objective, scientific interest was almost totally submerged in a great relief that I was spared the scenes depicted in those ancient tapestries.

If those aspects of the huge room which I could see in the glow of my lantern contributed to a sense of apprehension, consider the effect of the vast areas which remained concealed. I began to fill the darkened corners with fancy. What lurked there, just beyond the light, watching me? Did I hear whispering in the gloom above me, or was it only the sea breeze becoming reacquainted with these aged stones? Surely the latter was true, for I could smell afresh, with sharpened senses, the foetid odour of the "beach." Or was this scent original within the temple, caused by the same sudden decay of once-living flesh as had struck the objects which had been reduced to dust?

For the first time in my young life, I cursed the imagination which had always enriched physical experience for me. If I persisted in conjuring spectres to satisfy my straining senses...

I saw the altar.

It rested atop a long, shallow stairway which stretched the whole width of the aisle. From where I was, I could see three steps, a long platform, and another set of three steps. At the end of that second platform stood a massive block, only a rectangular shape at the edge of the light.

I recognized that it functioned as an altar because I could now sense the exact focus of the energies which had drawn me across the room. On the wall above and behind the altar was an idol. Not even its vaguest outline was visible to me, yet I knew it was there, and that when I looked upon it, I would know the truth.

At that moment I looked back across the blackness at the patch of grey gloom that was the only doorway, the only way in...or out. I knew that I had reached the only remaining moment of choice. To mount the first step toward the altar was to commit myself unremittingly to viewing what waited beyond it. I could turn back now, escape this dark and horrid place, return to the honest sunlight, however obscure.

But with my goal in sight, the hard stone step at the toe of my boot, I was shamed by the memory of my terrifying phantasies. I could not quite scoff at them, standing as I was almost within reach of what I could think of only as a *sacrificial* altar. But I argued with valid logic that the truth, whatever it might be, would dispel forever the lingering trauma of that fancy-ridden trek. So, with a grand and foolish determination, I turned and stepped upward.

As the altar loomed into the circle of light I carried with me, I could not repress a shudder of horror. Here was not the indestructible grey stone I had seen throughout the temple, but a giant block of scabrous white marble. Once smooth and gleaming, it had been etched and scarred by the elements of the air confined for—how long?—within these walls. The pattern of the marbled surface was lost beneath scattered patches that reflected an unhealthy white, as though some thin and pallid fungus were feeding on the evil, glistening stone.

I looked down at last upon the entire altar, and try as I did to resist, I was swept up in another eddy of phantasy. For what blasphemous rituals had this hideous altar been used? I could not shake the impression that living sacrifice had been offered here. In my mind's eye I could see a razor-sharp spearblade hovering ever nearer a terrified victim whose outline was blurred and unclear. And who—or what—held that threatening blade? Was this really only phantasy, or was I seeing a scene so often repeated that its impression had remained these countless thousands of years?

I knew the moment had come. I lifted high my lantern and looked upon the thing to which the ancient sacrifice had been made.

The carven image on that wall was never meant for our eyes. I am the only person who has ever seen it, and time has not yet erased my sense of utter revulsion when the light of my lantern exposed it at last. Numbed by the horror of it, I stood as if paralyzed for what seemed an interminably long time; then, driven nearly mad by that ghastly visage, I threw the lamp at it with all my strength, as though I could destroy the sight of it. I must have screamed, but I can remember only the echoing of my boots as I ran back to the welcoming gloom of the still-dark day, fled for my soul's sake from that revolting and nauseous vision.

Past that, my memory is unclear. I retain an impression still of the total panic in my mind, as my body ran back across the sandy level to the noxious sea-scudded rocks. Some thankful instinct guided me toward the White Moon. The joy that surged through me when I saw her masts above the slimy crest that marked the edge of the "beach" is totally indescribable. Those masts represented safety, refuge, security. To my unbalanced mind they represented wholesomeness. All I need do, so my mind ran, was reach the White Moon—there I would find forgetfulness. It would be as though I had never set foot in that gruesome temple; it would never have happened at all. And how I longed to escape the memory of that place, of the indescribable horror that ruled over that dishonourable altar!

I ran for the White Moon's masts, slipping and falling, heedless of the dangerous coral which cut repeatedly at my extremities. With a soulfelt sob of relief, I ran straight over the edge of the crest and plummeted to the beach below.

I do not remember the pain; all I remember is the shock of the blow that knocked the breath out of me. And then, gratefully, I gave myself up to the sweet oblivion of unconsciousness.

I was told later that I was unconscious for two days, and thus did not experience the second volcanic eruption and the resulting quake which allowed the merciful sea to flood over and cover again that horrid island and its tomb-like temple.

Some infection from the coral cuts must have invaded my body, for I was in a fevered delirium for the next five days.

But, delirium or no, I did not imagine that carven figure above that gruesome altar. No living thing has that much imagination, even in delirium.

I can still see it clearly in my mind's eye, although I would far rather forget it. It tells too much about the horrible and blasphemous rites which must have been performed in that evil place, rites practiced by monstrous beings that ruled this planet a quarter of a million or more years ago.

The hideous thing was almost indescribable, and I cannot, *will not*, bring myself to draw it. It was thin and emaciated-looking, with two tiny, deep-sunken eyes and a small mouth surrounded by some kind of bristles or antennae. The muscles were clearly visible, as though its flesh were all on the outside. It had only two arms, and these were flung wide. The horrible, five-fingered hands and the five-toed feet *were nailed firmly to a great stone cross!*

LOOK OUT! DUCK!

By Randall Garrett

This one is due primarily to Peg Campbell, John's lovely wife. She read a story in The New Yorker *by Peter de Vries, and in it was one line that tickled her fancy. It is the last line of* Look Out! Duck!

But both she and John objected to what Mr. de Vries had to say about "pulp" writers, and wanted me to prove him wrong.

I don't know whether I did or not, but I enjoyed writing the story. You wouldn't believe the research it took to find out about ducks.

By the way, all the names of the characters and the spaceships are taken from the New Yorker *story—with the exception of the hero's.*

And one other.

There were four men aboard the cargo ship *Constanza* when she made the voyage to Okeefenokee. Three of them were her regular crew: Joseph Dumbrowski, the captain; Donald Mac-Donald, the engineer; and Peter Devris, the astrogator.

The fourth man didn't show up until the *Constanza* was almost fully loaded and ready to take off. Dumbrowski was definitely reaching the peevish stage when the panel truck came rolling up towards the loading pit that housed the interstellar vessel.

Inside the truck, the driver pointed toward the shaft of silver that speared up from the pit. "That's the *Constanza*, ahead," he said.

Rouen Drake, M.D., D.V.M., looked at it, nodded, and looked back through the glass panel at the remaining cargo in the rear of the truck. "You can't see it, children," he said, "but your new home is just ahead. At least it will be your home for a while."

The cargo did not reply. The truck driver grinned. "You like

them ducks, eh, Doc?"

The doctor grinned back. "In a way. They're the product of ten years of genetic engineering. Besides being proud of them, I think they're kind of cute."

The truck pulled up beside the ramp of the *Constanza* and braked to a halt. "Here comes Captain Dumbrowski," the driver said. Dr. Drake climbed out and offered his hand to the man in the striking crimson-and-gold of the Interstellar Service. The officer took it in a bone-crushing grip.

"Dr. Drake? I'm Captain Dumbrowski. Where have you been?"

The captain was a thickset man with beetling brows, and a voice like a bellowing bull.

"I got here as soon as possible, captain," Drake said stiffly. "I'm sorry if I'm late."

"We're overdue now," the captain said. "MacDonald will help you get loaded." He turned to another crimson-and-gold clad man nearby. "MacDonald, here's our last entry. One Drake and a harem of ducks." And with that, he turned and went into the ship.

Drake's jaw muscles set a little, and his face flamed crimson under his blond complexion. The truck driver smothered a snicker, and MacDonald seemed to be trying to offer a friendly smile instead of an impish grin. He didn't quite succeed.

"Section Five has been set up for your...uh...ducks, Doctor," he said.

"Excellent," said Drake evenly. "Let's get them aboard as soon as possible." Then he added: "I'll check the rest of the cargo later."

Twenty minutes later, fifty ducks were safely ensconced in the specially rebuilt Section Five of the *Constanza*'s hold. Mac-

Donald leaned against a bulkhead and wiped his forehead with a handkerchief. "Hoo!" he said. "I'm worn out."

"It isn't very comfortable, is it?" Drake asked rhetorically. He, too, was streaming with perspiration, and his arms felt heavy as lead.

"Temperature, one hundred degrees Fahrenheit," MacDonald said in a dry voice. "Humidity, eighty-five per cent. Gravity, one point five. Why...if I may ask?"

Drake stuck a soggy handkerchief in his pocket. "We have to reproduce the environment of the surface of Okeefenokee as closely as possible," Drake explained. "That's what the ducks are bred for."

"What's this planet like?" MacDonald wanted to know. His eyes warily followed a duck that flapped its way through the hot, muggy air with apparent unconcern.

"Something like Earth was a few hundred million years ago. Mostly swamps and shallow seas. Plant life is pretty highly evolved—wind pollinated, though; there aren't any insects. Animals haven't gotten much above the crustacean stage. Oh, there are a few chordates, I understand, but no true vertebrates. There are some things that look like fish, but they're more closely related to the mollusks.

"That wouldn't be so bad, but it means the colonists wouldn't have the proper proteins. We've got to change the ecological setup. Therefore, the ducks."

"Why ducks?"

"Don't ask me; I'm not an ecologist."

"They're sure queer looking," MacDonald said as one of them waddled unconcernedly toward him.

"They're mutations," Drake told him. "Had to be. The surface gravity of Okeefenokee is half again as great as Earth's, and the air pressure and temperature are higher—as you've noticed. That necessitated modification of the duck's flying apparatus. And there were other changes; their diet isn't quite the same as that of ordinary Terrestrial ducks. They're still members of the *Anatidae*, but they aren't like any other duck on Earth."

The duck waddled closer and looked at the two men with apparent interest.

"What are you along for, Doc?" MacDonald asked. "Are you a veterinarian?"

"Yes. I also have an M.D. degree."

The duck looked him straight in the eye. "*Quack!*" it said distinctly.

MacDonald almost gagged.

Dr. Rouen Drake was a scholarly man who had the unfortunate luck to look like a scholar is supposed to look. He was lean and somewhat shorter than average height. His shoulders were slightly rounded, and his eyes had the faint telltale glitter which betrayed the lenses that corrected his myopia. His hair was blond and straight and had a pronounced widow's peak. Even his soft, measured, somewhat pedagogical voice betrayed him. It was the first time he had ever been aboard a spaceship in his life, and he felt somewhat out of place among the spacemen.

But he had a job to do, and he was determined to do it well.

After he and MacDonald left Section Five, they went back and checked over the other cargo. Item: One electric incubator, five thousand egg capacity. Item: Fifty electric brooders, one hundred duckling capacity. Item: Two hundred and thirty thousand pounds duckling rations, Types A and B. Item: Three thousand pounds adult duck rations, normal feeding. Item: Three thousand pounds adult duck breeding rations.

And, Item: Five thousand crash-frozen fertile duck eggs.

All in order.

Satisfied, Drake went up to the control blister in the nose to report to Captain Dumbrowski.

He was in a somewhat better mood now, possibly because there were still ten minutes until the scheduled take-off time. If Drake had been late—

"I'm all set, captain," Drake said. "The cargo is in excellent shape, and the live ducks are all taken care of."

"Good," said Dumbrowski. He turned to the other man who had been in the control blister with him. "Lieutenant Devris, this is Dr. Drake. Doctor, this is Devris, our navigator."

Devris was a good-looking man, quiet, efficient, and intelligent. His handshake was warm and friendly.

"All right, men," Dumbrowski said, "let's get settled. Take-off in eight minutes. MacDonald, show the doctor to his cabin."

Eight minutes later, the sixty-five meter long *Constanza* lifted her huge mass gently and easily from her pit and accelerated toward the sky. As she left the atmosphere, her course changed slightly, aiming her nose at a point near Shaula in Scorpio. Then the mass-time converters shifted in and the ship vanished. She was moving towards her destination at nearly ten thousand times the velocity of light. Okeefenokee was eighteen weeks away.

Time plodded on. The operation of the vessel was largely

automatic, requiring only occasional human judgment. Once every twenty-four hours, the mass-time converters were cut and the ship returned to normal space so that Devris could take positional readings.

Twice a day, Dr. Drake went down to Section Five to feed and care for his ducks.

Between times, the men read, played cards, or watched the new movies that had been brought along. And each night, Captain Dumbrowski issued each man a ration of two bottles of beer.

Dumbrowski himself was a storyteller of no mean ability, although the subject matter was rather monotonous.

"And then there was that time on Tripha," he would say, pouring himself a foaming glass. "Some disease had wiped out nine-tenths of the male population. They'd whipped it finally, but even the men who were left were in pretty sad condition. Naturally"—he chuckled knowingly—"we had to do our duty. There was one little blonde who had four sisters—good lookers, all of 'em. Well, they seemed to take a shine to me, so...."

Or: "I remember a red-headed dancer in Lunar City; she did a strip that was out of this world! What technique! Anyway, I was in this dive, and—"

And so on. MacDonald would try to top him, but he always came off second best. Neither of them ever repeated himself exactly, but after a few weeks there developed an overhanging pall of similarity about the tales.

Drake noticed that Devris usually listened to Dumbrowski for a while, and then got up and strolled quietly to the astronomical dome. One evening, he walked out as usual, but as soon as he was out in the corridor, he turned and made signals with his hands and fingers.

Drake realized the signals were for him, since neither the captain nor the engineer could see Devris from where he sat.

Drake nodded imperceptibly, and got up a few minutes later. He walked quietly out, mumbling something about his ducks. Behind him, Dumbrowski was saying:

"...Could be picked up without any trouble. So I..."

Drake headed for the astronomy dome. Devris was pouring a colorless liquid into a couple of glasses. He added ice and fruit juice and said: "I thought you might like to get away from Joe 'One-Note' Dumbrowski for a while. Here; have a drink." He handed one of the glasses to the doctor.

Drake sipped at the drink. It was smooth, but with a strange aura of power. "Isn't this against regulations?" he asked.

"Not exactly." Devris' smile was that of the triumphant loophole-seeker. " 'Articles of Interstellar Commerce,...' " he quoted, " 'Section VIII, Paragraph 4: No beverage alcohol shall be permitted aboard Service vessels except regulation five per cent beer, which shall be rationed to personnel at the rate of twenty-four fluid ounces per day, such rations not to be cumulative.' " He paused for a moment, then went on: " 'Section IX, Paragraph 3: Intoxication of personnel shall be punished by the commanding officer of the ship according to Section II, Paragraphs 7 and 8, dealing with endangering the lives and/or property aboard service vessels.' "

"Then what's this?" Drake asked, holding up his glass.

"Lens cleaning fluid," Devris said candidly. "I find absolute alcohol to be an excellent lens cleaner.

"Naturally," he continued virtuously, "no one in his right mind could consider lens cleaning fluid a beverage."

"Which proves," said Drake, taking another sip, "that I am not in my right mind."

"I'll drink to that," said Devris. They drank.

"Very neat," Drake said. "As long as you do not become intoxicated and do not have alcoholic beverages aboard, you are not disobeying the regulations. Does the captain know about this?"

"Probably. But we don't mention it. We have a tacit agreement. He doesn't check on my lens cleaner, and I don't ask him why he has an extra foot locker aboard."

"I see. No one checks on the captain. What about Mac-Donald?"

"He's satisfied with his beer ration, I guess. He isn't much of a drinker. He'd rather swap true confessions with Joe One-Note." He finished his drink and mixed another. "You know," he said philosophically, "I have done a little computation. Assuming that all of Joe's stories are true, and assuming that each of his conquests was completed in a minimum amount of time, and using Service tables to compute the average length of a voyage and the average time of stay on a planet—figuring all these in, I say, I have come up with a cubic equation."

Drake nodded. "I follow you. So?"

"I have come up with two real and one imaginary roots to the equation." He held up a hand and began counting them off on his fingers.

"Real Root One: Captain Dumbrowski is over nine hundred years old. Otherwise, he couldn't possibly have done all that work in the time allowed.

"Real Root Two: Captain Dumbrowski has psionic powers and is able to teleport himself from this ship every night to some suitable planet in the galaxy and get back within eight hours."

"Uh-huh. And the imaginary root?"

"Captain Dumbrowski's stories are imaginary. But, being imaginary, such a root is not allowable in a real situation."

"Naturally not," agreed Drake. "Pour me another drink."

As the navigator mixed, Drake asked: "I wonder why he lays it on so thick?"

"He married young," Devris said oratorically. "His wife is a small, birdlike woman to whom he is intensely devoted. She is, as far as I can determine, a simpering prude."

"So he tells sea stories like Long John Silver, eh?"

From then on, Drake managed to get away from Dumbrowski early and have a chat with Devris in the evening. The navigator proudly displayed his instruments, and even let the doctor compute their position one day. Drake got one of the factors confused, and Devris respectfully informed him that he had better tell the captain to turn around, because the ship was heading towards Alhena in Gemini, dead away from their target.

Drake, in turn, took the navigator to Section Five to show him his ducks.

"Why live ducks, anyway?" Devris asked. "Why not just ship them all as eggs?"

"Well, remember, these aren't going to be domestic ducks; they'll be allowed to go wild on Okeefenokee. One of the most important things a duck can learn is how to be a duck. It isn't all instinct, you know. So we have a live adult duck for every hundred eggs. The old duck teaches the younger ones the duck business."

"Been in the family for generations, eh?" Devris asked.

"We hope so. Believe me, we hope so."

"You hope so? I'd think any duck could learn the duck profession. It ought to be easy as duck soup."

Drake winced. "Not necessarily. These ducks, like most domestic ducks, are descended from the *Anas boschas*—the mallard. But domestic ducks have been inbred and crossbred for meat and egg qualities. In several strains, the brooding or nest-sitting instinct has been bred right out. Such a species wouldn't survive in the wild; the duck would lay her eggs and then walk off and leave them.

150

"We went back to the original wild mallard to get *Anas okeefenokias*, here. The genetic engineers worked hard to get the bird they wanted, but a couple of strains turned out to be absolutely worthless. One strain was a failure because the opposite sexes refused to have anything to do with each other—no mating instinct."

"Tell that to Captain Dumbrowski. He'll have a duck fit," said Devris calmly. He ducked just in time.

Seventeen weeks slipped by. It was on the fourth day of the eighteenth week, two days' flight from Okeefenokee, that Drake found a sick duck.

It wasn't really very ill; it had managed to get a scratch near one eye, and the scratch had become slightly infected. It took him a couple of minutes to snare the duck, then he picked it up and looked at it.

"Not too bad at all," he said. "I'll take it up to my cabin and put something on that. And I guess I'd better take a good look at the others; they may have been fighting."

Devris mopped the perspiration from his dripping brow. "You want me to take it up, doc? I have to go make my positional check, anyway. MacDonald is going to stop the ship in a few minutes."

"Sure. Thanks." Drake handed the duck to the navigator. "Keep her close to your body, and when you get her up to my place, put a blanket around her. These ducks have a higher body temperature than normal, and that air out there is pretty cold to them."

"Can do," said Devris. And he left, with the duck cradled securely in his arm.

Fifteen minutes later, a loud-speaker blared in the room. The dense air, coupled with Dumbrowski's booming voice, made a thunderous noise in the compartment. Squawking, flapping ducks fled from the voice.

"DRAKE! GET UP HERE TO THE CONTROL BLISTER! AND I MEAN *FAST!*"

Drake made it fast. There must be something badly wrong for Dumbrowski to give an order like that.

The first thing that struck him oddly when he entered the control blister was the peculiar odor. There was the acrid smell of burnt insulation, the biting, metallic effluvium of vaporized copper, the stench of burnt feathers, and—beneath it all—the tasty, tantalizing aroma of roast duck.

151

Devris was standing at rigid attention in the middle of the room, listening to Dumbrowski bellow.

"...and I don't give a damn what the doctor asked you to do!"

"He didn't ask me, captain; I volunteered."

"Shaddup! You had no right to volunteer! He—"

"What about me, captain?" Drake asked.

Dumbrowski whirled. "Oh, *there* you are! What do you mean, letting one of your blasted ducks out of their Section? You dumb cluck, do you realize you've wrecked a multi-million dollar spaceship?"

MacDonald was kneeling over an open panel from which heavy clouds of smoke were still pouring.

It seemed that MacDonald had been inspecting the circuits, giving them a final check before the last two days of the drive. The mass-time converters had been shut off so that Devris could make the daily position check.

MacDonald had had the panel open, and had stepped across the room to get a meter of some kind.

And a duck walked in.

MacDonald had tried to shoo it out, but the duck, stubborn to the end, had shooed in the opposite direction. Instead of fleeing through the open door, she had headed for the darkened cabinet which housed the control circuits.

She had landed across a couple of leads which came directly from a high-voltage, high-amperage, direct-current generator. MacDonald had been afraid to try to get her out, and afraid not to. She had flapped and quacked and fluttered about, jiggling loose wires and cracking other equipment. Then the insulation on the DC leads had broken, and all hell busted loose.

The unfortunate thing was that the leads had been between the generators and the circuit breakers. There was no load on them at that point and no reason to think there would be a short. But short there was.

The duck had died instantly, and had carbonized an instant later. The arc established had blazed its way back to the generator, destroying everything in its path. Carried by the ionized metal between the leads, the arc had not stopped until it reached the point where the leads were separated by a high-test ceramic insulator.

"And the worst of it," MacDonald said, "is that we can't replace it. We're not equipped to repair a burned out generator and all that other stuff. We don't carry that many spares. Things

152

like this just don't happen on board a spaceship."

"I'll say they don't!" Dumbrowski bellowed. "And if it hadn't been for this duck doctor here, it wouldn't have happened at all!"

Drake clenched his teeth and said nothing.

"Do you know what this means?" Dumbrowski asked in a subdued roar. "It means we will have to call all the way back to Earth and tell them we're marooned here, two days' time from our destination. And that means we'll have to sit here and wait for eighteen weeks for the ship to get here with the necessary parts!"

"Couldn't we get a ship here from Okeefenokee?" Drake asked, forcing his voice to keep calm.

Dumbrowski sneered. "Hardly. That's a Class C colony; it isn't really a colony yet. It isn't self-supporting. There isn't a ship any closer than Earth."

He stood there for a moment, and evidently his anger subsided a little. "All right; it's happened. We'll have to make the best of it. We've got enough food on board, and the paragravity units didn't go—thank Heaven."

MacDonald, rummaging around in the smouldering mass of fused equipment, said: "The only thing gone is the control system of the mass-time converters and the drive thrust." He scrabbled around a bit more, then: "And all the leads to the cryogenics section."

It took a full two seconds for that to hit Drake. "You mean the refrigerator? The one my eggs are in?"

"Yeah," said MacDonald, his voice muffled by the cabinet.

"Five thousand rotten eggs on our hands!" bellowed Dumbrowski. He turned to Drake. "We might as well start dumping them now."

It was all Drake could do to hold his temper. Part of him wanted to throw a punch straight into Dumbrowski's teeth; part of him whispered that it might be not too sensible. Dumbrowski outmassed him by fifteen kilos.

Discretion won by a narrow margin. "I'm afraid I can't let you do that, captain," he said stiffly. "At least not until we check with the Interstellar Commission. They might frown on our dumping those eggs without doing everything in our power to save them."

"Look, Doc," Dumbrowski said coldly, "I've dumped cargo before if it was going to spoil. I once dumped five tons of powdered eggs because a leaky water pipe damped them down. When eggs begin to stink, they really stink. Hydrogen sulfide isn't too congenial an aroma.

"If I ask the Commission, they'll just tell me to dump 'em. So why bother?"

"Now you look, Dumbrowski." Drake's voice was rapidly becoming brittle. "In the first place, those aren't ordinary eggs. They are fertile, mutant duck eggs. In the second place, I am quite sure that the Commission won't tell you to dump five thousand eggs worth two thousand dollars each!"

Dumbrowski's heavy brows shot up. "Two thou— You mean those eggs are worth *ten million dollars?*"

"Exactly."

"But what else can we do? MacDonald!" He swung around to the engineer, who was still probing in the ruins. "Is there any chance we can get the refrigerator going again?"

"None, skipper. Everything in here is gone."

Dumbrowski turned back to Drake. "See? What else can we do?"

"What do you normally do with fertile eggs?"

"You mean—?"

"I mean we incubate them. Check with the Commission." And Drake turned on his heel and walked out.

Drake blamed himself for the escape of the duck. He'd forgotten to tell Devris that they were stronger than an average duck because of the high gravity they lived under. Devris had wrapped the duck securely in a blanket and left it on Drake's bed. The door to the doctor's cabin had been left open a crack, and after the duck had wriggled herself loose from the blanket, she had gone out for a stroll.

Well, he had to agree with Dumbrowski on one thing: there was nothing to be done about it now; they'd just have to make the best of it.

He went down to Section Twenty, where the refrigerators were. The egg cases would have to be removed and thawed properly, at just the right rate. Then they'd have to go into the incubator. He figuratively spat on his hands and got to work.

When Lieutenant Devris came down an hour or so later, the eggs were in the slow warmer. Drake looked up as the sound of boots echoed along the corridor and into the room.

"Hi, Pete. What's up?"

Devris grinned lopsidedly. "The captain told me to bring this to you. He's too furious to bring it himself." He handed Drake a flimsy.

Drake looked at it and grinned. It read: "Okeefenokee duck eggs must not be allowed to perish. Incubate and hatch. Every effort short of actual danger to crew must be expended to save ducks. Crew of the *Constanza* is instructed to give Dr. Rouen Drake full co-operation."

Devris said: "I'm sorry about that duck, Doc."

"Forget it. It could have happened to anyone. What are the chances that it would walk into the control blister? Pretty small, I'd think."

"Yeah. Pretty small. But it happened."

"I'll say it did. What a mess." He paused and looked up at the navigator. "Pete?"

"Yeah?"

"Pete, why does Dumbrowski have it in for me?"

Devris looked uncomfortable. "I don't know, Doc. It's just his way. He yells at everybody. Don't ask me why he picked you to rib. You can't always explain the queer quirks in a guy's mind." Then he turned and went out.

Drake looked at the door for a long time. Then he shrugged and went on with his work.

The eggs went into the big automatic incubator. Normal duck eggs are incubated at 101° to 103° Fahrenheit for twenty-eight days, but the Okeefenokee duck eggs required 129° F. for only twenty-one days.

Every ten hours, the incubator automatically turned the eggs; the atmosphere inside was kept properly humid and warm. On the sixth day, Drake candled the eggs to see if any were infertile.

Thirty-two of them showed no sign of life; they went into the disposal unit. The others went on incubating.

Dumbrowski calmed down quite a bit during the next couple of weeks. Drake didn't go out of his way to avoid the man, but he didn't seek the captain out, either. The feeling seemed mutual.

Still, Drake dreaded the day when he would have to tell Dumbrowski the whole truth. He had spent his time getting the exact measurements of the ship—and the ship wasn't quite big enough.

Eighteen weeks until help would come from Earth. Eighteen weeks of floating in emptiness, fifty-four light-years from their destination, thirty-four hundred light-years from Earth, and nine light-years from the nearest star.

The eighteen weeks became seventeen, then sixteen, and then fifteen. And the duck eggs were ready to hatch.

Two days before the hatch was ready, Drake went to Captain Dumbrowski. For over a week, things had looked calm on the surface, but underneath, the situation was about as touchy as dry nitrogen iodide in a sandstorm.

Dumbrowski was playing cribbage with MacDonald. "Fifteen-two, fifteen-four, pair six, pair eight," he said, pegging his hand. He looked up as Drake entered. "Hello, Doc. How're the eggs?" His voice was carefully modulated.

"They hatch day after tomorrow, captain. I'll need some room for the brooders. They're all knocked down for shipment, and I'll have to put them together."

"I see." Dumbrowski shuffled the cards slowly. "About how much room will you need?"

"There's fifty of 'em," Drake said. "They're square, two meters on a side."

"I see." He tamped the cards on the table, cut the deck, and shuffled again—slowly. "That's two hundred square meters of floor space."

"A little more," Drake said. "They can't be crowded together too much."

Dumbrowski sighed gustily. "Well, I reckon we can find space here and there in different sections. It'll take a little moving around, but I guess it can be done."

"I'm afraid that won't do, captain. You see, those ducks have to be raised under one point five gees, at high pressure and high temperature and high humidity—just like the rest of the ducks."

Dumbrowski stopped shuffling. "I see," he said at last. "They're going to hatch in two days and we have to shift the cargo around so that you can have another section. Then we have to reset the paragravity units under the floor. And set up the heaters and the humidifiers and the pressurizers. I see." He put the cards down carefully on the table and looked up at Drake. "All right, Doc. MacDonald and I will tend to it. Meanwhile, I'd appreciate it if you'd stay out of my sight for a while."

Drake swallowed and said nothing for a moment. Then: "You hate my guts, don't you, Dumbrowski?"

"I would if you had any," the captain said evenly. "You get 'em; I'll hate 'em."

That evening, Drake went up to the navigation dome. Devris was punching figures into a small computer, so the doctor sat down and waited quietly until he was through.

After several minutes, a relay clicked, a typer rattled a little, and a white sheet covered with figures slid out. Devris took it, stared at it, and snarled four words.

"Is that what's known as a 'deep space oath'?" Drake asked mildly.

"Huh? Oh, hello, Doc. Didn't see you come in." He looked back at the paper. "If you mean an oath directed towards space, yes. So far, I can't pin our exact position down without an error of plus or minus one light-month. That's a little over four minutes' flight time."

"That sounds pretty good."

"Oh, it is; but I want it better. My ambition is to be able to get it down plus or minus an inch, but I think the noise level is a bit too high."

"Hm-m-m. Where's Dumbrowski and MacDonald?"

Devris looked up from his paper. "Didn't you know? They're working on Section Six."

"Oh?" Drake blinked. "I'd have thought they'd have that cleared out hours ago."

Devris let his mouth hang open for a second, then snapped it shut. "Oh, joy, joy. What you know about a spaceship could be printed in newsface headline print on half-inch osmium plate and it would consist entirely of the fifteenth letter of the alphabet."

"What do you mean?"

"I mean that the paragravity units under the floor have to be completely reblocked. You don't just wave your hand to get an extra half gee out of 'em."

Drake swallowed—hard. "Why...why, I thought all you had to do was turn a dial or something, like a thermostat."

"You did? Is that why you waited until two days before the hatching to tell Dumbrowski? He'll be up all night and all day tomorrow, he and MacDonald. I'd be down there helping them, except there isn't room between the deck plates for three men."

Drake buried his face in his hands. "This is horrible! No. Nononono!"

Devris looked a little alarmed. "Oh, now, Doc, it isn't as bad as all that. You didn't know."

The doctor looked up. "It's worse than that! I need that little bitty space for ducklings—*ducklings*, mind you! But do you realize that those birds will be adult ducks by the time the rescue ship gets here? An adult duck needs eight thousand square centimeters of space; those ducks will need four thousand square meters of floor area by the time they grow up!"

"Four thousand square meters," Devris said in a thoughtful tone. "That's pretty nearly the whole deck area of the ship. Interesting." He got up and went over to the bottle marked "Lens Cleaner" and began mixing a stiff drink.

He was humming to himself, and it took Drake a second or two to recognize the tune.

> *I heard one day*
> *A gentleman say*
> *That criminals who*
> *Are cut in two*
> *Can hardly feel*
> *The fatal steel*
> *And so are slain*
> *Without much pain.*
> *If this is true,*
> *It's jolly for you;*
> *Your courage screw*
> *To bid us adieu—*

Devris stirred the drink vigorously and handed it to the doctor. "You'd better go down and tell Dumbrowski now, before he gets too much more done on that section. Drink that—you'll need it."

Drake finished the glass in short order and headed for Section Six.

The stairway to Section Six was closed, and a big sign glowed on its surface.

DANGER! THE P-G UNIT IN THIS SECTION IS OFF! USE EXTREME CAUTION!

Drake opened the door carefully and peered down the stairway. The lights were on, and everything looked normal. He started down the stairs.

Halfway down, something tugged at his insides and sudden

158

nausea hit him. He stumbled down two more steps, and the ship seemed to do a prodigious loop. There seemed to be a pull from above. He was falling up the stairs! He lurched out and grabbed at the railing. He missed, and the ship whirled about him. He did a queer somersault, while his stomach flipped in the opposite direction. He twisted frantically, trying to regain his balance and his sense of orientation. His stomach flipped back in place, twisted around, joggled, gave up in despair, and emptied itself of its contents in one titanic upheaval.

Drake passed out, colder than a fritter.

He was being shaken. A voice was saying: "Come on, Doc; snap out of it. You're all right, Doc; come on."

In the background, he could hear Dumbrowski's bellowing laughter.

As if in a dream, he opened his eyes blearily. "What happened?" Then: "Where am I?"

"You're in Section Seven, Doc," said MacDonald. "You stepped across the barrier field into no-gee, and went haywire."

"Boy!" said Dumbrowski, "did you look funny!" And again he burst into laughter.

Drake found himself lying on the floor. His clothes were a mess, and his head still felt dizzy.

"But I've stepped across barrier fields hundreds of times," he protested feebly. "It never did that before."

"Sure," MacDonald said. "You've gone from one and a half gees to one gee and vice versa. But all you felt was a weight shift. But total absence of pull is the limit; you lose all your orientation."

"You flipped, man; you *really* flipped!" Dumbrowski had subsided to a rumbling chuckle, punctuated by gasps.

"How do you feel?" asked MacDonald with a broad grin.

"I feel fine." Drake's voice was cold. He sat up, pulled a handkerchief from his pocket and began dabbing at his face. His stomach still felt a little queasy, but otherwise he was all right.

"Didn't you know the Olympics were being held in Madagascar this year?" Dumbrowski asked. "Or did you have some other purpose than trying to win the fancy-diving championship?"

"I came down to tell you something." The ice in the words almost liquefied the air, but Dumbrowski didn't seem to notice.

"Really? Well, I must say you attracted my attention. What was it?"

Drake told him. He told him in detail and with precision. And, inside himself, he enjoyed every second of watching Dumbrowski's expression change. *Laugh at me, will you? Laugh now.*

Go ahead and laugh.

Dumbrowski didn't laugh. His face darkened a little, and he said: "You don't think very far ahead, do you, *Doctor? You're* supposed to take care of those ducks, not me. You wanted 'em hatched; my orders are to co-operate. Well, you haven't told me a thing. I don't know what kind of orders you think you're giving, but I've had just about enough of 'em. I'm tired of walking around blind on my own ship, wondering when you're going to come up with another half-baked idea."

It had the effect of an emotional thermite bomb. In a phenomenal energy gain, Drake's nerves went from frigid to boiling. "Now, listen here, you thickheaded ape...you...you dumb lowbrowski! You haven't even offered to co-operate! You haven't even asked any questions! How am I supposed to know everything when you don't tell me and don't ask me?"

"*Me?*" bellowed the captain. "*Me?*" How am I supposed to know what kind of questions to ask about ducks? Who ever heard of raising ducks on a spaceship, anyway? You and your eggs, you egghead! You and your filthy rotten eggs!"

They were on their feet now, glaring at each other. MacDonald was looking from one to the other apprehensively, wondering what was going to happen and when.

"My eggs are cleaner than your filthy stories!" Drake snarled. "At least I don't bore everybody to death with imaginary tales."

That was enough for Dumbrowski. He snarled back at Drake, then, with a bellow of mingled rage and pain, he came at him.

He was heavier than Drake, but they were more evenly matched than might be supposed. The doctor had been working with his ducks in a one-point-five gee field for several years, at least an hour a day. His muscles were harder and tougher than they looked.

Drake stepped aside, and the captain's blow missed. But his other arm, flailing out, caught Drake in the ribs. The doctor grunted and drove a fist into Dumbrowski's abdomen at short range. The spaceman's hard-muscled middle gave a little, and his arms went around Drake. They went down together, rolling over and over on the tough plastic covering that sheathed the steel deck.

MacDonald ran forward to break up the battle, but one of the combatants swung out a leg at just the wrong moment and caught the engineer across the shin. He staggered back, off balance, and dropped, landing hard. He got up and limped toward the intercom while the Battle of Section Seven went on.

He jabbed the general call button and bawled: "Pete! Come down to Seven! These two blockheads are tryna kill each other! On the double!"

Devris barreled down the stairway and tried to help Mac-Donald break up the tussle—without noticeable success. Both of them got punches for their pains.

Finally, Devris ran over to the wall and pulled out the emergency fire hose. He almost turned it on before MacDonald yelled: "Hey! Pete! Water—not carbon tet!"

Devris looked at the selector dial. It pointed at CCl_4. He twisted it past CO_2 to H_2O and flipped the switch. A high-velocity stream of water splattered into the tangled bodies on the floor.

They broke up, sputtering.

"Now both of you stop," Devris commanded, "or I *will* use the carbon tet!"

But it wasn't needed; the water had done the job.

"How's your nose?" Devris asked.

Drake stood before the mirror in his room and surveyed himself. One eye was bruised a little and his nose was badly swollen. "Id hurds," he said, "bud I thig ids gwid bleedig. I'll dage the pagging oud." He pulled the packing from his nostrils and reached into his kit for a little spray gun. He directed the cloud of mist into his nostrils for a second.

"There; that's better."

MacDonald stuck his head in the door. "You all right, doc? Anything broken?"

"I'm O.K.," Drake told him. "For a while I though I'd busted a hand on Dumbrowski's head, but I took a look at it under the transparency, and it's only bruised."

"Well...uh...You *sure* you feel, O.K.?" MacDonald's tone was hesitant. "Uh...the...uh...the captain has a pretty bad eye. I wonder if you'd take a look at it."

Drake hesitated. "I doubt it he'd let me in the room."

MacDonald grinned and relaxed a little. "He said that if you didn't come, I was to tell you that you caused the damage and you had better get up there and fix it or the skipper will confiscate your med kit, report you to the TMA, and personally come down here and beat you in a fair fight." He shrugged. "I'm quoting, you understand."

In spite of the fact that it hurt his lip, Drake grinned. "I'll be right up. And you tell him that if he gives me any trouble I have a hypo here that will put him to sleep for a week."

"Righto!" MacDonald vanished.

As the doctor packed his kit, Devris said: "I see you've learned one thing about Dumbrowski."

"Yeah? What's that?"

"That he doesn't expect anybody to believe what he says when he exaggerates."

Drake paused to let that sink in. "You mean—"

"Yeah. Those stories of his. They bore me, but he and MacDonald have a lot of fun with them. Everybody doesn't have the same tastes, Doc."

Drake closed his kit slowly. "You're right; they don't." He picked up his kit and headed toward the captain's room, wondering what he was going to say.

When he went in, Dumbrowski was sitting in a chair with his shirt off, scratching his hairy chest. His face was a mess. He'd obviously washed it once, but there was still blood pouring from a cut under his eye. With his free hand—the one that wasn't scratching—he was holding a gauze pad to the cut, but it had already become bloodsoaked.

The two men looked at each other without smiling. "You hurt?" Dumbrowski asked levelly.

"Yeah." Drake pointed at his nose. "Slightly busted," he lied. "You?"

Dumbrowski removed the pad, and blood poured from an inch-long cut directly over his cheekbone. "I'm bleedin' to death, you butcher."

Drake walked over and looked at the wound. "I'll put a tourniquet around your neck."

"You would."

Drake took antiseptics and healing agents from his bag and did things with them. Dumbrowski sat stolidly through it all. Finally, the doctor sprayed dermiseal over the cut and pinched it together while the proteinoid plastic polymerized, sealing the edges of the wound.

The eye was badly swollen and purpling. Drake took a hypogun out of his case and fired three minuscule shots into the tissue around the eye and then stood back.

"You'll live," he said.

"Thanks, Doc." He turned to MacDonald. "Mac, go down and get Pete, and you two put that Section Six peegee unit back together. We'll have to work on the main generator coils instead."

When MacDonald had gone, Dumbrowski got up and walked over to his foot locker, from which he extracted a one-liter bottle

162

of amber fluid. "I hope you like Irish," he said. "It's as good for settling a brawl as it is for starting one." He poured two and added ice water. Then he said: "We've got to figure out how we're going to handle these ducks."

He never mentioned the fight again.

"I really don't think I can stand this much longer," Devris said. "I've gone along this far just for the gag, but I have almost reached my limit."

The heat was oppressive. The air was so wet that it seemed to splash as they slogged through it. And at one and a half gravities, even the effort to lift a foot was annoying and tiring.

Drake took a scoopful of duckling food from a fifty-kilo drum and dumped it into the feeding troughs near the brooder.

"Wakwakwak!" chortled a hundred little balls of feathers as they scrambled around the heating unit of the brooder.

Devris poured water into the drinking pans. It ran abnormally fast and splashed queerly under the extra pseudogravitational acceleration. "Yes, sir," he repeated, "just about reached my limit."

"What are you griping about?" Drake asked.

"Oh, nothing, nothing. It's just that for the past two weeks, I have been bumbling around under a gee pull that makes me feel like I was made of lead. I seem to have spent all my life feeding ducklings stuff that acts like bird shot and pouring them drinks that flow like mercury."

"There's not that much difference," Drake objected.

"In addition," the navigator went on, ignoring the interruption, "I have to lug this grossly heavy corpse of mine around through a fever-swamp atmosphere that is gradually driving me to the verge of acute claustrophobia." He wiped at his forehead. "And, as I said, I have just about reached my limit."

"What are you going to do when you reach it?"

"Take a taxi and go home," Devris said, with an air of finality.

Drake finished filling the feeder and dusted off his hands. "That's the last one for today," he said. "Let's go up to your place; I want to look up something in that book of regulations of yours."

Devris set down his bucket of water. "How did you know I had a reg book?"

"Simple deduction."

"He can't even use a word without 'duck' in it," Devris whispered in a hoarse aside. "O.K. How?"

"I reasoned that no one would be able to quote from regula-

163

tions the way you do without having studied them extensively. Whence, it follows that you must own a copy of your own, since it would be inconvenient for you to borrow the captain's all the time—and bad politics, besides."

"Marvelous, Holmes! Absolutely marvelous! You figured it out with only those few clues?"

"Almost," Drake admitted modestly. "Of course, there was one additional bit of evidence."

"Which was?"

"I saw the book in your room."

"Holmes, you are phenomenal; let's go."

The two men plodded their way up the stairs. The entire ship was under one hundred and fifty per cent of a Standard Gee now; the power coils had had to be rebuilt, but it was easier than redoing each floor singly.

They finally pushed their way into Devris' cabin and sat down.

"Whooo!" Devris said. "At least it's cooler in here."

MacDonald had rigged up individual air-conditioners for the sleeping rooms, but nothing could be done about increased pressure and gravity. The air was cooler and less humid, that was all.

Drake took the copy of the Interstellar Commission Regulations and began leafing through it.

"What's the trouble?" the navigator asked.

"Space," Drake said. "We haven't got enough floor area on the ship to take care of the ducks unless we jettison some of the cargo. This is a pretty big ship, but it's not big enough."

"Cargo?" Devris put a finger to his chin and stared at the ceiling. "You want to get rid of non-perishable cargo. Hm-m-m." He rubbed his chin with the finger. "Try Section XIX, Paragraph...uh...seven, I think."

Drake turned to that section and began reading.

"The cargo officer shall be responsible for all damage to the ship due to shifting cargo, since it shall—"

"Nope," Devris interrupted, "that's for bigger ships, with four or five men in the crew. Wrong paragraph. Try Seventeen."

Drake flipped over several pages. "If, in case of emergency, it shall become necessary to jettison cargo, such cargo shall be that which is the least—"

"I can boil that down for you," Devris said. "There are orders of precedence. The idea is to junk the cheapest, most useless cargo first, and work your way up. Suppose you have a hundred kilos of oxygen and a hundred kilos of diamonds, and you have to get rid of a hundred kilos of something. What do you get rid of?

"Well, if it's space you need, you get rid of the oxy, because a hundred kilos of diamonds can be broken up and stashed here and there in out-of-the-way places. Even if they couldn't, they'd be kept because they're a bit more expensive than oxy.

"On the other hand, if the ship is low on oxy, you jettison the diamonds. See?"

"Who decides which to drop?" Drake asked.

"The captain, always—even if there's a cargo officer aboard. It's the captain's decision, because his job is to protect life first and property afterwards."

Drake nodded. "That's what I wanted; I'm going up to see Dumbrowski."

As he was toiling his way up the stairs, he met Dumbrowski toiling his way down.

"Oh, there you are," the captain said. "I wanted to know if you needed that incubator any more."

"Just what I was going to talk to you about. I was looking things up in the regulations, and I found we can toss out a lot of stuff—a lot of the cheaper cargo."

Dumbrowski nodded slowly. "You looked it up, eh? That's good. But, you know, I hate to throw anything away—and I don't think I will."

"But, captain—"

"Will you kindly go back down those stairs? I'm getting tired of just standing here. Let's go to Devris' room."

Drake retreated obediently. They went to the navigator's compartment, and Dumbrowski knocked resoundingly on the door. "Pete! It's me."

"Come on in, skipper," Devris said.

Dumbrowski looked at the doctor. "I wouldn't want to open the door while he was cleaning lenses," he said. "It might get dust on them if I opened the door too suddenly."

"I see," said Drake.

They pushed the door open and sat down.

"Now, about this jettisoning cargo," Dumbrowski began. "I don't think it's necessary. Besides, we just couldn't dump all the stuff we'll need. We couldn't get rid of all your duck food, could we?"

"No-o-o; we couldn't."

"But we'll need that space. So, I have an idea. Look; we're a good long way from the nearest large gravitational body. Is that right, Pete?"

"I haven't detected anything in the past five weeks. We're nine light-years from the nearest star. It's a blue-white; you can't miss it if you look out the ports."

Dumbrowski nodded and looked back at Drake. "So here's what we do: We take all the stuff we can and cart it outside and attach it to the hull with magnaclamps. That includes all those drums of duck food, and everything else. The brooders, too, when you're through with 'em.

"Then, if we need anything, all we have to do is go out and get it. Follow?"

Devris just nodded, but Drake felt rather dazed. It had never occurred to him that it was possible to throw something overboard without throwing it away.

I'm just not used to thinking in terms like that, he thought. *I keep thinking of aircraft.* Then he thought of something else. "What do we do when the rescue ship comes?"

"Well, they'll be able to take part of the cargo, and we'll haul back in the rest. Those ducks can be crowded for a couple of days, can't they?"

"Sure; two days won't matter." After all, he decided, it wouldn't really crowd them much. By that time, all the feed would be gone—or at least most of it would.

"Good," said Dumbrowski. "Good. There's one other problem. Who's going to clean up after the ducks?"

Drake smiled a sickly smile. "I guess we'll all have to work at it. It'll all have to be carted to the disposal."

"Three cheers." Dumbrowski stood up. "Well, MacDonald and I will start hauling stuff outside." And with that, he heaved himself up and walked out.

"You know," Drake said, looking at the closed door, "that guy worries me. For the past couple of weeks, I thought that... well—" He stood up and looked at his hands, frowning. "I thought we'd arrived at an understanding." He looked up at Devris. "But he still seems worried about something."

"Well, sure he is," Devris said. "He's not going to be in the best of odor with the Commission."

"Why not?"

"You mean you don't know?" Devris sat down again on a nearby chair. "Why, man, he's in trouble. So am I, and so is MacDonald—although neither of us is in as bad a jam as the skipper is."

"Why?"

"Because the ship has been disabled. We don't have any reasonable explanation for it. I'm in a jam because he had the control panels open when the duck walked in. But Dumbrowski is in a jam because he's captain, and all this is his fault. He's directly responsible for the whole thing."

Devris wasn't looking at Drake now; he was looking at his fingernails. "Maybe you wondered," he said, "why the skipper was so sore at you after the accident. Maybe I should have told you before this, but here it is.

"The *Constanza* is Dumbrowski's whole life. Sure, his little wife is a nice gal, but she's not something you can anchor your life to. Dumbrowski's pinned his life to *Constanza.*"

Drake chewed at his lower lip. "I can see that. Sure. But what did I do?"

Devris looked up from his fingernails. "It isn't something you did. It's something you can't be held responsible for.

"The ship has been wrecked. For the first time in his career, Dumbrowski has had to call for help because his ship was out of commission. *His* ship. The *Constanza.*

"I'm responsible because I brought the duck up. And Mac, as I said, is responsible because he shouldn't have let the duck get in. But Dumbrowski may never get another promotion—it's his ship that was wrecked."

"I see," Drake said slowly. "And I'm not responsible at all?"

"Not as far as the Commission is concerned. It couldn't be shifted on to you, even if you wanted it to be." Devris smiled a little. "And I know you well enough after all these weeks to know that you'd take responsibility if you could. But it won't wash. It can't be done. We've *had* it—that's all."

Heat. Damp, soggy, broiling heat. Unpleasant, miserable heat, from which there was no escape. And a great burden of weight that sapped the strength rapidly in the hot, wet air.

MacDonald lifted another shovelful and dumped it into the wheelbarrow. He was stripped to the waist, clad only in a pair of sport shorts and his boots, and the perspiration ran down his neck and chest and back, soaked into the shorts, ran on down his legs, and collected in soggy pools in his boots. His hands were slippery on the handle of the improvised shovel, making it difficult to work.

Across the room, Drake was surrounded by hundreds of

awkward little birds who chorused their monotonous *wakwak-wak.*

MacDonald stopped shoveling for a moment and said: "I'm glad I'm not the feed man around here; I'm perfectly happy to handle the other end of the operation."

"I don't follow you," said Drake.

"No, but the ducks follow you," the engineer pointed out. "It would drive me nuts to have them underfoot all the time."

Drake put more feed in the pans. "You mean you think they follow me around just because I feed 'em?"

"Well, don't they? You give 'em their goodies; I just clean up after 'em."

"It isn't that," Drake said. "Even if you fed them, they'd still follow me; I'm the first moving thing they saw after they hatched. It's a built-in reflex. They think I'm their mother."

MacDonald plied his shovel again. "In that case, I am gladder than ever. Imagine being mama to thousands of ducks." He lifted the scoop and dumped it into the wheelbarrow. "Imagine. Thousands and thousands of ducks. Following you. Loving you. 'Mama! I stubbed my little webby foot, Mama. Kiss it and make it well.' "

"Stop!" Drake said. "You make it sound nauseating."

"It *smells* nauseating!" boomed a voice from the door. "This whole ship is beginning to smell like a chicken coop!"

"Duck coop," MacDonald corrected as Captain Dumbrowski came on in.

"Where are you taking that?" Dumbrowski asked, pointing at the wheelbarrow.

"To the disposal. Why?"

"Well, we can stop that right now! You're an engineer, it says here; you ought to be able to figure it out."

MacDonald stopped and wiped his forearm over his dripping brow. "You mean clogging the disposal? Nah. There isn't that much."

"There will be; there will be. Drake! Are these figures you gave me on feeding correct?"

Drake dusted crumbs of feed from his fingers, and walked toward Dumbrowski. "I'm pretty sure they are—why?" As he walked, the ducklings followed lovingly.

"According to this, each one of those ducks will eat approximately seventeen kilos of feed in the next fourteen weeks. At the end of that time, they'll mass about four kilos each."

"That's right."

MacDonald dropped his shovel. "By the Seven Purple Hells of Palain! Nearly sixty-five thousand kilograms! The disposal won't take it—not by a long shot!"

Drake said: "Well, I'll admit there'll be more per day as the ducks grow, but—" Then he stopped. "What can we do?"

"Do? There's only one thing we *can* do. Dehydrate the stuff and dump it overboard!"

Drake looked down at the ducklings clustered around his feet. "But we can't do that! We've got to reclaim the grit!"

"Grit? What do you mean *grit*?" Dumbrowski asked.

"Sand and gravel. Ducks don't have any teeth, so they have to eat a certain amount of grit to grind up the food in their crops. Without it, they'll die. But there isn't enough on board. We were going to hatch these birds on Okeefenokee, where there'd be plenty of it, so we didn't bother to bring any along."

"Then what the devil have you been doing?"

"Re-using what we have. It isn't digested, of course, so I've been reclaiming it as fast as it's eliminated, sterilizing it, and giving it back to them."

Dumbrowski put a hand over his eyes. "Let me think."

MacDonald and Drake stood there silently while the captain

cerebrated. Finally, he took his damp hand away from his eyes and looked at MacDonald. "The A stage will have to be disconnected and used separately. We can dehydrate the stuff and take the sand out, but the organic section—well, that simply can't be overloaded. It'll have to go outside."

"I can do it," said MacDonald. "But it'll mean we'll have to dump it out the air lock at least once a day."

"You can do it when we go out to get new cans of food. Make it all one operation," said Drake.

"Yeah," said Dumbrowski. "You know," he went on, with a touch of bitterness in his voice, "this isn't a spaceship—it's a sea anemone!"

"I see what you mean," said Drake.

Overhead, two ducks flapped by.

Two men stood in the decompression room of the air lock while the pumps labored to reduce the pressure to zero. Their spacesuits swelled a little as the air left the room, and between them, a box of grayish powder churned softly as the atmospheric gases between the particles of powder worked their way out.

"Are you sure you'll be all right, Doc?" MacDonald asked.

"I think so. With this nylon rope to anchor me, if I get nauseated again, you can pull me back."

"Well, it will be easier with two of us, but Devris could have gone instead."

"He's got to keep shoveling. I can't scrape up the stuff from the floors," he explained.

"Oh? Why not?"

"Because I can't keep the ducks away from me. Every time I lift up a scoopful, I get three or four ducks with it!"

MacDonald shook his head inside the bubble of his space helmet. "Poor mama duck. Or should I say Papa Drake?"

"You should say nothing of the kind," the doctor said.

The "all clear" light winked on, and MacDonald opened the outer door.

"You go out first, Doc. Ease yourself past the barrier field slowly. Keep a hand on the edge of the door. And remember, you're not falling. Just keep your eyes open."

Drake did as he was told, and, in a few seconds, he was outside the ship and outside the paragravity field.

"How do you feel?" MacDonald's voice came over the phone.

"All right. A little confused, but I'm not sick. And everything isn't spinning around."

"O.K.; I'll be right with you." He came out, dragging the heavy box with him. "Now, can you clamp your boots onto the hull? They'll come on automatically; all you have to do is put them flat on the metal." He demonstrated, and Drake followed suit.

"I'm O.K., now," he said. "Here—let me carry the box while you get the food."

"Fine." MacDonald raised a gloved finger and pointed. "The dumping ground is right back there near the tail."

Drake looked around him. Here and there, spread over the outer hull of the ship, were fantastic-looking shapes—various pieces of the cargo which had had to be taken outside. He could see the incubator looming queerly in the dim illumination of the far-off stars.

MacDonald was making his way toward a jungle of steel drums which held the duck food. Drake watched him for a moment, then started walking toward the tail of the ship.

It was an eerie feeling; the ship was big, but it wasn't big enough to make one feel one was walking on a planet. The horizon was much too close. His boots were a little difficult to handle at first; the magnetic soles stuck tenaciously to the hull and had to be pulled off with each step. Finally, he found it easier to shuffle along, sliding the magnets over the hull.

Ahead of him, he saw a huge white patch on the hull. His helmet light gleamed off its surface. The dumping ground. He shuffled into the area, his boots raising clouds of the stuff, which only settled very slowly under the feeble pull of the ship's orthogravitational mass.

When he reached a spot near the middle of the heap, he turned the box upside down to dump it.

Nothing happened. The stuff just stayed in the box.

Sure, he thought to himself, grinning; *not enough pull to make it fall out of the box.*

Well, that was easily solved. With the box still held upside down, he shoved down hard, and then stopped the box. The powder, with its inertia undiminished, went on out, moving toward the hull. It hit—and splashed!

Like a liquid, the powder sprayed out in all directions, enveloping Drake in a white cloud.

He tried to back away from it, but instead of backing, he jumped. His boots came loose from the hull. He was drifting, weightless, in a cloud that was as impenetrable as heavy fog. His helmet light illuminated the particles a few feet in front of his face, but beyond that, there was nothing.

For a moment, nausea threatened to further complicate matters, but he forced it down. "Mac," he said steadily into his phone, "I think I'll need a little help."

"Yeah? What happened?"

Drake told him.

"Have you still got the box?" MacDonald asked.

"Yes."

"O.K." There was a feeling of stifled laughter in MacDonald's tone. "I'll go back to the lock and pull you in on the nylon rope."

A minute or so later, Drake felt a slight tug on his rope. And that was all. Just the first slight tug, then nothing. Had his rope broken?

"Mac!" he yelled frantically. "I think my rope broke! I'm lost!"

"Take it easy, Doc; take it easy. You're O.K. I just gave enough pull on the rope to get you started in this direction. You'll drift on in. I'm taking up slack now."

Drake didn't feel as though he were moving. "Taking up slack? Are you sure? Why don't you keep pulling?" His voice sounded strained, and it boomed loudly inside the helmet.

"If I kept pulling, I'd accelerate you. I don't want to brain you or something. Ahhh! Here you come!"

The white cloud was thinning, now, soon Drake could see that he was, indeed, drifting toward the air lock.

He moved in near MacDonald. The engineer reached out, grabbed his legs and pushed them down toward the hull. The boot magnets grabbed hold.

"Let's get inside," MacDonald said. "This suit is beginning to itch."

"Itch? Hell, this is the first time I've been comfortable in five weeks!"

"Yeah? Well, I itch. Say—how come you walked out into the middle of that to dump the box? That won't settle for days."

"It looked higher out in the middle—I thought that's what you had been doing."

"Naw! I walk up to the edge and give the box a shove. The stuff slides along the hull plates and piles up in just about the middle. Didn't you see the drift marks?"

Drake nodded. "Sure, but I thought it was just the wind—" He stopped and felt his face going a bright red.

How stupid can you get? Wind? *In space?*

But MacDonald only said: "Boy, will I be glad to get this suit off and scratch."

The next day, MacDonald was sick. His eyes were swelled almost shut, and his skin was covered with red, blotchy patches that itched like fire.

While Dumbrowski and Devris labored over the feeding and the cleaning, Drake labored over MacDonald. The man was feverish and miserable. The high temperature and the humidity hadn't helped any.

Dumbrowski, worried, got the ducks fed in short order and hurried up to MacDonald's cabin as fast as a one-point-five gee would let him.

Drake had pumped several shots into the engineer's blood system, and sprayed his skin with a soothing semi-anaesthetic lotion. The swelling was beginning to go down a little.

Dumbrowski stood at the door, waiting for him to finish; when he was, the captain motioned with his hand.

"What's the matter with him? Is it contagious?"

Drake shook his head. "No. Simple allergy reaction, that's all. He'll be all right."

"Something he ate?"

"No—he's allergic to duck feathers."

Dumbrowski leaned against the wall, and said nothing for a long moment. "I think I could cry," he said after a bit. "I honestly think I could cry. Can't cure him, I suppose?"

"Not with what I have on board. All I can do is keep the reaction down. He'll have to stay away from the ducks from now on."

Dumbrowski looked at Drake. "You know," he said philosophically, "when this trip is over, I think I shall apply for a vacation in the Martian uranium mines. I understand it's very pleasant."

Drake listened to the *scrape, scrape, scrape* of the shovel as Dumbrowski pushed it over the deck. It was a good thing the decks were covered with plastic; it would have been impossible to keep bare steel clean by scraping alone.

The doctor had put a small amount of the sterilized grit into a test tube and added hydrochloric acid. He held it up to look at it. Behind him, he could hear Dumbrowski's heavy breathing.

"No bubbles," Drake said. "No lime."

"What?" the captain asked wheezily.

Drake turned around. "There's no lime left in the grit. It's supplied in the form of crushed oyster shell; the birds need it for bone formation now and egg formation later. It dissolves slowly,

173

so most of the oyster shell is excreted intact. But this grit has been reprocessed so many times that there's no lime left."

Devris pushed open the door and trundled in a can of feed on the improvised wheelbarrow. He listened for a moment to the gasping breath of the captain and watched the worried look on Drake's face. "How much of this can the human system stand?" he asked, of no one in particular. "Mac has eczema, the skipper is coming down with asthma, Drake has ducks, and I have the galloping heebie-jeebies."

Dumbrowski ignored him. "What about this lime, Doc? Can they do without it?"

"Not at this stage of the game; it'd kill them to go without it for very long."

"I will gladly sacrifice my useless bones to be ground up for duck food," Devris volunteered. "Or, if that seems drastic, we can all pull each other's teeth."

"Very funny," said Drake sarcastically.

"It isn't so funny, at that," Dumbrowski told him. "We haven't got any lime on board. Why didn't you think of this before?"

"It's never come up before," Drake said, irritated. "We know how much oyster shell to give them, but the amount that's actually absorbed has never been computed because there's no necessity for it, usually."

"Well, you still should have mentioned it before now!" Dumbrowski's voice was tight.

"Hey! Hey!" Devris interrupted. "Don't go flying off the handle, you two! That fire hose, you know, still works." He set the can of feed gently on the floor, shooing ducks out of the way.

"You know the trouble with you two guys?" he continued. "You, Doc, know everything about ducks and nothing about spaceships. And the skipper knows everything about spaceships and nothing about ducks. And neither of you knows which bit of information is vitally necessary for the other. And you both think the other is playing it dirty by withholding information."

"You're right," said Dumbrowski, cooling perceptibly. "I'm sorry, Doc; now, let's think about this.

"Lime, you say. I'm not much of a chemist; isn't that calcium oxide?"

"Not in this case. 'Lime' can be calcium oxide, or calcium hydroxide, or calcium phosphate, or calcium carbonate, depending on who's doing the talking. In this case, it's the carbonate."

"You couldn't use calcium chloride, I suppose. We've got plenty of that in the emergency air purifiers."

"I'm afraid not. It'd have to be the carbonate."

174

"Hey!" Devris said suddenly. "I'm no chemist, either, but couldn't we add carbon dioxide to it or something?"

"Not unless we had plenty of sodium hydroxide or the like—"

"We do!" said Dumbrowski. "We've got that in the air purifiers, too! It takes the CO_2 out!"

"Then we've got it!" Drake was excited. "We run enough carbon dioxide through it to make sodium carbonate; then we mix the calcium chloride with it! The calcium carbonate formed will drop to the bottom because it's insoluble, leaving sodium chloride in solution! It's perfect!"

Then his face fell. "But we can't tamper with the air purifiers, can we?"

Devris and Dumbrowski both grinned. The navigator said: "That proves my point—you don't know enough about spaceships."

Dumbrowski said: "These are the emergency purifiers. As long as the electronic purifiers work, we don't use the chemicals—too inefficient. We only have 'em aboard in case the electronics go out—and they're in good condition. Besides, we shouldn't have to use all the chemicals. About how much would you need?"

"I'll have to figure it out from the lime removed from the grit, but it shouldn't be too much."

"Good! We're all set, then."

More weeks passed. The brooders were taken outside to make more room as the birds increased in size and need for living space. By the end of the sixteenth week, the *Constanza* was full of ducks. From engine room to control dome, there were nothing but ducks—ducks that waddled and quacked and flapped their way freely through the huge ship. All the doors were left open now, except those which sealed off the engines and the control rooms and the sleeping compartments. Everywhere else, there were ducks. Thousands of ducks.

It had been hard work, but the pressure was beginning to let up a little as the hour of their rescue approached. None of the men had had too much sleep, and all had lost weight. Even Dumbrowski was beginning to look hollow-cheeked.

To Drake, everything was fine; his ducks were in fine fettle, all of them. The tanks that had been built and flooded for swimming purposes were being used as the older ducks taught the young ones to swim. Everything was fine except for one thing—he still didn't understand the odd aloofness that concealed Dumbrowski's anger. Why should the captain be sore at Drake *before* the accident happened? The remark about "Drake and his harem of ducks" still rankled.

He didn't understand it until one evening when Devris broke into song. Dumbrowski was not in the little common room when it happened; he was in his own cabin.

Devris was singing: "Old MacDonald had a ship, E,I,E,I,O! And on this ship, he had some ducks, E,I,E,I,O! With a *Quack! Quack!* here and a *Quack! Quack!* there, here a *Quack!* there a *Quack!* everywhere a *Quack! Quack!* Old MacDonald had a ship, E,I,E,I,O-O-O-O!"

When he'd reached the part where he said "here a *Quack!*" he'd indicated Drake with a thumb. The doctor grinned good-humoredly. MacDonald was laughing uproariously.

Devris had started with the second verse: "Old MacDonald got the itch, E,I,E,I,O!"

"That's a lie!" bellowed Dumbrowski's voice from the door. They all stopped and looked at him. It was quite obvious that he had been hitting the Irish bottle.

"No it isn't, skipper," Devris said. "He does have the itch."

"I mean about the ship! This is *my* ship! It ain't Old Mac-Donald's ship, or Drake's ship, or the ducks' ship! It's my ship, and I'm captain here!" He swung around to Drake. "You understand that, Quack?"

Drake didn't mind Devris calling him that, but when Dumbrowski did, it made him see red. He stood up. "What makes you think I care who runs this dirty tub?"

"Dirty tub! Who made it dirty? You! You and your *carte blanche* orders from the Commission!"

MacDonald and Devris were both on their feet, moving to block off the captain.

But Drake said: "Wait a minute! What's all this about? What *carte blanche?* I don't know what you're talking about!"

Dumbrowski said something foul. Then he added: "And I don't care what the Commission does, either! I'm captain here! See!" He turned back into his cabin and came out again with two sheets of flimsy. "Here!" He threw them at Drake. Then he slammed the door, leaving the three men alone.

Drake picked up the papers and read them.

"What does it say, Doc?" MacDonald asked.

Drake looked up slowly. "He must have got this before take-off. It says that Dr. Rouen Drake is entirely responsible for the cargo, and that any orders pertaining to the cargo should be obeyed."

Devris whistled softly. "Wow!"

"No wonder he's been sore!" MacDonald said.

Drake swore, borrowing some of Dumbrowski's vocabulary.

"How stupid can they get! I swear to you, I didn't ask for any such thing. I thought I was just bucking the skipper's bullheadedness. I wonder why he didn't say something about this before?"

"He probably assumed you knew," Devris said. "He should have said something about it though."

"I'm glad he didn't," Drake said softly. "I've learned a lot in the past eight and a half months."

"What do you mean?"

"I was so stupid then that I might have tried to give orders." Drake's voice was very low.

The captain of the cargo ship *Stramaglia* looked out of his control blister at the mass ahead.

"It most certainly does *not* look like the *Constanza*," he said. "I wonder what those things are sticking out all over it? And why is it painted white?"

"May as well find out," said his engineer. He held his helmet globe under his arm. "Jones and I will go over and take a look."

Captain Dumbrowski and his crew were waiting for the men from the *Stramaglia* as soon as they came in from the air lock, their spacesuits coated with white powder.

Martin, the engineer, and Jones, the navigator of the rescue ship, were confronted by three tired-looking, almost emaciated men. The newcomers found one-point-five gees difficult to bear, but the men from the *Constanza* seemed to be used to it.

"Don't take your helmets off just yet," Dumbrowski said. "The air pressure in here is pretty high. Let it leak in."

"O.K.," said Martin. "By the way, what is that white stuff we got all over us?" At the same moment he cracked his helmet just a little, and a hissing jet of the ship's atmosphere hit him in the face. He flinched. "And what's that smell?"

"Duck excrement," said Dumbrowski, answering two questions with two syllables.

"These two men are Lieutenant Devris, my navigator, and Dr. Drake, in charge of ducks. My engineer, MacDonald, is confined to quarters for being allergic to ducks."

"Uh...I...uh, yeah. Sure. Are you ready to start work on the control systems?"

"Let's go," said Dumbrowski. "And mind the ducks."

"Huh?"

"Never mind—come along."

"This place isn't so bad," said Devris. "It isn't nearly as hot as I thought."

Dumbrowski looked around him at the scenery of Okeefenokee. Overhead hung drifts of clouds, through which a bright yellow sun blazed. "It isn't as hot as it was on the ship. This is in the southern hemisphere; the ducks are to be set free farther north, nearer the equator."

"Have they got the ducks unloaded yet?"

"Yeah," said Dumbrowski. "Now they're airing it out and washing it down."

The *Constanza* and the *Stramaglia* towered high over the little cluster of buildings around the planet's one small spaceport. So far, the planet only had a population of eighty, and these were mostly ecologists and biologists studying the planet. It wouldn't be fit to really colonize for a while yet.

They had been on the planet less than twenty-four hours, but they had been ordered to return to Earth as soon as practicable—which meant immediately.

MacDonald was walking toward Dumbrowski and Devris, holding a sheet of paper in his hand. "Communication from Earth," he said, handing the sheet to the captain.

Dumbrowski read it and said: "What the devil? Listen to this: 'Excellent job on preserving shipment to Okeefenokee. Citation is being placed in your promotion file for job above and beyond call of duty. Congratulations.'" He looked wonderingly at MacDonald and Devris. "How could that be?"

"Devris—tell him," said MacDonald.

"Drake worked it out," Devris explained. "That stupid order wasn't his idea. He didn't even know anything about it. So he wrote a report that ought to keep the top brass from ever pulling a stunt like that again."

"But...but...*how?*"

"They'd put him in charge of the cargo, hadn't they? Well, remember Section XIX, Paragraph Seven?"

"No."

"Well, Drake did after seeing it once. It says that the cargo officer is responsible for all damage due to shifting cargo, because it's his job to make sure it doesn't shift—follow? Well, technically, a duck is cargo in this case, and if it shifted—or walked, or flew—in such a way as to damage the ship, it's the cargo officer's fault. And that message you got from the Commission technically appointed him cargo officer. And that's against regs, because the *Constanza* only rates a three-man crew. Drake tied 'em up good."

"But what will they do to him?" MacDonald asked.

Dumbrowski grinned. "Nothing. What can they do? He's not a member of the Space Service."

"They could give him a commission and then bust him," Devris said helpfully.

The voyage home would be pure vacation. It would be cool and comfortable, and a one-gee pull all the way. Nothing to do but loaf and get soft after eighteen weeks of hell.

The *Constanza* lifted comfortably from the surface of Okeefenokee and speared Earthwards at ten thousand light speeds.

"Ahhhh!" said Dumbrowski. "Feel that air! Smell that air! Deelightfull! Open another beer."

"Glad to," said Drake. "I am going to enjoy this trip."

Dumbrowski hadn't apologized, and Drake hadn't even worried about it. Each knew how the other felt.

"I'm going to have to juggle my books," Drake said, sipping at his beer. "Otherwise, I'll get hell when we get home."

"How's that?" Devris asked interestedly.

"Evidently my egg count was off. I know how many ducks died *en route*—about average. But I must have miscounted the number of eggs that didn't hatch. I was one short."

"What'll they do? Charge you two thousand bucks for it?"

"Nope. I'll just add one to my bad egg count, that's all."

"Damn!" said MacDonald. "I itch?" He scratched furiously at his arm.

"Maybe there's a duck feather around," said Devris.

Then they heard a far-off sound, and all four men stared at each other in horror. They knew, then, why MacDonald itched, and what had happened to the extra duck.

The sound came again.

Somewhere a duck quacked.

MASTERS OF THE METROPOLIS

By Randall Garrett and Lin Carter

Well, you see, it was like this:
    Lin Carter and I were having a few drinks one night.
More than a few.
Several.

We were discussing Hugo Gernsback's classic, Ralph 124C41+, the first novel written as science fiction, back in 1912. The term "science fiction" had not been invented yet, and would not be until Hugo Gernsback himself invented it in the Thirties. (He had previously invented the word "scientifiction," but it didn't work out right. If you want to research this, see the several works of my friend, Sam Moskowitz, one of the outstanding historians of science fiction.)

Anyway, Lin pointed out that the trouble with Ralph was that the folk of the future were always so amazed at what was going on about them, whereas we, in the mid-fifties, were not. Lin was right. We, today, take scientific miracles for granted. The man on the street does not gawp at flights to the moon or the fantastic things computers can do.

But—suppose he did!

CHAPTER I

The Journey Begins

It was in the Eighth Month of the Year 1956 that Sam IM4 SF+ strode down the surging, crowded streets of Newark, one of the many cities of its kind in the State of New Jersey. He had just left his apartment in one of the vast, soaring pylons of the city. There, living in universal accord, hundreds of families dwelt side by side in the same great tower, one of many which loomed as many as forty stories above the street.

He paused to board a *bus* which stopped at regularly-spaced intervals to take on new passengers. The *bus*, or Omnibus, was a streamlined, self-propelled public vehicle, powered by the exploding gases of distilled petroleum, ignited in a sealed cylinder by means of an electrical spark. The energy thus obtained was applied as torque to a long metal bar known as the "drive-shaft," which turned a set of gears in a complex apparatus known as the "differential housing." These gears, in turn, caused the rear wheels to revolve about their axes, thus propelling the vehicle forward smoothly at velocities as great as eighty miles every hour!

Dropping a coin into the receptacle by the driver's cubicle, and receiving a courteous welcome from the technician employed to pilot the machine, he took his seat inside the vehicle. Marveling anew at the luxurious comfort of the form-fitting seats, Sam IM4 SF+ gazed out of the window at the gorgeous spectacle of the city as it raced past.

Within a very few moments, the vehicle decelerated to a smooth stop before Pennsylvania Station, a mammoth terminal where the far-flung lines of public transportation converged.

Entering the great building, he paused to marvel anew at the inspiring architectural genius capable of erecting such an imposing monument to modern civilization—a building which would have struck with awe the simpler citizens of earlier times.

Threading his way through the crowds which thronged the vaulted interior of the terminal, he came to a *turnstile*, an artifact not unlike a rimless wheel, whose spokes revolved to allow his passage. He placed a coin in the mechanism, and the marvelous machine—but one of the many mechanical marvels of the age—recorded his passage on a small dial and automatically added the value of his coin to the total theretofore accumulated. All this, mind, without a single human hand at the controls!

Once past the *turnstile*, Sam IM4 SF+ followed the ingenious directional signs on the walls, which led him to a vast, artificially-lighted underground cavern. There he waited for his second conveyance to arrive.

Sam IM4 SF+, a typical citizen of his age, towered a full six feet above the ground. His handsome face was crowned by a massive, intellectual forehead. His hair was dark and smooth, neatly trimmed to follow the contours of his skull. He was clad in complex and attractive garments, according to the fashion of his century. His trousers were woven of a fabric synthetically formulated from a clever mixture of chemicals, as was his coat, for these favored people no longer depended upon herds of domesticated quadrupeds for their raiment. These garments were fastened, not by buttons, but by an ingenious system of automatically interlocking metallic teeth known as a *zipper*.

Suspended from his ears, a frame of stiff wires supported a pair of polished lenses before his eyes, which served not only to protect those orbs from the rushing winds that were a natural hazard of this Age of Speed, but also to implement his vision, lending it an almost telescopic power.

As he stood on the platform, his sensitive ears detected the distant roar of a *subway train*. Gazing down the dark tunnel by whose egress the platform stood, he observed the cyclopean glare of the artificial light affixed to the blunt nose of the onrushing all-metallic projectile. The entire cavern reverberated to the roar of the vehicle as it emerged from the tunnel with a mighty rush of wind and braked smoothly to a dead stop before his very feet.

The marvel of modern transportation which was to bear him on his journey to the great Metropolis of New York had arrived!

CHAPTER II

Aboard the *Subway Train*

The automatic door slid open, and our hero entered the car and was offered a seat by one of the courteous, uniformed crewmembers.

Pausing to marvel anew at this miracle of modern science, Sam IM4 SF+ turned to a fellow traveler and remarked conversationally: "Ah, fellow citizen; is it not wonderful to reflect that the same Energy which propels us through the very bowels of the Earth is identical with the lightning that flames in stormy skies, far above these Stygian depths? For thousands of years, the simple peasants of a ruder age looked upon the lightning bolt as the awesome weapon of angry gods; little did they surmise that their descendants would one day chain this Gargantuan power and harness it to serve their will!"

"How true!" remarked his companion. "And could one of them now be with us as we speed through this fantastic system of tunnels, would he not be struck dumb with terror and think us gods?"

"Would he not, indeed," smiled Sam, "commonplace though it is to us."

As they were speaking, the *subway train* sprang to life and plunged into the ebon mouth of another tunnel. In an instant, the vast, lighted cavern was lost to view, and the car was swallowed in the blackness of the tunnel, illuminated only by the colored lights set at intervals along the cavern walls as signals to the pilot.

The mighty engine thundered through the darkness like some mythical monster of a bygone age. Sam, however, experienced no difficulty in observing his fellow passengers, since the interior of the vehicle was brilliantly illuminated by ingenious artificial lighting. These *light bulbs* consisted of cleverly blown globes of glass which contained a delicate and intricate filament of tungsten wire. Upon the application of sufficient electrical current, the wire heated up to many hundreds of degrees, thus emitting a bright and pleasant light. Indeed, so great was the temperature at which they operated, the globes were filled with inert gas in order to prevent even the highly refractive tungsten from burning in the air!

Sam spent his time pleasantly by reading the various colorful and informative signs within the car. These advertisements portrayed the many necessities and luxuries which all citizens of this age might acquire. Each told of its own product in glowing, descriptive terms. Here, a poster told of a harmless chemical mixture which, when applied to the skin, destroyed the unpleasant body odors with which earlier ages had been plagued; there, another card told of a confection which, when masticated, acted as a tooth-cleansing agent, thus serving as an aid to the buoyant health of the people of this era.

Within a few minutes, the vehicle had passed beneath the rolling waters of the mighty Hudson River, and emerged from the darkness into another vast cavern, larger than, though similar to, the one in which our hero first boarded the conveyance.

As the passengers emerged in orderly rows from the *subway train*, Sam joined them and thus beheld the awe-inspiring vastness of Grand Central Station. Breathtaking was the panorama that greeted his dazzled orbs as he joined the motley throng that surged and eddied beneath the tremendous dome. A traveler from an earlier age would have been confused and lost in the orderly chaos of the great terminal. Level upon level, tier upon tier, exit upon exit met the eye at every turn.

But Sam IM4 SF+ was no stranger here; indeed, he gave scarcely a glance to the confusion through which he made his way. In a very few moments, he left the building to gaze in awe at the fantastic sight of the great Metropolis of New York, the hugest city ever constructed—vast, even on the mammoth scale of other cities of this advanced age.

CHAPTER III

Through the Vast Metropolis

All about him soared the incredible towers, spires, pylons, monuments, buildings, palaces, temples, cathedrals, domes, and other breath-taking constructions of the Metropolis. Through its broad streets moved the traffic of the great city. Row on row of metallic projectiles called *automobiles* passed smoothly, silently, and swiftly through the streets. Powered by the same "internal combustion engine" that powered the Omnibus, they were marvels of mechanical genius. So common were they to the favored children of this Mechanical Age that the gayly-costumed passersby scarcely gave them a glance, even when crossing the streets through which the *autos* ran.

Sam lifted his nobly-sculptured head and gazed enthralled at the towers that rose, rank upon serried rank, as far as the eye could see. Their smooth, regular sides of artificial stone literally blazed with hundreds of illuminated windows. Their lofty tops seemed to touch the very sky itself—for which reason, let me remark in passing, the inhabitants called them *Sky-Scrapers*.

"Ah, madam," exclaimed Sam to a lovely young woman, who, curiously attired in the daring fashions of the age, stood near him, also gazing in awe at the spectacle, "how much vaster is our great Metropolis even that storied Nineveh, or Tyre, or mighty Babylon with its famed hanging gardens, or Carthage of yore!"

"Truly, good sir," she responded modestly. "And is it not wonderful that we are here to see it all? Ah, would not some proud Caesar or Attila of old have given all his treasures for such a privilege?"

Before them, in multicolored grandeur, blazed hundreds of vast advertising displays, each shining with a light that dazzled the eye of the beholder. These sign-lights were ingeniously wrought tubes of glass of no greater diameter than a common lead-pencil, but many feet in length. The tubes were curved to form the various letters and symbols which made up the great illuminated signs, and were filled with various gases under low pressure. When electrical energy of tremendous voltage was applied to electrodes at the ends of the tubes, the gas within glowed brilliantly with colored light, just as the atmosphere glows when a bolt of lightning passes through it during a thunderstorm. By filling these tubes with diverse gases, all the hues of the rainbow could be duplicated.

Sam IM4 SF+ turned his admiring gaze from the breathtaking displays and started to cross the street. By a clever contrivance of flashing signal-lamps, the flow of mechanical traffic was periodically halted, to thus allow unmounted citizens to pass from one side to the other in complete safety. Sam strode across the street as the traffic halted in strict obedience to the signal-lamps. Once on the other side, he started off through the byways of the city. On either side stretched mercantile establishments of divers sorts, selling luxuries and commodities undreamed of by earlier peoples. He strode past a theater of the age which, instead of living actors, displayed amazing dramas recorded on strips of celluloid and projected by beams of light on tremendous white surfaces within the darkened theater. Ingeniously recorded voices and sounds, cleverly synchronized to the movement of the figures on the screen, made them seem lifelike.

"Ah, the wonders of modern science!" Sam marveled anew.

CHAPTER IV

The Threat of the Mind Masters

Not even the varied panorama of the Metropolis could keep Sam IM4 SF+ from thinking of his mission to the city. He had constantly kept a sharp look-out, watching those who might betray too much interest in his person, being careful that no one was following him.

For Sam IM4 SF+ knew that danger was afoot in New-York; a secret group known as the Mind Masters was plotting to take over the Government, using super-scientific devices, about which Sam could only conjecture. There was no proof, unfortunately, with which our hero could have gone to the rulers of this enlightened country and denounced the scoundrels for the criminals they were. Only Sam IM4 SF+ knew of the existence of this evil band—Sam, and a few loyal cohorts that he had gathered to combat the menace.

For Sam, like few others across the world, had a Sixth Sense, which enabled him to detect certain emotional responses which were, to others, non-existent.

Thus, Sam proceeded carefully to his destination, for he knew full well that if he were discovered, death would be his reward.

Little did he know that, in a secret room, many miles away, the Mind Masters were, at that very moment, plotting his destruction. Twelve men in black hoods were seated about a table. Eleven of them were listening to the twelfth speak.

"Even now," he said, in a voice that reeked with evil, "our agents are following IM4 SF+, clad in invisibility suits. Fear not, my friends, we shall destroy that prying Sixth Sense of his. When our agents close in at last, they will use the hyper-decerebralizer ray. The fool has no chance!"

To Be Continued

WILL THE CABAL DESTROY SAM'S WONDER SENSE?

WHAT OF COUNTESS TAMARA AND THE HIDDEN LEGION?

WILL DR. DOOM PERFECT HIS ROCKETSHIP IN TIME TO ESCAPE?

CAN DALE ARDENT SURVIVE THE MIND-FREEZING MACHINE?

READ THE SECOND PART OF THIS AMAZING SERIAL AND SEE!

Both Lin and I apologize for the fact that these questions have no answers. However, dear reader, if you come up with answers of your own, rest assured that we would be glad to see them. Those questions have been bothering us, too.

MUSTANG
By Randall Garrett

*I believe the term "horse opera" is, like "soap opera," some-
what older than "space opera," which is logical. Ned Buntline
(Edward Zane Carroll Judson) was writing at the same time as
Jules Verne, but in those days, as today, more people understood
horses than understood space. But which is more important? If all
the horses were to vanish suddenly tonight, the human race
would muddle through somehow, but if space were to vanish,
where would we be?*

*Personally I like horses, and I like Zane Grey. Now if you just
add a touch of the strange and come up with the Old Switcheroo—*

Beautiful? Hell yes, she was beautiful!

You ever see one of them golden palominos? Beautiful, right?
Well, this mustang was that golden color all over—almost a
blonde, you might say.

Whadda y' mean?

The Kid? Well, hell yes. There's a dozen men and more on the
Turkey Track Bar who'll swear to it. He was still wet behind the
ears, but we all saw him do what none o' the rest of us could do.

All right. You think the Kid is a sissy. All right, go ahead—we
thought so, too, on the Turkey Track Bar. But let me tell you, that
don't prove nothin'. Not one way or another.

Naw; I'll buy. Hey, Sam! Just leave the bottle here; I reckon
me and Morty can pour our own. Thanks.

Anyhow, where was I? Oh, yeah.

It was the Kid who spotted the mustang in the first place.
Now, I been Tad Jenkins' foreman at the Turkey Track Bar for
twelve years, and I got no complaints. He pays a good wage and
lets me do my job without always ridin' herd on me, like some

bosses do. Tad's a tough old buzzard, and the only weak spot he's got is the way he spoils that kid of his. So when the Kid comes ridin' in after an all-day jaunt, all het up about this golden mustang he seen runnin' with the herd, I could see we were gonna have us a time of it.

Now, don't get me wrong. I like Tad Junior, and so do most of the boys, but he just ain't what you'd call a man's man, if you see what I mean. Spends most of his time readin' books, and don't give a damn for the ranchin' business.

Hell, when I was seventeen, I'd been workin' on my own for two years, and I joined the Marine Corps before I was eighteen, back in '42. But that don't make no never-mind.

Anyhow, the Kid comes back, all het up, as I said, about this here horse he seen. He come ridin' like there was a twister chasin' him, which is doin' pretty good on that horse his old man gave him. She's an old bay; gentle as mother's kiss, and damn near as old as the Kid is, seems like. The Kid likes 'em gentle—he ain't exactly what you'd call a bronco buster.

He scoots up to the ranch house, hops off'n that bay, and runs inside, a-yellin' for his dad. I'd've figured there'd been an accident or something, except that the Kid's got a big happy grin on his face, so I didn't pay no more attention.

Fifteen, twenty minutes later, the Old Man comes moseyin' out toward the corral, where I was oiling some bridles.

"Frank," he says, "you been payin' any attention to them mustangs lately?"

"I got an eye on 'em," I says. "I know pretty well where they are."

He nods, easy-like. He just keeps that mustang herd because his own daddy kept horses. Once in a while, we cut out a few of 'em for the rodeo business, and when we thin out the herd, we shoot the old ones and sell the carcasses to the dogfood packers, but horseflesh ain't what it was worth twenty, thirty years ago, so it don't pay to keep any real close watch on 'em.

The Old Man says, "You didn't happen to notice a big palomino stallion runnin' with 'em, did you, Frank?"

I thought for a minute and had to allow that I hadn't. "Mostly browns, greys, and bays," I told him. "Course," I went on, "I ain't seen 'em all. I figure, long as I know about where they are and about how many we got, why, if we need any more information, we know where to get it."

"Sure, that's right, Frank," he says. "But young Tad was ridin' up near Smoky Bend, and he saw this mustang. Now, that herd ain't bred a palomino for as long as I can remember, so I figure that maybe someone's horse run away and joined up with my herd."

"A stallion?" I said, sort of questionin' like.

"Well, young Tad seemed to think so," the Old Man says. "But he didn't get too close. Likely he couldn't be too sure." Then he sort of looks off up at the sky as if he was figurin' the weather, which he wasn't. "Tad's got another idea, though. He thinks, what with all the bomb-testin' and stuff they've been doin' in these parts, he thinks maybe we got a mutation on our hands."

What? Well, Mort, the way I understand it, a mutation is an animal that don't turn out exactly like his folks—sort of a freak, you might say. This here radiation from the atom bombs is supposed to cause it.

Anyway, the Old Man says, "Tad says this mustang looks different, somehow." And he sort of looks off towards the hills. "Why don't you round up some of the boys, Frank, and we'll go have us a look."

That's when I got the whole picture. The Kid had taken a notion that he wanted that horse, and the Old Man was going to give it to him. Well, it wasn't any of my business—I don't mind cuttin' out a horse for the Kid any more than I mind cuttin' one out of the herd for a rodeo. In fact, I sort of cherished the idea of watchin' the Kid try to ride a wild mustang. Might be worthwhile watchin'.

Well, me and some of the boys saddled up and rode out with the Old Man and the Kid to find this here golden horse.

Morty, let me tell you that we had the dangdest time catchin' that ornry animal. He was skittish as a new bride and a damn sight faster on his feet.

We spotted the herd out near Smokey Bend and reined up a quarter of a mile away to look 'em over. We were on that little rise just north of the river and we could look down on the mustangs and see most of 'em.

Naturally, we spotted the palomino right off. You couldn't of missed him. The Old Man got his field glasses out and took a good, long look, and passed 'em to me.

Well, sir, I never seen a horse like that'n before. I could see what the Kid meant when he said it was different. It was a golden blonde all over, except for a white spot on its forehead and the dark hooves. And it wasn't just the color, either—the neck and head were just a shade too long to look natural on a horse, and his chest was as broad as a Percheron's. And there was one other thing queer about him that I didn't notice until I'd looked for a while.

Now, you mightn't believe this, Mort, but that mustang's

eyes were as blue as sapphires! Yes, sir, just as pretty a blue as you'd ever want to see.

Oh, you'd heard, eh?

Well, anyway, I handed the glasses back to the Old Man and said, "Pretty eyes."

"Mighty pretty," he says, looking at me peculiar. "Mighty pretty."

We both knew right then that this wasn't no horse that had strayed off from nobody's ranch and gone wild. If anybody had ever had a blue-eyed blonde for a horse, we'd of heard about it, and if anybody'd lost such an animal, there'd of been a reward out, you can sure bet.

The Old Man looks for a mite longer, then he says, "Okay, boys, let's corral that beauty. And watch yourselves. Anybody causes that animal to break a leg, I'll shoot him instead of the horse."

So we started down the slope gentle-like, so's not to spook the herd. The Kid stayed back on the rise to watch.

Well, sir, I tell you that horse didn't no more want to be caught than a bar of soap in a bathtub. We tried to box her up by goin' in easy, but she was the first one to notice what we was up to, and she spooked the rest of 'em. She—

What?

Well, sure I said, "she." The Kid thought she was a stallion, and so did the rest of us until we got close up and down level with her. But she wasn't—she was the biggest, toughest-looking mare you ever seen.

And run! We couldn't even get close to her if she didn't want us to. Every time we got up near, that horse would take off like a stray piece of lightning, left our nags so far behind that we knew we'd just have to find a better way.

The trouble was, that horse was smart. She knew that we didn't intend to hurt her, so we couldn't scare her any. She'd just as soon come at us as run away, and she was slick as buttered glass. And the damn critter didn't really try to run very far. She'd only circle around, stayin' just out of range.

Pretty soon, the rest of the herd was so spooky that they took off down toward Barton's Creek, but that mare didn't go with 'em. She just stuck around to laugh at us poor fools tryin' to catch her.

Well, finally, we circled around her and started closin' in. We figured we had her this time, but she just waited until we were really close—just stood there, chompin' grass until we were almost on top of her—and then she took a flyin' leap between me and the Old Man and tore up the rise toward the Kid.

Well, danged if that Kid didn't have his rope out. That mare is comin' at him at a full gallop, and he just sits there, waitin', with his lasso ready.

The Old Man bellows at him "Tad! Don't you rope that horse. She'll break a leg at that speed!"

But the stupid young sprite don't even hear—all he sees is that horse.

And when she gets close enough, he throws the loop over her neck.

Now, you know as well as I do that that would have killed any ordinary horse. But not this baby. She comes down on all fours and skids herself to a stop as if she'd had air brakes. Didn't even tighten the loop much. Then she just stands there, meek and peaceful as you please, while we ride up.

The Old Man tries to chew the Kid out for usin' a rope, but there ain't much he can really say. That horse had made fools out of the rest of us, and the Kid had caught her slicker'n a whistle, so the Old Man had to pretty much let it go.

Well, we led that mare back to the ranch and put her in the corral, and the Old Man gave orders to break her to saddle.

Three days later, there wasn't a man on the ranch that didn't have bruises all over him. Jake Moffat had a busted arm, Ed Lowey had a dislocated shoulder, and I had a sprained ankle. There wasn't a man in the outfit that had stayed on that mare more than thirty seconds.

The Kid wanted to try—he was the only one who could get close enough to her to put a saddle on her. But the Old Man said No, and he said it loud and hard.

And then, one mornin', we hear a ruckus at the corral. I limp over on my game leg as fast as I can, and the rest of the boys come, too, as best their bruises will let 'em.

And there's the Kid, sittin' on that golden horse, holdin' on for dear life, while she cavorts around the place. But he sticks with her, and finally she gentles down and trots around as nice as you please. Some of the boys said she wasn't buckin' as hard by a long shot as she had when they were on her, but I figure that's just a mite of jealousy creepin' in.

Well, of course, when the Old Man hears about it, he gives the Kid all kinds of hell for disobeyin' orders, but, again, there ain't much he can really say. Actually, he's pretty proud of the Kid, and he can't help showin' it.

That evenin', a bunch of the boys decide they're gonna take the Kid in to town and show him a real good time. They figure it's worth a little celebration.

Oh, you saw it, Morty? Yeah, they had him in here, all right. Sam knows the Kid ain't old enough to drink, but he let on that he didn't.

The Kid said something about losin' a few bucks at Blackjack. Said it wasn't his lucky night.

Where'd they go from here, Mort? Oh? Well, I guess that bunch *really* painted the town red, eh? Bet Mabel and the girls were glad to see 'em, huh?

Yeah, I know he did a lot of braggin' about his gold horse. That's why he decided to ride her into town the next day—just to show off that horse.

What happened? Well, that night in town hadn't done him much good, I guess, 'cause he climbed on, that filly took one leap into the air, and the Kid hit the ground. Knocked colder than an Amarillo blizzard—busted his collar bone and his left arm and had a concussion for a week.

The horse cleared that corral fence like she was flyin' and took off. We ain't seen her since.

Was she a mutation? Well, she must've been. The Kid said that that spot on her forehead was the nub of a horn, and who in the *Hell* ever heard of a horse with a horn?

...NO CONNECTIONS
By Randall Garrett

Isaac Asimov is, I think I dare say, more widely known to the general public than any other science fiction writer,* but not, I fear, for his science fiction. For the past two decades his straight science articles and other works, ranging from Biblical commentary to learned discussions of Shakespeare, have outgrossed his science fiction wordage by a ratio of—at a guesstimate—something like a hundred to one.

Twenty years ago, he was merely one of the top science fiction writers in the world. For my money, he still is.

The basic gimmick of this story actually was given to me by John Pomeroy, whose "Progress Report" belongs in a collection like this one. I think the gimmick came from Dr. Albert Einstein's remark, "If I had it to do all over again, I'd have become a plumber."

When John suggested it, I thought, "Mmmmm. Given a hundred thousand years, that ought to put the action somewhere in the middle of Isaac's Second Empire. What the hell—why not?"

---

*His only rivals are Ray Bradbury and Arthur C. Clarke. A. B. C.?

"Imitation," said Ducem Palver, "is supposed to be the sincerest form of flattery, isn't it?"

Dr. Nikol Buth inspected what was left of his cigar and decided that between the ash and the chewed stub there was not enough tobacco to make further puffing worthwhile. He dropped it into the disposal and watched the bright flash of light that marked the question that Palver had asked.

"In a way, I suppose—if you can call it imitation to take a hint from a myth and develop something from it."

Ducem Palver leaned back in his chair. His blue eyes seemed to twinkle beneath his slightly arched brows, although there was no obvious trace of a smile on his round face. "Then," he said, "you consider mathematical treatment of vast numbers of human beings to be a myth?"

Dr. Buth considered that for a moment. He hardly knew how to speak to his visitor. Palver, he knew, occupied some small post in the Imperium—Imperial Librarian, Third Class—but Buth wasn't sure just how important the man was nor exactly why he had come. Nor did he know how much Palver knew of archaeology.

Buth said: "I realize that people once believed in such a thing—seven or eight hundred years ago. But the barbaric period of the Interregnum, before the establishment of the Second Galactic Empire, was hardly a period of vast scientific knowledge." He gestured with one hand. "Oh, I'll grant you that there may just possibly be something to the old story that a mathematical treatment of the actions of vast masses of human beings was worked out by a scientist of the First Empire and then lost during the Interregnum—but I don't believe it."

"Oh?" Palver's face was bland. "Why not?"

"It's ridiculous on the face of it. Discoveries are never lost, really. We still have all the technological knowledge that the First Empire had, and much more; myths and legends, on the other hand, have no basis, except in easily explained exaggerations."

Palver looked the slightest bit defensive. "Why do you call them legends? It seems to me to be a bit too pat to say that those arts which were not lost were real and that those which *were* lost are legendary."

Dr. Nikol Buth had long since made up his mind that Ducem Palver was nothing but another small-time, officious bureaucrat who had decided, for some reason, to make a thirty thousand light-year trip from the Imperial capital just to get in his, Buth's, hair. Inwardly, he sighed. He had walked on eggs before.

Outwardly, he was all smiles. "I'll admit it sounds odd when you put it that way. But look at it from another angle. We have fairly accurate information on the history of the First Empire; the last ten thousand years of its existence are very accurately documented, thanks to the information found in the old Imperial Library. And we have no mention of 'lost arts' or anything else like that. None of the records is in the least mysterious. We know that one nonhuman race was found, for instance. Nothing mysterious there; we know what happened to them, how they escaped the First Imperial Government, and their eventual fate."

Dr. Buth fished in his pocket for another cigar and found none. He got up and walked over to the humidor on his desk, saying: "On the other hand, the records of the Interregnum are scanty, inaccurate, and, in some cases, patently falsified. And it is during the Interregnum that we find legends of supermen, of mental giants who can control the minds of others, and of 'lost' sciences which can do wonders."

Buth lit his cigar, and Ducem Palver nodded his head slowly.

"I see," the librarian said at last. "Then you don't believe that a mathematical treatment of the future actions of a mass of people could be formulated?"

"I didn't say that," Dr. Buth said, somewhat testily. "I said that I did not believe it was ever done in the past." Then he forced a smile back onto his face and into his voice. "Not having any such thing as a mathematical system of prediction, I can hardly predict what may be done in the future along those lines."

Ducem Palver steepled his hands pontifically. "I'm inclined to agree with you, Dr. Buth—however, I understood that you had evolved such a system."

Dr. Buth exhaled a cloud of smoke slowly. "Tell me, Mr. Palver, why is the Imperial Government interested in this?"

Palver chuckled deprecatingly. "I *am* sorry, Dr. Buth. I didn't intend to lead you to believe that the Imperium was interested. In so far as I know, they are not." He paused, and his blue eyes seemed to sparkle for a moment with an inner, barely hidden mirth. "Ah, I see that you're disappointed. I don't blame you; it would be quite a feather in your cap to have your work recognized by the Imperium, would it not? I'm truly sorry if I misled you."

Buth shook his head. "Think nothing of it. As a matter of fact, I should be...uh...rather embarrassed if my work came to Imperial notice at this time. But..."

"...But, then, why am I here?" Palver finished for him. "Purely out of personal curiosity, my dear sir, nothing more. Naturally, the records of your published works are on file in the Imperial Library; my position at the Library is that of Keeper of the Files. Have you ever seen the Files?"

Dr. Buth shrugged. "No—but I've read descriptions."

"I'm sure you have. It's a vast operation to feed all the information of the galaxy into that one great machine to be correlated, cross-indexed, filtered, digested, and abstracted so that it may be available at any time. Only about one billionth of the total information flowing into that machine ever comes to my direct notice, and even then it is fleetingly glanced over and forgotten.

"But my hobby, you see, is History." He pronounced the word with a respect touching on reverence. "I'm especially interested in the—as you pointed out—incomplete history of the Interregnum. Therefore, when your mathematical theories of archaeology came to my attention, I was interested. It happens that my vacation period came due some weeks ago, so I decided to come here, to Sol III, to...ah...have a chat, as it were."

Dr. Buth dropped some cigar ash into the dispenser and watched it flare into oblivion. "Well, I'm afraid you may find you've come for nothing, Mr. Palver. We're not investigating Interregnum history, you see."

Ducem Palver's blue eyes widened slightly and a faint look of puzzlement came over his cherubic face. "But I understood that you were working on pre-Imperial civilization."

Dr. Nikol Buth smiled tolerantly. "That's right, Mr. Palver. Pre-*First*-Imperial. We're digging back more than thirty thousand years; we're looking for the origin of the human race."

Palver's face regained its pleasant impassivity. "I see. Hm-m-m."

"Do you know anything of the Origin Question, Mr. Palver?" Buth asked.

"Some," admitted Palver. "I believe there are two schools of thought, aren't there?"

Buth nodded. "The Merger Theory, and the Radiation Theory. According to the Merger Theory, mankind is the natural product of evolution on all worlds with a water-oxygen chemistry and the proper temperatures and gravitational intensities. But according to the Radiation Theory, mankind evolved on only one planet in the galaxy and spread out from that planet after the invention of the first crude hyperspace drive. I might point out that the Merger Theory has been all but abandoned by modern scholars."

"And yourself?" Palver asked.

"I agree. The Merger Theory is too improbable; it requires too many impossible coincidences. The Radiation Theory is the only probable—one might almost say the only possible—explanation for the existence of Man in the galaxy."

Palver leaned over and picked up the carrying case which he had placed beside his chair. "I transdeveloped a copy of your 'Transformations of Symbolic Psychology and Their Application to Human Migration.' It was, in fact, this particular work which decided me to come here to Sol III. I'm not much of a mathematician, myself, you understand, but this reminded me so much of the old legends that...well, I was interested."

Dr. Buth chuckled. "There have been, I recall, legends of invisibility, too—you know, devices which would render a human being invisible to the human eye so that he could go where he pleased, undetected. If you had heard that I had written a paper on the transparency of glass, would you be interested?"

"I see the connection, of course," said Ducem Palver. "Just how does it apply here?"

"The legend," Buth said, puffing vigorously on his cigar, "concerns a mathematical system which can predict the actions of vast masses of people—the entire population of the galaxy.

"My work has nothing to do with prediction whatever— unless you want to call it prediction in reverse. I evolved the system in order to work backwards, into the past; to discover, not what the human race was *going to do*, but what it *had done*. You see, there is one fatal flaw in any mathematical prediction system; if people know what they are supposed to do, they will invariably try to do something else, and that can't be taken into account in the system. It becomes a positive feedback which automatically destroys the system, you see."

Palver nodded wordlessly, waiting for Dr. Buth to continue.

"But that flaw doesn't apply to my work because there can't be any such feedback into the past. What I have done is trace the human race backwards in time—back more than thirty millennia, through the vast migrations, the movements through the galaxy from one star to another, taking every lead and tracing them all back to their single focal point."

"And have you found that focal point?" Palver asked.

"I have. It is here—Sol III. My system shows positively that this is—*must be*—the birthplace of the human race."

Ducem Palver looked out the transparent wall at one end of the room. "I understand that archaeologists have always supposed the Origin Planet to be somewhere here in the Sirius Sector, but I wouldn't have thought such a bleak planet as this would be the one. Still"—he laughed pleasantly—"perhaps that's why they left."

Dr. Buth allowed his gaze to follow that of his visitor to the windswept, snow-covered terrain outside. "It wasn't always like this," he said. "For reasons we haven't nailed down exactly as yet, this planet shows a definitely cyclic climate. There appear to be long ice ages, followed by short periods of warmth. Perhaps, in the long run, the cycle itself is cyclic; we're not too sure on that score. At any rate, we're quite sure that it was fairly warm here, thirty to fifty thousand years ago."

"And before that?" Palver asked.

Buth frowned. "Before that, another ice age, we think. We've just barely started, of course. There is a great deal of work yet to be done."

"No doubt. Ah—what have you uncovered, so far?"

Dr. Buth stood up from his chair. "Would you like to see? I'll show you the lab, if you'd like."

"Thank you," said Ducem Palver, rising. "I'd like very much to see it."

A well-equipped, operating archaeological laboratory is like no other laboratory in the galaxy. This one was, if the term can be used, more than typical. Huge radiodating machines lined one wall, and chemical analyzers filled another. Between them were other instruments of all sizes and shapes and purposes.

The place was busy; machines hummed with power, and some technicians labored over bits of material while others watched recorders attached to the machines in use.

Dr. Buth led his visitor through the room, explaining the function of each instrument briefly. At the end of the room, he opened a door marked: SPECIMEN CHAMBER and led Ducem Palver inside. He waved a hand. "Here are our specimens—the artifacts we've dug up."

The room looked, literally, like a junk bin, except that each bit of junk was carefully tagged and wrapped in a transparent film.

"All these things are artifacts of Man's pre-space days?" Palver asked.

Buth laughed shortly. "Hardly, Mr. Palver. This planet was a part of the First Empire, you know. These things date back only ten or eleven thousand years. They prove nothing. They are all from the upper layers of the planet's strata. They've been duly recorded and identified and will doubtlessly be forgotten.

"No, these are not important; it is only below the D-stratum that we'll find anything of interest."

"The D-stratum?"

"We call it that. D for Destruction. There is an almost continuous layer over the land of this planet, as far as we've tested it. It was caused, we believe, by atomic bombardment."

"Atomic bombardment? *All over the planet?*" Ducem Palver looked shocked.

"That's right. It looks as though uncontrolled atomic reac-

198

tions were set off all over the planet at once. Why? We don't know. But we do know that the layer is nearly twenty-five thousand years old, and that it does *not* antedate space travel."

"How so?"

"Obviously," Buth said dryly, "if such a thing had happened *before* mankind discovered the hyperspace drive, there would be no human race today. Man would have died right here and would never have been heard of again."

"Of course, of course. And what have you found below that...uh...D-stratum?"

A frown came over the archaeologist's dark eyes. "Hardly anything, as yet. Come over here."

Ducem Palver followed his host across the room to a pair of squat objects that reposed on the floor. They looked like pieces of grayish, pitted rock, crudely dome-shaped, sitting on their flat sides. From the top of the irregular dome projected a chimney of the same material. They were, Palver estimated, about thirty-six centimeters high, and not quite that big in diameter at their base.

"We haven't worked on these two yet," Dr. Buth said, "but they'll probably turn out the same as the one we've already sectioned."

"What are they?" Palver asked.

Buth shook his head slowly. "We don't know. We have no idea what their function might have been. They're hollow, you notice—you can see the clay in that chimney, which was deposited there during the millennia it lay in the ground.

"See this flange around the bottom? That's hollow, too. It's a channel that leads to the interior; it's connected with this hole back here." He pointed to another hole, about the same size as that in the top of the chimney, but located down near the base. It was perhaps seven centimeters in diameter.

"And you haven't any definite idea what they were used for?" Palver said.

Buth spread his hands in a gesture of temporary bafflement. "Not yet. Ober Sutt, one of my assistants, thinks it may have been some sort of combustion chamber. He thinks that gases—hydrogen and oxygen, for instance—might have been fed into it, and the heat utilized for something. Or perhaps they were used to synthesize some product at high temperatures—a rather crude method, but it might have been effective for making...oh, ammonia, maybe. I'm not a chemist, and Sutt knows more about that end of it than I do."

"Why does he think it's a high-temperature reaction chamber? I mean, why *high*-temperature, specifically?"

Dr. Buth waved his cigar at the objects. "They're made out of a very crude ceramic, a heavy mass of fired silicon and aluminum oxides, plus a few other things. They're eroded, of course, and rather fragile now, but to stand up under all the abuse of three or four hundred centuries, they must have been pretty strong when they were made."

"Perhaps the ceramic was used because of its structural strength?" Palver said, half questioningly.

"That's doubtful. We know they used metals; there are oxides of iron, copper, zinc, chromium, and aluminum everywhere, in deposits that indicate the metals once formed artifacts of some kind. It wouldn't be logical to use a ceramic, brittle as it is, when metals were used."

"So you think the combustion chamber idea is the most likely?"

Dr. Buth took a long pull at his cigar and looked abstractedly at the glowing ash. "Well, Ober Sutt puts up a good argument for it, but I don't know..." He waved again with the cigar. "Those things don't have any bottom, either, and I don't think they ever did—not connected directly, at least. Sutt counters that by saying that they must have sat on a ceramic plate of some kind, but so far we haven't found any of those plates, if they exist."

Palver looked carefully at the two objects, then shrugged. "What else have you found?"

"Aside from a few shards," Dr. Buth said carefully, "that's all we've found below the D-layer. However, as I said, we've just begun."

Back in Buth's office, Ducem Palver picked up his carrying case, snapped it shut. "Well, I'm sorry to have bothered you, Dr. Buth," he said. "I must admit, however, that the solution of the Origin Question holds little interest for me. The history of the latter part of the First Empire, and that of the Great Interregnum —ah, those are deeply interesting. But, as to how Man came to be spread throughout the galaxy—" He lifted his eyebrows and cocked his head to one side. His blue eyes seemed very deep for a moment. "Well, Man is here. I will leave it to others to find out how he got here, eh?"

Dr. Buth smiled tolerantly. "It's just as well that we're not all interested in the same thing, isn't it?" He walked over to the transparent wall and looked out at the bleak whiteness of the windswept snowscape. "But to me, the fascinating thing about Man is his peculiar drives. Imagine a time when men had no spaceships, no modern instruments of any kind. What must it have been like to look out at the stars and feel trapped on one single planet?"

Behind him, Ducem Palver's voice said: "Perhaps you could draw a parallel from the planet Kaldee. During the Interregnum, they were cut off from the rest of the galaxy; they lost all their history—everything. They knew nothing of the spaceship, nor of the stars themselves. They thought those lights in the sky were nothing more than bits of glass, reflecting the light of their sun. They believed the night sky was a black bowl a few miles above their heads, upon which these pieces of broken glass were fixed."

"Oh?" said Dr. Buth without turning. "And how did they feel about their isolation?"

"They didn't know they were isolated. They were quite happy, all things considered. They had no burning desire to leave their planet—indeed, they reserved that privilege for the dead."

Dr. Buth's brows drew together. "Then what made primitive Man want to leave? Why wasn't he happy on one planet? What happened?"

And suddenly, it seemed as if his whole mind came to a focus on that one question. *Why had they decided to conquer space? Why? What caused that odd drive in Man?*

"I've got to know," he said—aloud, but very softly.

Ducem Palver didn't even seem to hear.

After nearly a full minute, Ducem Palver said quietly, "I must be going now. I wish you success, Dr. Buth."

"Yes," said Buth, still looking at the icy plain outside. "Yes. Thank you very much, Mr. Palver. Very much. Good-by."

Ducem Palver left him that way, standing, staring at the whiteness of the landscape of Sol III.

It was an old planet, civilization-wise. Not, thought Dr. Nikol Buth, as old a planet in that respect as Sol III, but old, nonetheless. Before the Interregnum, it had served as the capital of the First Empire, and before that, as the nucleus from which the First Empire had grown. It had once been a mighty world, sheathed in metal and armed with the might of the Galactic Fleet, the center of strength of the First Galactic Empire. And then that Empire had fallen, collapsed in upon itself, and with it had collapsed its capital.

It had been great once. And now?

Now it was beautiful. The capital of the Second Empire was far away in space, and this old planet was of no consequence whatever. But it was beautiful.

It was a garden planet now, filled with green forests and broad sweeps of grass and fields of flowers. It was a place where a young man could relax for a few weeks before returning to the busy work of maintaining the Empire, a place where an old man, freed from the seemingly eternal grind, could find peace in doing other, less strenuous work.

Dr. Nikol Buth was such a man. He was old now, and the years had not treated him kindly; now, after thirty years of driving himself towards an unattainable goal, he sought only peace. Here, on this garden world, he would find it.

It wasn't easy to become a permanent resident here. The planet was an Imperial Protectorate, the personal property of the Emperor himself, although His Imperial Majesty never visited it. Tourists were allowed access to certain parts of it, but there were vast estates reserved for those who had earned the right to spend their last years in quiet and solitude. The right to live here had to be earned, and it had to be granted by the Emperor in person. In his pocket, Dr. Nikol Buth carried a precious document—a signed, sealed Imperial Grant.

He had landed at the terminal—like all spacesport terminals, a busy place, even here—and had supervised the shipping of his personal effects to his new home at a little village called Mallow and then had taken an aircar there himself.

At the air depot at Mallow, he had been met by a pleasant young man who had introduced himself as Wilm Faloban— "General factotum and chief of police—for all the need they have of police here."

He had quietly checked Buth's identification papers and his Imperial Grant, then he'd said casually: "You haven't seen your home yet, I take it?"

Buth shook his head. "Not directly. Full stereos, of course; it's quite what I want. I—" He stopped, realizing that he wasn't making much sense to the young man. He started again: "I really don't see how I managed to get a place here; think how many must apply each year—hundreds of billions, I suppose."

"About that," agreed Faloban. He opened the door of his ground car. "Hop in," he said. "I'll drive you out to your place."

Buth nodded his thanks and stepped carefully inside the little machine. He had to move carefully these days, had to remember that old bones are brittle and old muscles tear easily. "And how many are accepted?" he continued. "Only a few?"

Faloban slid into the driver's seat. "An average of ten thousand a year," he said. "Not many are chosen."

"I don't know what I ever did to deserve it," Buth said.

Faloban chuckled as he trod on the accelerator and the little vehicle slid smoothly out to the road. "You really great men are all like that. You never think you've done anything."

"No, no," said Dr. Buth, "it's not like that at all. I really never did do anything."

Faloban just chuckled again. "You'll have to talk to your neighbor, old Ducem Palver, on that score. He's always saying he never did anything, either. Amazing, isn't it, how the Emperor never picks anyone but ne'er-do-wells?"

But Dr. Nikol Buth wasn't listening. *Ducem Palver,* he was thinking, *Ducem Palver. Where have I heard that name before?*

And then he remembered. Aloud, he said: "Yes, I will have to see Mr. Palver. He's a near neighbor, you say?"

"Just a kilometer away. We'll go right by his place on the way to your new home," Faloban said.

It was a woman who opened the door, a short, round, pleasant-faced woman whose halo of white hair seemed almost silvery. She was old, yes, but her face still held the beauty of her youth, modified by the decades of life so that it was changed into a graciousness—almost a regal queenliness.

"Yes?" Her voice was soft, and her smile kindly.

"I—" Buth felt the hesitation in his voice and tried to overcome it. "I'm looking for Mr. Ducem Palver. My name is Buth—Dr. Nikol Buth. I . . . I don't know if he remembers me, but—"

The woman stood aside. "Come in, Dr. Buth, come in. I'm Mrs. Palver; I'll see if my husband is busy."

She led him to a chair and made sure he was comfortable before she left to find her husband.

Queer, thought Buth, *I'd never thought of Palver's having a wife. Still, it's been thirty years; maybe he married after—*

"Ah! Dr. Buth! How good to see you again!"

Buth covered his slight start at hearing Palver's voice by rising quickly to greet his host. A slight twinge in his back warned him against moving quite so rapidly.

Palver himself had changed, of course. His hair, which had been thick and black, was now thin and gray. His face was still full and round, although it tended to sag a bit, and his eyes seemed to have faded somewhat. Buth had the feeling that they weren't quite the deep blue they had been three decades before.

But he showed that he still had the same brisk way about him as he extended his hand and said: "Am I the first to welcome you to Mallow and Forest Glade?"

Buth took his hand. "Except for a young chap named Faloban, yes. Thank you."

"You liked cigars, I think?" Palver went to a panel in the wall, slid it aside, and took out a small cigar humidor. "I don't use them myself," he said, "but I like to keep them for friends."

Buth accepted the cigar, lit it carefully. "I have to limit myself on these," he told Palver. "I'm afraid I overdid it for too many years. My lungs aren't what they used to be."

"Well, well"—Palver pulled up a chair and sat down—"how have you been? I didn't think you'd even remember me—a nobody. What did you ever find on Sol III? I haven't been following your work, I'm afraid. They kicked me upstairs to rot a while back, you know; haven't been able to keep up with anything, really."

"There wasn't much to keep up with," Buth said. "Sol III was a dead end. I couldn't prove a thing."

Palver looked blank. "I don't think I quite understand."

Dr. Buth settled himself more comfortably in his chair. "There's nothing to understand. I'm a failure, that's all. No joke, no false modesty—no, nor bitterness, either. I spent thirty years of my life looking for something that wasn't there to be found, trying to solve a problem that couldn't be solved."

Ducem Palver looked somewhat uncomfortable. Buth noticed it, and realized that it was perfectly possible that Palver didn't have even the foggiest notion of what he was talking about. Thirty years is a long time to remember a conversation that only lasted an hour. Even Buth himself hadn't remembered it until Faloban had mentioned Ducem Palver's name.

"If you recall," Buth said swiftly, "my group and I were digging on Sol III, searching beneath the D-layer for anything that might show us that Sol III was the original home of mankind. Above the Destruction Stratum, everything was post-space-flight; it proved nothing. But we did have hopes for the artifacts below that layer."

"I see," said Palver. "It turned out that they, also, were post-space-flight?"

There was a trace of bitterness in Buth's short laugh. "Oh, no. We didn't prove anything—not *anything*. We don't know, even now, whether those artifacts we found were pre- or post-space-flight. We don't even know who made them or how or why."

"What about those ceramic things?" Palver asked. "Were

those all you found?"

Buth laughed again, bitterly, almost angrily. "It depends on how you mean that question, 'Were those all you found?' If you mean, did we find any more, the answer is an emphatic yes. If you mean, did we find anything else, the answer is almost no. We found plenty of them—to be exact, in thirty years we uncovered twelve thousand four hundred and ninety-five of them!"

He paused for breath while Palver blinked silently.

"After the first few thousand, we quit bothering with them. They got in the way. We had classified some two hundred different varieties under about nine group headings. We were beginning to treat them as animals or something, classifying them according to individual and group characteristics." His voice became suddenly angry. "For thirty years, I worked, trying to find some clue to the mind of pre-spaceflight Man. It was my one drive, the one thing on my mind. I dedicated my life to it.

"And what did I find? Nothing but ceramic mysteries!"

He sat silently for a moment, his lips tight, his eyes focused on the hands in his lap.

Palver said smoothly: "You found nothing else at all?"

Buth looked up, and a wry smile came over his face. "Oh, yes, there were a few other things, of course, but they didn't make much sense, either. The trouble was, you see, that nothing but stones and ceramics survived. Metals corroded, plastics rotted. We did find a few bits of polyethylene tetrafluoride, but they had been pressed out of shape.

"We couldn't even date the stuff. It was at least twenty thousand years old, and possibly as much as a hundred and fifty thousand. But we had no standards—nothing to go by.

"We found bones, of course. They had thirty-two teeth in the skulls instead of twenty-eight, but that proved nothing. We found rubble that might have been buildings, but after all those thousands of years, we couldn't be sure. In one place, we found several tons of gold bricks; it was probably a warehouse of some kind. We deduced from that evidence that they must have had ordinary transmutation, because gold is pretty rare, and it has so few uses that it isn't worth mining.

"Obviously, then, they must have had atomic power, which implies spaceflight. But, again, we couldn't be sure.

"But, in the long run, the thing that really puzzled us was those ceramic domes. There were so many of them! What could they have been used for? Why were so many needed?" Buth rubbed the back of his neck with a broad palm and laughed a little to himself. "We never knew. Maybe we never will."

"But see here," said Palver, genuinely interested, "I thought you told me that one of your men—I forget his name—had decided they were used for high-temperature synthesis."

"Possibly," agreed Dr. Buth. "But synthesis of what? Besides, there were samples which weren't badly damaged, and they didn't show any signs of prolonged exposure to high temperatures. They'd been fused over with a mixture of silicates, but the inside and the outside were the same."

"What else would you have to uncover to find out what they were?" Palver asked.

Buth puffed at his cigar a moment, considering his answer.

"The connections," he said at last.

"Eh?"

"They were obviously a part of some kind of apparatus," Buth explained. "There were orifices in them that led from some sort of metallic connection—we don't know what, because the metal had long ago dissolved into its compounds, gone beyond even the most careful electrolytic reconstruction. And there are holes in flanges at the top and bottom which—" He stopped for a moment and reached into his pocket. "Here...I've got a stereo of our prize specimen; I'll show you what I mean."

The small cube of transparency that he took from his pocket held a miniature reproduction of one of the enigmatic objects. He handed it to Ducem Palver. "Now that's the—No, turn it over; you've got it upside down."

"How do you know?" Palver asked, looking at the cube.

"What?"

"I said, how do you know it's upside down?" Palver repeated. "How can you tell?"

"Oh. Well, we can't, of course, but it stands to reason that the biggest part would be at the bottom. It would be unstable if you tried to set it on the small end, with the big opening up. Although" —he shrugged—"again, we can't be sure."

Palver looked the little duplicate over, turning it this way and that in his hands. It remained as puzzling as ever. "Maybe it's a decoration or something," he said at last.

"Could be. Ober Sutt, my assistant for twenty years, thought they might have been used for heating homes. That would account for their prevalence. But they don't show any signs of heat corrosion, and why should they have used such crude methods if they had atomic power?" Again he laughed his short, sharp laugh. "So, after thirty years, we wound up where we started. With nothing."

"It's too bad you didn't find traces of their writing," said Palver, handing the stereo crystal back to his visitor.

"We did, for all the good it did us. As a matter of fact, we found engraving on little tiles that we found near some of the domes. Several of the domes, you see, were surrounded by little square ceramic plates about so big." He held up his hands to indicate a square about eight centimeters on a side. "We thought they might have been used to line the chamber that the domes were in, to protect the rest of the building from the heat—at least, we thought that at first, but there weren't any signs of heat erosion on them, either.

"They must have been cemented together somehow, because we found engravings of several sets that matched. Here, I'll show you."

He took out his scriber and notebook and carefully drew lines on it. Then he handed it to Ducem Palver.

"Those lines were shallow scorings. We don't know whether that is printing—writing of some kind—or simply channels for some other purpose. But we're inclined to think that it's writing because of the way it's set down and because we did find other stones with the same sort of thing on them."

"These are the engravings you found near the mysterious domes?" Palver asked.

"That's right."

"They make no sense whatever."

"They don't. They probably never will, unless we can find some way of connecting them with our own language and our own methods of writing."

Palver was silent for several minutes, as was Dr. Buth, who sat staring at the glowing end of his cigar. Finally, Buth dropped the cigar into a nearby disposer, where it disappeared with a bright flash of molecular disintegration.

"Thirty years," said Buth. "And nothing to show for it. Oh, I enjoyed it—don't think I'm feeling sorry for myself. But it's funny how a man *can* enjoy himself doing profitless work. There was a time when I thought I might work on my mathematical theories— you remember?—and look how unprofitable that might have been."

"I suppose you're right," Palver said uncomfortably. He handed the notebook back to Dr. Buth.

"But still," Buth said, taking the notebook, "a man hates to think of wasting thirty years. And that's what it was."

He looked at the lines he had drawn. Meaningless lines that made a meaningless pattern:

EMPLOYEES MUST WASH
HANDS BEFORE LEAVING

"Waste," he said softly, "all waste."

ON THE MARTIAN PROBLEM

By Randall Garrett

I took in Edgar Rice Burroughs early in my life, washing him down with great draughts of mother's milk.

Mother, needless to say, did not approve when she found out what sort of "trash" I was reading. For some reason I could never understand, The Wizard of Oz was good fare for children, but A Princess of Mars was not. (After I was grown up and had become a selling writer, I asked my beloved mother why she had differentiated between the two. "I was younger then," she said, as though that explained it. Maybe it did.)

There are those who like the Tarzan series—certainly the most famous; there are those who like the Pellucidar series; and so on. Me, I love John Carter, Warlord of Mars.

Of late—like the past thirty years—there have been those who have said that the John Carter stories are not "true science fiction" because they lack scientific verisimilitude and because the latest scientific investigations have proven Burroughs wrong.

I have done my best to correct that erroneous attitude.

I am not at liberty to reveal whence I obtained the Xerox copy of this letter, nor why it was specifically sent to me rather than, say, Mr. Philip José Farmer, who would be far more qualified than I for the honor of putting it before the public. My duty, however, was clear, and with the kind co-operation of Dr. Isaac Asimov and Mr. George Scithers, it is herewith submitted for your perusal.

The letter itself is written in a bold, highly legible, masculine hand. The heading shows that it was written in Richmond, Virginia, and it is addressed to a numbered postal box in Nairobi.

The bracketed notes after certain of the writer's expressions were added by myself, and I have appended a conversion table of

209

equivalent units in three measuring systems.

—Randall Garrett

My dear Ed,

Since your secret retirement to Africa, we have had much less communication than I would like, but, alas, my duties at home have kept me busy these many years. It is, however, a comfort to know that, thanks to the Duke's special serum, you will, barring accident or assassination, be around as long as I.

I am sorry not to have answered your last letter sooner, but, truth to tell, it caused me a great deal of consternation. I fear I had not been keeping up with the affairs of Earth as much as I perhaps should have, and I had no idea that the Mariner and Viking spacecraft had sent back such peculiar data.

One sentence in your last letter made me very proud: "I would rather believe that every man connected with NASA and JPL is a liar and a hoaxer than to believe you would ever tell me a deliberate lie." But, as you say, those photographs are most convincing.

Naturally, I took the photoreproductions you sent to a group of the wisest savants of Helium, and bade them do their best to solve the problem. They strove mightily, knowing my honor was at stake. Long they pondered over the data, and, with a science that is older and more advanced than that of Earth, they came up with the answer.

The tome they produced is far longer and far heavier than any book you have ever published, and is filled with page after page of abstruse mathematics, all using Martian symbolism. I could not translate it for you if I wished.

In fact, I had to get old Menz Klausa to explain it to me. He is not only learned in Martian mathematics, but has the knack of making things understandable to one who is not as learned as he. I shall endeavor to make the whole thing as clear to you as he made it to me.

First, you must consider in greater detail the method I use in going to Mars. There are limitations in time, for one thing. Mars must be almost directly overhead, and it must be about midnight. To use modern parlance, my "window" is small.

At such times, Mars is about 1.31×10^6 *karads* [4.88×10^7 miles] from Earth.

I call your attention to my description of what happens when I gaze up at the planet of the War God. I must focus my attention upon it strongly. Then I must bring to the fore an emotion which I

210

can best describe as *yearning*. A moment's spark of cold and dark, and I find myself on Mars.

There is no doubt in my mind that I actually travel *through* that awful stretch of interplanetary void. It is *not* instantaneous; it definitely requires a finite time.

And yet, for all that I travel through nearly fifty million miles of hard vacuum naked, or nearly so, I suffer no effects of explosive decompression, no lack of breath, no popping of the eardrums, no nosebleed, no "hangover" eyeballs.

Obviously, then, I am exposed to those extreme conditions *for so short a time that my body does not have the time to react to them!*

Consider, also, that the distance is such that light requires some 296 *tals* [262 seconds] to make the trip. Had I been in the void that long, I would surely have been dead on arrival. Quite obviously, then, when I make such trips, *I am traveling faster than light!*

There is, unfortunately, no way of telling *how* much faster, for I have no way of timing it, but Menz Klausa is of the opinion that it is many multiples of that velocity.

Now we must consider what is known to Earth science as the "time dilation factor." I must translate from Martian symbols, but I believe it may be expressed as:

$$T_v = T_0 \, [1-(v^2/c^2)]^{1/2}$$

where T_v is time lapse at velocity v, T_0 is the time lapse at rest, v is the velocity of the moving body, and c is the velocity of light.

The Martians, however, multiply this by another factor:

$$[(c-v)/(c^2-2cv+v^2)^{1/2}]^{1/2}$$

Thus, the entire equation becomes:

$$T_v = T_0[1-(v^2/c^2)]^{1/2} \cdot [(c-v)/(c^2-2cv+v^2)^{1/2}]^{1/2}$$

As you can clearly see, as long as the velocity of the moving body remains below the velocity of light (443,778 *haads* per *tal*), the first factor is a positive number, and the second factor has a value of +1. This, I believe, is why it has never been discovered by Earth scientists; multiplying a number by +1 has no effect whatever, and is not noticeable.

When v is exactly equal to c, both factors become zero; in other words, the moving body experiences zero time. Its clock stops, so to speak.

However, when v exceeds c, the equation assumes the form:

$$T_v = T_o (xi)(i)$$

where i is the square root of minus one, and x is a function of v.

If the second, or Martian, factor is neglected, it is obvious that the experienced time of the moving body would become imaginary, which is unimaginable in our universe.

However:

$$(xi) \, (i) = xi^2 = -x$$

In other words, if the body is moving at greater than the velocity of light, the elapsed time becomes negative. *The body is moving backwards in time!*

According to the most learned savants in Helium, this is exactly what happened to me. Indeed, so great was my velocity that I traveled an estimated 50,000 years into the past!

Thus, the Mars that I am used to has, in Earth terms, been dead for fifty millenia.

This explanation seemed perfectly sound when Menz Klausa first elucidated it, but suddenly a thought occurred to me.

Why did I always go forward in time when I returned to Earth?

For surely that must be so, else I could not be here today. If that formula I quoted were true, when I returned the first time, I should have found myself a hundred thousand years in the past, in about the year 98,000 B.C. Considering the number of trips I have made, I should, by now, be somewhere back in the Miocene.

However, that, too, is explained by our Martian theorists. Another factor comes into play at ultralight velocities, that of gravitation field strength. At light velocity, this factor accounts for the gravitational red-shift of light when it is attempting to escape from a strong gravitational field, and the violet-shift when the light is falling toward the gravity source.

At velocities greater than that of light, the factor becomes +1 when the direction of travel is from a greater gravitation field force to a lesser one, and -1 when the direction is from a lesser to a greater. Thus, when I return to Earth, the negative time factor becomes positive, and I go into the "future" of Mars, which is your "present."

I trust that is all very clear.

Unfortunately, there is no way I can translate the gravity

factor into Earth's mathematical symbolism. I can handle simple algebra, but tensor calculus is a bit much. I am a fighting man, not a scientist.

By the way, it becomes obvious from this that the Gridley Wave is an ultralight and trans-time communicator.

Another puzzle that the photos brought out was that they show no trace of the canals of Mars. And yet, Giovanni Schiaparelli saw them. Percival Lowell not only saw them, but drew fairly accurate maps of them. I can testify to that, myself. And yet they do not show on the photographs taken from a thousand miles away. Why?

The answer is simple. As you know, certain markings that are quite unnoticeable from the ground are easily seen from the air. An aerial photograph can show the San Andreas Fault in California quite clearly, even in places where it is invisible from the ground. The same is true of ancient meteor craters which have long since weathered smooth, but have nonetheless left their mark on the Earth's surface. From an orbiting satellite, more markings become visible when there is a break in the cloud cover.

Many modern paintings must be viewed from a distance to understand the effect the artist wished to give. Viewed under a powerful magnifying glass, a newspaper photo becomes nothing but a cluster of meaningless dots. One is too close to get the proper perspective.

Thus it is with the canals of Mars, long since eroded away, from your viewpoint in time. In order to see those ancient markings properly, you have to stand back forty or fifty million miles.

But what is going to happen to the Mars I love? Or, from Earth's viewpoint, what *did* happen to it?

According to Menz Klausa, that is explained by one significant feature on the photos you sent.

Remember, even "today" (from the Martian viewpoint), Mars is a dying planet. Our seas have long since vanished; our atmosphere is kept breatheable only by our highly complex atmosphere plant. Martians have long since learned to face death stoically, even the death of the planet. We can face the catastrophe that will eventually overtake us.

From Earth's viewpoint in time, it happened some forty thousand years ago. A great mountain of rock from the Asteroid Belt—or perhaps from beyond the Solar System itself—came crashing into Mars at some 24 *haads* per *tal* [10 miles per second]. So great was its momentum that it smashed through the planetary crust to the magma beneath.

The resulting explosion wrought unimaginable havoc upon

the planet—superheated winds of great velocity raced around the globe; great quakes shook the very bedrock; more of the atmosphere was literally blown into space, irretrievably lost.

But it left no impact crater like those of the Moon. The magma, hot and fluid, rushed up to form the mightiest volcano in the Solar System: Mons Olympus.

And the damned thing landed directly on our atmosphere plant!

However, we won't have to worry about that for another ten thousand years yet. Perhaps I won't live that long.

Give my best regards to Greystoke. Your Aunt Dejah sends her love.

All my best,
Uncle Jack

REFERENCE TABLE
MARTIAN/ENGLISH AND MARTIAN/METRIC

DISTANCE:	Martian	English	Metric
Circumference	360 karads	13,392.6 miles	21,551.38 km
1 karad	100 haads	37.20167 miles	59.86494 km
1 haad	200 ads	1964.248 feet	59,864.94 cm
1 ad	10 sofads	9.82129 feet	299.3247 cm
1 sofad		11.78555 inches	29.93247 cm

TIME UNITS:	Martian	Terran
1 day	10 zodes	24 hours, 37 minutes, 22.58 seconds
1 zode	50 xats	2 hours, 27 minutes, 44.26 seconds
1 xat	200 tals	2 minutes, 57.26 seconds
1 tal		.886291 seconds

VELOCITY OF LIGHT:

ENGLISH: 186,282 miles per second
METRIC: 2.99793×10^{10} centimeters per second
MARTIAN: 443,778 haads per tal

SURFACE GRAVITY OF MARS:
ENGLISH: 12.9 feet/second^2
METRIC: 392 centimeters/second^2
MARTIAN: 1.27 ads/tal^2

PREHISTORIC NOTE
By Randall Garrett

Sprague, in his more serious moments, writes historical works. Since I don't want to make this introduction longer than the piece itself, I will merely say that it is a touch of Robert E. Howard as by L. Sprague de Camp with a soupçon of Ferdinand Feghoot.

Of all the antedeluvian empires, perhaps the most stable and longest-lived was the Double Kingdom of Mekh-Pyget.

The two kingdoms were forcibly combined (c. 1250 BD) through the able generalship of Prince Ahlmos, eldest son of the then King of Mekh. The Prince presented the King with the crown of Pyget, thus making his father the first ruler of the Double Kingdom.

Within the year, the old King died, and his son then reigned as the first King Ahlmos. (There were fourteen of that name.) The father's name, unfortunately, has not come down to us, for his grandson, Vekos I, hated the old man and had his name excised from the histories and effaced from all monuments.

The sixty-one kings following Vekos I, including their names and genealogies, are well documented. It is only as we approach the end of the Antedeluvian Age that another void appears.

The naval architect Zuizudras built his great vessel during the reign of King Damnir, fifteenth and last of his name. King Damnir XV died only ten months before the onset of the Great Catastrophe, leaving his only son as heir. But since this sovran had no opportunity to build monuments to himself, as was the custom, his name has not been preserved.

Nonetheless, because of this custom of monument building

or a millenium and a quarter, we have a nearly complete list of
he Kings of Mehk-Pyget, from Ahlmos I to Damnir the Last.

—*The Annals of Unrecorded History*

"REVIEWS IN VERSE"
By Randall Garrett

I started writing these things in 1951, with no notion whatever that they were publishable, except perhaps, in a fanzine. (A "fanzine," for those of you who do not dig the slang of science fiction fans, is a "little" magazine published by a fan or fans in order to get things in print which the professional magazines ("prozines") won't buy. Many of them are very good. Those which are not die quickly and are called "crudzines." Back in '51, most of them were mimeographed or even hectographed. Today, most are offset. With the exception of a very few, payment is in free copies of the issue in which one's work appears. Nearly every professional author has had offbeat work appear in a fanzine.)

My inspiration for this work was a New Yorker named Newman Levy. By profession, he was a lawyer, but as a hobby he constructed light verse. (And "construct" is the word! Good light verse is an engineering problem, since, unlike "serious" poetry, it should be absolutely perfect in meter, rhyme, and sense.) During the Roaring Twenties, Newman Levy turned out dozens of them, and many were, like mine, "Reviews in Verse"—although he never used that phrase that I know of.

Levy's Opera Guyed, published by Alfred Knopf, is almost a textbook on How To Do It. So is his Theater Guyed. Many of his works are quoted and printed today (the copyright has run out) without giving the author's name. Do you remember "Thais"?

One time in Alexandria, in wicked Alexandria,
    Where nights were wild with revelry, and life was but
      a game,
    There lived, so the report is, an adventuress and courtesan,
    The pride of Alexandria, and Thais was her name.

217

Or his takeoff on W. Somerset Maugham's "Rain," the story of the Immor(t)al Sadie Thompson, which begins:

On the isle of Pago Pago,
Land of palm trees, rice, and sago,
Where the Chinaman and Dago
   Dwell 'mid natives dusky-hued.
Lived a dissolute and shady
Bold adventuress named Sadie;
Sadie Thompson was the lady,
   And the life she lived was lewd.

And the final line is an absolute smasher!

Levy was a master of double and triple feminine rhyme, and of mosaic rhyme ("report is, an"—"courtesan"). His stuff rolls off the tongue.

So I decided to try to do for science fiction what Newman Levy had done for opera and the theater.

One evening, at a party in New York, someone asked me to recite one of my reviews for the group. Since I am about as bashful and modest as Isaac Asimov, and for similar reasons, I acceded to the request.

There is an old one-liner: "He asked me if I like card tricks; I said no; he showed me ten."

I think I had to be shut up with a fire extinguisher.

But sitting in that crowd was a gentleman named Robert A. W. "Doc" Lowndes, who was then editor of Original Science Fiction Stories, Future Science Fiction, *and* Science Fiction Quarterly.

Doc Lowndes, bless 'im, said: "If you'll type those up and bring them to my office, I'll buy 'em."

And he did.

WARNING: IF YOU HAVE NOT READ THE ORIGINAL STORY, PLEASE DON'T READ MY VERSE FIRST. GO OUT AND BUY, BEG, OR BORROW A COPY OF THE ORIGINAL WORK AND READ IT. THEN READ THE VERSE.

AFTER ALL, WHO WANTS TO KNOW THE WHOLE PLOT OF A STORY BEFORE READING IT?

ISAAC ASIMOV'S
"THE CAVES OF STEEL"
By Randall Garrett

Many years ago, John Campbell made the flat statement that it was impossible to write a science fiction detective story. The hero can always whip out his hyperinductivizer and re-create the scene of the crime in toto, or he can get into his handy-dandy time machine and go back to watch the murder being committed, or he can read all the suspects' minds, or...

In other words, since anything can happen in a science fiction story, the job is too easy. No suspense. And no need for a detective.

Now, every time John made a flat statement like that, at least one of his authors would try to prove him wrong. And very often succeeded. The idea was to prove John wrong and make him pay for it. It was a game we all loved.

The first to succeed at the detective story game was Hal Clement, with "Needle." The question was: "Where is the alien hiding?" It was strictly fair; all the clues were given and the reader had a fair, honest chance of finding out where the critter was hidden before the author told him.

But...It wasn't a formal detective story.

In the strictly formal detective story, there must be a detective, either amateur or professional, and he must solve the crime —usually murder. In "Needle" the crime is an alien one, and so is the detective. There is no murder, and the detective does not solve the puzzle. His host, a human boy, does. Don't get me wrong; it's a good story, but you have to stretch things pretty thin to call it a formal detective story.

However, "Needle" paved the way. You can write a formal detective story of science fiction, but first you must define your parameters! You must make it perfectly clear that the detective *can* not *pull rabbits out of hats or superscience gadgets out of his home lab.*

Even in a society where good old-fashioned magic works, the job can be done. I've done it myself, in Too Many Magicians *and other Lord Darcy stories.*

But the man who showed me how was Isaac Asimov in The Caves of Steel.

In the future, when the towns are caves of steel
   Clear from Boston, Massachusetts, to Mobile,
There's a cop, Elijah Baley, who's the hero of this tale. He
   Has a Spacer robot helper named Daneel.

For it seems that there's some guys from Outer Space
   (They're descendants of the Terran human race),
And all over Terra's globe, it seems they're giving jobs to robots,
   Which are hated by the people they replace.

So a certain Spacer, Sarton, gets rubbed out,
   And the Chief says to Elijah: "Be a scout;
Go and find out just whodunit, and, although it won't be fun, it
   Will result in your promotion, without doubt!"

The assignment puts Elijah on the spot.
   He must do the job up right; if he does not,
It not only will disgrace him, but the robot will replace him
   If the robot is the first to solve the plot.

In the city, there's a riot at a store.
   R. Daneel jumps on a counter, and before
Baley knows it, pulls his blaster. Then he bellows: "I'm the master
   Here, so stop it, or I'll blow you off the floor!"

So the riot's busted up before it starts,
And Elijah's wounded ego really smarts.
"Well," he says, "you quelled that riot, but a *robot* wouldn't try it!
Dan, I think you've got a screw loose in your parts!"

Baley doesn't see how R. Daneel could draw
Out his blaster, for the First Robotic Law
Says: "No robot may, through action or inaction, harm a fraction
Of a whisker on a human being's jaw."

Since Daneel, the robot, has a human face,
And he looks exactly like the guy from space
Who has been assassinated, Mr. Baley's quite elated,
For he's positive he's solved the murder case!

"The Commissioner," he says, "has been misled,
'Cause there hasn't been a murder! No one's dead!
Why you did it, I don't know, but I don't think you are a robot!
I am certain you are Sarton, sir, instead!"

"Why, that's rather silly, partner," says Daneel,
"And I'm awful sorry that's the way you feel."
Then, by peeling back his skin, he shows Elijah that, within, he
Is constructed almost totally of steel!

Well, of course, this gives Elijah quite a shock.
So he thinks the whole thing over, taking stock
Of the clues in their relation to the total situation,
Then he goes and calls a special robot doc.

Says Elijah Baley: "Dr. Gerrigel,
This here murder case is just about to jell!
And to bust it open wide, I'll prove this robot's homicidal!
Look him over, doc, and see if you can tell."

So the doctor gives Daneel a thorough test
While the robot sits there, calmly self-possessed.
After close examination, "His First Law's in operation,"
Says the doctor, "You can set your mind at rest."

That leaves Baley feeling somewhat like a jerk,
But Daneel is very difficult to irk;
He just says: "We can't stand still, or we will never find the killer.
Come on, partner, let us buckle down to work."

Now the plot begins to thicken—as it should;
It's the thickening in plots that makes 'em good.
The Police Chief's robot, Sammy, gives himself the double
        whammy,
    And the reason for it isn't understood.

The Commissioner says: "Baley, you're to blame!
Robot Sammy burned his brain out, and I claim
That, from every single clue, it looks as though you made him
        do it!"
    Baley hollers: "No, I didn't! It's a frame!"

Then he says: "Commish, I think that you're the heel
Who's the nasty little villain in this deal!
And I'll tell you to your face, I really think you killed the Spacer,
    'Cause you thought he was the robot, R. Daneel!"

The Commissioner breaks down and mumbles: "Yes—
I'm the guy who did it, Baley—I confess!"
Baley says: "I knew in time you would confess this awful crime.
        You
    Understand, of course, you're in an awful mess!"

The Commissioner keels over on the floor.
When he wakes up, R. Daneel says: "We're not sore;
Since the crime was accidental, we'll be merciful and gentle.
    Go," he says in solemn tones, "and sin no more!"

Then says Baley to the robot, with a grin:
"It was nice of you to overlook his sin.
As a friend, I wouldn't trade you! By the Asimov who made you,
    You're a better man than I am, Hunka Tin!"

ALFRED BESTER'S
"THE DEMOLISHED MAN"
By Randall Garrett

This "Review in Verse" was taken from Bester's original magazine version, which appeared in Galaxy. It differs somewhat from the book version. For instance, "the author, Mr. Bester, doesn't specify the year" in the magazine version, whereas, in the book version, he does. Another change was his lessened use of shortcut symbols. In the original, "Tate" was spelled "T8"; in the book, it's spelled out. Also, there's a character in the original called "$$son." Now, I could have sworn that was "Dollarson" and I wrote the verse accordingly. But when the book came out, it was spelled "Jackson."

"Obscure, Alfie," says I.

"That's why I changed it," says he.

At any rate, when you read it—and it must be read aloud for full effect—pronounce the symbols as though they were words. "@" is pronounced "at," so "f@" is pronounced "fat." The trouble is that the twelfth letter of the alphabet and the figure "one" look pretty much alike in print, so, in Verse 14, when you come to the word "18," pronounce it "late," not "eighteen."

"*" is "asterisk," "%" is "percent," and "(" is "parenthesis."

Now you're on your own.

In the far & distant future—you can pick the d8 2 suit your-
    Self, the author, Mr. Bester, doesn't specify the year—
There's a fellow named Ben Reich, a rich investor who's no piker,
    Who has dreams about a Faceless Man in nightmares odd &
        queer.

Craye D-Courtney is his rival. Says Ben Reich: "While he's alive, I'll
　　Never rest, so I must rub him out the best way th@ I can!"
But, according 2 report, neither Ben Reich nor old D'Courtney
　　Knows the other well enough 4 Ben 2 h8 the older man.

Now, despite his wealth & power, Ben Reich still does not see how ar-
　　Ranging old D'Courtney's death can be achieved with grace & ease.
If he gets in2 a mess, perception by an expert Esper
　　Will eventually happen, 4 these lads are thick as fleas.

But since Reich remains determined 2 extermin8 th@ vermin, d-
　　Rastic action must be taken 2 make sure he won't get caught.
So he calls Augustus T8, a doctor who, we find, is r8ed
　　As a 1st Class Esper Medic. Reich is sure he can be bought.

"Gus, D'Courtney is a bird I rather think I'd like 2 murder,
　　& I'll pay an even million if you'll help me kill the slob!"
T8 says: "I don't like it, still you never know—an even million?
　　Th@'s an awful lot of money, Ben; I think I'll take the job!"

Next he needs some brain protection from the Espers' keen detection;
　　Just a song th@ he can think of so they cannot read his mind.
So he calls a gal named Duffy, who is just a bit of fluff he
　　Knows, who has a music shop th@ carries songs of every kind.

"Just a song with rhythm in it?" Duffy frowns & thinks a minute.
　　"Well, we have all kinds of songs, but if you simply must have 1
Th@ keeps running through your head, the best we have is '10ser, said the
　　10sor, 10sion, apprehension & dis¢sion have begun!' "

Now the fireworks really start; he hears from T8 about a party
　　At the Beaumonts'. Craye D'Courtney will be there without a doubt.
Ben Reich packs his g@ & goes there, smiles @ everyone he knows there,
　　　& sneaks up 2 old D'Courtney's room when all the lights are out.

Craye says: "Ben, I'm sick & feeble!" Says Ben Reich: "You can't
 make me bel-
 Ieve a word of all th@ guff!" & then he shoots Craye through
  the head.
But Ben's planning's all 4 naught; around comes old D'Courtney's
 daughter,
 & she grabs the g@ & runs off when she sees her father dead.

Now comes Powell, a detective, whose main job is 2 collect ev-
 Aders of the law, who ought 2 know th@ they can not
  succeed.
He's an Es% by the police 2 peep @ all the people
 @ the party 2 determine who has done this dreadful deed.

His Lieu10ant, known as $$son, is hot beneath the collar.
 "What's the motive? Where's the witness? Who's the killer?
  Where's the gun?
Ben Reich's mind cannot be read, the best I get is: '10ser, said the
 10sor, 10sion, apprehension & distortion have begun!' "

"It's a tough 1," murmurs Powell, "& I really don't see how I'll
 Get the evidence I need 2 take this murder case 2 court.
& I may be wrong, but still, I really think Ben Reich's the killer.
 If he is, 2 take him in will prove 2 be a bit of sport."

Ben says: "This'll be a b@tle, & I'm much afraid the f@'ll
 Soon be in the fire unless I find the young D'Courtney dame."
Likewise, Powell's biggest worry is 2 get his hands on her, he
 Knows he'll really have 2 scurry, 4 Ben Reich's goal's just
  the same.

Babs D'Courtney is loc8ed by Ben Reich, but he's 2 l8, a d-
 Ame who's known 2 all as Chooka tells friend Powell where
  she's @.
Ben Reich's chances would be gone, except th@ Babs is c@@onic,
 & the 3rd° can't make her tell where she got Ben Reich's g@.

Powell still has 1 more chance. A Reich employee has the answer
 2 a note Ben sent D'Courtney 2 conclude a business deal.
Powell's sure th@ Ben Reich's motive 4 the murder's in this note,
 he v-
 Ows 2 get it from this Hassop, even if he has 2 steal.

Then, 2 Powell's consternation, Ben Reich goes 2 a space station

Known as Ampro, a resort with tropic jungles grown inside.
Ben goes in with Hassop. "Now I'll have 2 find them," mutters
      Powell.
    "Mr. Hassop has gone in2 th@ mor* his hide!"

Since he knows th@ Ben won't pass up this big chance 2 murder
      Hassop,
    He & several other Pee%er Ampro 4 the search.
But when the note's collected, it's not what the cop expected,
    & the case just falls apart, which leaves poor Powell in the
      lurch.

Powell mutters: "I'll get dirty! Though Ben thinks he can't be hurt,
      he
    Still has dreams about a Faceless Man who wakes up
      screaming screams."
Espers of the 1st Class r8ing start their minds 2 con¢r8ing—
    Ben begins 2 see the Faceless Man come stalking from his
      dreams!

Powell has the famed "last laugh"; he drives poor Ben completely
      daffy,
    & they take him 2 a nuthouse, where he's out of Powell's hair.
Though they've gone and caught the villain, I'm inclined 2 think
      it's still un-
    Necessary 4 policemen 2 be quite so damned unfair.

There's a part of the plot I completely forgot;
    I'll insert it down here, if you like.
Craye D'Courtney & Barbara, respectively, are
    The (ter of Reich.

L. SPRAGUE DE CAMP'S "LEST DARKNESS FALL"

By Randall Garrett

There are some books one reads over and over again, and, for me, Sprague's Lest Darkness Fall *is one of them. Like* Slan, *the* Lensman *series, the* Foundation *trilogy, and a handful of others, Sprague's book is an old friend that is always showing me something new.*

I first read it in John Campbell's Unknown, *a World War II casualty. I literally wore that issue of the magazine out by re-reading that one story. When it finally came out in book form, years later, I was overjoyed. It had been expanded and was much richer.*

It was the first history I ever read that made me realize that history could be interesting.

Thank you, Sprague.

The reader's tossed into this tale with great impetuosity.
The hero, struck by lightning, sees a burst of luminosity!
His vision clears, and he is overcome with curiosity—
    The lightning's tossed him back in Time to ancient Gothic
        Rome!
At first, poor Martin Padway thinks he's stricken with insanity,
To find himself immersed in early Roman Christianity,
But finally he buckles down to face it with urbanity;
    He knows that he's forever stuck and never will get home.

Now, Europe's just about to start the Age of Faith and Piety,
And such an awful future fills our hero with anxiety,

So he begins to bolster up this barbarous society
　　　With modernistic gadgets that the Romans haven't got.
A moneylending Syrian of singular sagacity
Succumbs, in time, to Mr. P's remarkable tenacity,
And, though he makes remarks decrying Martin's vast audacity,
　　　Proceeds to lend him quite a lot of money on the spot.

Now, in return, our hero starts, in manner most emphatical,
To show the banker how to solve his problems mathematical.
And one clerk gets so sore he ups and takes a leave sabbatical;
　　　"I can't take Arab numerals," he says; "I've had my fill!"
But Mr. Padway takes the resignation with passivity.
The other men have shown a mathematical proclivity,
So, confident the system will increase their productivity,
　　　He takes his borrowed money and goes out and buys a still.

Then, trading in on what he knows about historiography,
Our Martin Padway next invents the art of mass typography.
He hires a bunch of Roman scribes (He's fond of their
　　　chirography),
　　　And makes them all reporters for his paper: *Roman Times.*
Because of a Sicilian he fired without apology,
He gets in lots of trouble on a charge of demonology.
But, using all the very best of Freudian psychology,
　　　He gets himself released from prosecution for the crimes.

The Roman city governor, a certain Count Honorius
(A man who is notorious for actions amatorious),
Is then convinced by Padway, in a very long, laborious,
　　　And detailed explanation of how corporations work,
That he (the Count), in order to insure his own prosperity,
Should use his cash to back, with all expedient celerity,
A telegraphic system Padway's building for posterity.
　　　The Count proceeds to do so, with an avaricious smirk.

But while our hero is engaged in projects multifarious,
An army of Imperialists under Belisarius
Invades the Goths, who find that their position is precarious,
　　　So Padway has to help the Gothic army win the fight.
He saves the King from being killed, to win his royal gratitude,
And though our hero's hampered by the King's fogheaded
　　　attitude,
He gets appointed Quaestor, which affords him lots of latitude.
　　　He whips the Greek invaders in the middle of the night.

The King becomes so useless that he's almost parasitical,
And Padway finds himself up to his neck in things political;
He has to learn to tread with care, and not be hypercritical
     Of how affairs are run in the Italo-Gothic state.
The Byzantines send in another army with rapidity,
And Bloody John, the general, attacks with great avidity.
Because the Gothic nation lacks political solidity,
     The Byzantines march northward at a very rapid rate.

The Greeks go up through Italy with thundering and plundering;
The Gothic troops, as always, just continue with their
          blundering,
While Martin Padway, at their head, is worrying and wondering
     Just what the Hell he's gonna do and where he's gonna go!
At last he comes in contact with Joannas Sanguinarius!
(The battle's very bloody, but de Camp makes it hilarious.)
And just as he's about to lose, the turncoat Belisarius
     Comes charging in with cavalry and quickly routs the foe.

Now, though all through the novel we've been jollied with
          jocundity,
The story's ended on a note of very great profundity:
The Roman-Goth society's been saved from moribundity!
     For two years, Padway's been in Rome—and things have
          sure changed since!
The greatest fighting man in Rome since Emperor Aurelian,
The sneaky little tricks he pulls are quite Mephistophelian;
Though modest and retiring once, he's changed like a chameleon
     To something like a character from Machiavelli's "Prince"!

A.E. VAN VOGT'S "SLAN"
By Randall Garrett

Like many of the other stories I mention in this book, I first read Slan in the magazine version. In those far-off and ancient days, science fiction was a genre rarely found between book covers, either hard or soft. If you wanted to read science fiction, you went to the magazines, or you did without. And in 1940, the best of them all was John Campbell's Astounding Science Fiction. And towards the end of that year, in the last three issues, Slan exploded like fifty kilos of lithium hydride. Nothing even remotely like it had ever been written before.

Much of my magazine collection was lost during the war, and the Arkham House edition, which came out in 1946, somehow got lost, too. For years, all I had was the paperback edition of Slan, which was slightly different from the original.

But I remembered the original, and it is from the magazine version that I wrote the verse.

Two days ago, as I write this, I received in the mail a present from A. E. Van Vogt. It was a personally autographed copy of the Nelson Doubleday edition of Slan, from the original magazine version.

Lord love you, Van. I know I do.

> Our tale begins with Jommy Cross,
>   A Slan lad who's pursued
> By Petty, Secret Service boss,
>   A fellow mean and shrewd.
> It seems, you see, that any Slan
> Is somewhat of a superman,
> So humans have pronounced a ban,
>   Which starts an awful feud.

Young Jommy, who's a telepath,
    Escapes and meets old Gran,
Who feeds him, makes him take a bath,
    And then begins to plan.
She hates to live in filth and grime;
She don't like starving all the time;
And so she plans a life of crime,
    For which she needs a Slan.

The scene now shifts some miles away,
    Where, in a palace grand,
A plot is laid to murder Gray,
    The ruler of the land.
The plot is foiled by sweet Kathleen,
A female Slan, the heroine,
Whose telepathic mind has seen
    How Gray's demise was planned.

With Katy's aid, the entire gang
    Is mopped up neat and clean.
Says Gray: "You done that with a bang,
    So bend an ear, Kathleen,
The law says all Slans must be shot
And that puts you upon the spot.
But since you helped me foil that plot,
    I could not be so mean."

Meanwhile, young Cross, against his will,
    Has started stealing, which
Has helped Gran fill the coffers, till
    The two of them are rich.
Unknown to Granny, Jommy's found,
In someplace hidden underground,
A gun his father left around,
    Concealed there in a niche.

One day, while thinking of his woes,
    He bumps into a pair
Of older Slans, to whom he shows
    The tendrils in his hair.
There are two types of Slans, we find—
The tendrilless and tendrilled kind.
(The former cannot read your mind.)
    Well, these two don't play fair.

They chase him! Jommy runs like hell!
    He hears them call him "snake."
He says, "They don't like tendrils. Well,
    That's more than I can take.
Although I'm in an awful mess,
Since them two Slans is tendrilless,
If I escape, they'll see, I guess,
    They made a bad mistake!"

Without delay, he gets away
    And starts in making plans
To search until he finds, some day,
    The true or tendrilled Slans.
For this he needs a space ship, so,
Since he knows just the place to go,
He quickly packs up all his dough,
    And also most of Gran's.

The Slans (*sans* tendrils) have a lair,
    And Jommy knows they've got
A hot-rod space ship hidden there;
    He sneaks off to the spot.
And giving all the guards the slip,
He climbs into the rocket ship,
Sits down and gives the switch a flip,
    And takes off like a shot.

The Slans' gigantic super ships
    Are cruising all around.
Says Cross: "I'll hide from all these drips
    Where I cannot be found.
They think they got me on the run;
Well, brother, watch me have some fun!"
He turns on Pappy's atom gun
    And dives into the ground.

The space ship's now well-hidden, so
    He says, "I'll never rest.
Until I find true Slans, I'll go
    And do my very best."
He knows, no matter where they are,
They can't have gone so very far,
And so he builds a super car
    And starts out on his quest.

Now let's get back to sweet Kathleen.
    She's double-crossed by Gray.
She's told, in manner quite serene,
    That on that very day
She must become the mistress of
A gentleman she doesn't love.
"Oh, hell," says Kate, "I guess I'll shove."
    And quickly runs away.

She's chased by Petty. (You know him,
    The Secret Service Boss.)
She flees into a cavern dim,
    All full of dust and moss.
Now to an author, nothing beats
All these coincidental feats,
So whom do you suppose she meets?
    You guessed it! Jommy Cross!

So down the cavern halls they walk.
    "Gee, this is great!" says he.
(Of course, instead of normal talk,
    They use telepathy.)
She says, "I ran from Petty, but
He'll never find me here, the mutt."
And Jommy Cross, the stupid nut,
    Says, "Yes, dear, I agree."

He really pulls a boner then,
    A stunt I can't condone.
He leaves her. Petty and his men
    Find Katy all alone.
So Petty shoots her through the head;
He fills her noggin full of lead;
And sweet Kathleen falls over dead;
    She doesn't even groan.

Poor Jommy slams his auto door
    And drives away in tears.
Of course, he gets away once more.
    We now skip seven years.
The Slans are up to their old tricks.
They raid his hideout in the sticks.
Poor Jommy's in an awful fix,
    In trouble to his ears.

With rays they blast his hideout, and
    He runs out into space.
Although they have the upper hand,
    They're led a merry chase.
I hardly think I need to say
That once again he gets away.
He does it twenty times a day;
    By now it's commonplace.

He goes to Mars because he thinks
    True Slans are hidden there.
He soon finds that idea stinks;
    They aren't there anywhere.
"A most disgusting state," says he,
"The only place that they can be
Is highly dangerous to me;
    I wonder if I dare?"

So, back on Earth, he sneaks into
    The offices of Gray.
He's caught, and Gray says, "This won't do.
    I fear you'll have to pay."
For Gray, it seems, is not a man;
Instead we find that *he's* a Slan.
Says Gray: "I do not think you can
    Expect to get away."

Then Jommy shrugs and says, "Pooh-pooh,"
    And gives his head a toss.
Gray grins and shouts, "Hurray for you!
    You must be Jommy Cross!
My daughter Kathleen Layton Gray
Is somehow still alive today!"
Poor Jommy nearly faints away,
    He's thrown for such a loss.

The story's ended at this spot;
    I trust you get the gist.
This is a Dickens of a plot;
    The point cannot be missed.
The story of a little boy
Pursued by all the *hoi polloi*—
And so Van Vogt, we note with joy,
    Gives us a brand new Twist.

POUL ANDERSON'S "THREE HEARTS AND THREE LIONS"

A Calypso in Search of a Rhyme

By Randall Garrett

I said earlier that constructing light verse is like an engineering project, and that the rhyming must be precise. But rules are made to be broken; you just have to know what you're doing.

This is the only one of these Reviews in Verse that was written to be sung. (The others have been sung to various tunes at science fiction conventions, but that's not my doing.)

The first time Poul Anderson heard this one sung, he laughed. Now he just looks pained. Too much of a good thing.

The song is, as the subtitle says, a calypso. It sounds best when done with a broad Jamaican accent.

Here's a tale of knighthood's flower
And of one man's finest hour:
    The story of a most strange land,
    Of Holger Carlsen's little band,
    Of fights with trolls and giants, and
    The winning of a swan-may's hand.
By one of Denmark's noblest scions.
(Chorus) *Three Red Hearts and Three Gold Lions!*

Holger Carlsen's fighting Nazis;
While he's dodging their pot-shots, he's
    Wounded badly in the head,
    But he does not fall down dead,
    Nor go to hospital bed,
    But to Middle World instead.
Magic here holds sway, not science.
(Chorus) *Three Red Hearts and Three Gold Lience!*

When he wake up, there beside him,
Stands, for Carlsen to ride him,
    A horse with armor, shield and sword,
    Clothing and misericord,
    Fine enough for any lord;
    Holger Carlsen climb aboard.
Hungry, he must search for viands.
(Chorus) *Three Red Hearts and Three Gold Liands!*

Holger rides up to a cottage,
Where an old witch offers pottage.
    "How can I get home?" says he.
    "Well," the witch says, "seems to me
    That thou ought to go and see
    Good Duke Alfric in Faerie.
He will aid in gaining thy ends."
(Chorus) *Three Red Hearts and Three Gold Ly-ends!*

Off he rides to land of Faerie
With Hugi, a dwarf who's very
    Dour and speaks much like a Scot
    (Which he may be, like as not),
    Though ofttimes he talks a lot.
    Next the sex come in the plot.
(Please don't take offense at my hints.)
(Chorus) *Three Red Hearts and Three Gold Ly-hints!*

Here she is, named Alianora;
Holger really does go for her.
    She can change into a swan
    And go flying on and on.
    She make friends with doe and fawn;
    He feel love about to dawn.
But he's pure, so pardon my yawns.
(Chorus) *Three Red Hearts and Three Gold Ly-yawns!*

Off to Faerie they go quickly,
Where the light is dim and sickly.
    Alfric and Morgan-le'Fe
    Ask Holger to spend the day
    'Neath Elf Hill not far away;
    He is saved by his swan-may;
Beneath that hill, one night is eons.
(Chorus) *Three Red Hearts and Three Gold Leons!*

Off they flee across the border;
Spooks pursue on every quarter;
    First a dragon overhead—
    Holger Carlsen kill him dead;
    Next a giant huge and dread
    Who is looking to be fed.
Holger holds him in abeyance.
(Chorus) *Three Red Hearts and Three Gold Leyance!*

"Fight with riddles," says the giant;
Holger Carlsen's quite compliant.
    So they fight with quip and pun
    Till the U-V of the sun
    Hit that giant like a gun.
    "He's stoned!" says Holger, "Now let's run."
All the air is filled with ions.
(Chorus) *Three Red Hearts and Three Gold Lions!*

Next they ride into a village
Where a werewolf's bent on pillage.
    Who the warg is, folks can't guess.
    Holger Carlsen solves the mess,
    And he makes that warg confess
    She's the local young princess.
"Now," he says, "it's out of my hands."
(Chorus) *Three Red Hearts and Three Gold Ly-hands!*

When the village folk release 'em
On to Tarnberg go the threesome.
    By a good mage they are told
    They must find a very old
    Sword, that's worth its weight in gold
    At St. Grimmin's-in-the-Wold.
He found this out at a seance.
(Chorus) *Three Red Hearts and Three Gold Leance!*

Meanwhile, they have met a knightly
Saracen, with manners sprightly.
    Northward they all head apace,
    Searching for that dreadful place.
    But the swan-may's pretty face
    Is hurting Holger's state of grace.
"Should I," says he, "yield to my yens?"
(Chorus) *Three Red Hearts and Three Gold Ly-yens!*

Holger's kidnapped by a nixie
(That's an underwater pixie).
   Nixie, who is on the make,
   Drags Holger beneath the lake.
   "This is more than I can take!"
   Holger says, "I'll make a break.
Come on," says he, "let us flee hence!"
   (Chorus) Spoken: *Flee hence?*
   Spoken: Uh—fly hence?
(Chorus) *Three Red Hearts and Three Gold Ly-hence!*

Now to blast their hopes asunder,
They find that they must go under-
   Neath a mountain, where a troll
   Lurks in his disgusting hole.
   They kill him and head towards their goal;
   Holger says, "Now, bless my soul,
That was worse than fighting giants."
(Chorus) *Three Red Hearts and Three Gold Liants!*

Now, though it's no place for women,
They come to church of St. Grimmin.
   Round the altar they all flock;
   Holger pries up big stone block
   There is sword beneath the rock;
   Holger says, "Now, this I grok!
We found it, though surrounded by haunts."
(Chorus) *Three Red Hearts and Three Gold Ly-haunts!*

End of story! Jesu Christe!
Seems to me it's kind of misty.
   He should be belted and earled,
   But through space-time he is hurled,
   And, un-knighted and un-girled,
   He ends up in our own dull world.
His future's vague as that of Zion's.
(Chorus) *Three Red Hearts and Three Gold Lions!*

POUL ANDERSON'S *THREE HEARTS AND THREE LIONS*
A Calypso in Search of a Rhyme

Words and Music by
Randall Garrett

Arrangement by
Vicki Ann Heydron

Broad Calypso tempo

1. Here's a tale of knight-hood's flo-wer And of one man's fin-est ho-ur: The sto-ry of a most strange land, Of Hol-ger Carl-sen's lit-tle band, Of fights with trolls and gi-ants, and The win-ning of a swan-may's hand. By one of Den-mark's nob-lest sci-ons

CHORUS: THREE RED HEARTS AND THREE GOLD LI-ONS!

THREE RED HEARTS AND THREE GOLD LI-ONS!

JOHN W. CAMBELL'S "WHO GOES THERE?"

By Randall Garrett

John Campbell had his first story published in 1931, in the old Hugo Gernsback Amazing Stories. During the next seven years, he not only began to rival E. E. Smith as a writer of far-out space opera, but, under the pen name "Don A. Stuart," wrote some very perceptive and sensitive stories in quite another style. He became editor of Astounding in 1938, and wrote very little thereafter except for his thought-provoking (and often just plain provoking) editorials for the magazine.

Who Goes There? was published in 1938 under the Stuart by-line, and when I first read it, I didn't know Stuart was Campbell. What I did know is that it scared the daylights out of me. It still does.

A very bad movie called The Thing from Outer Space was presumably based on it about 1950, but the resemblance was slight. James Arness stalked through it, looking like a cross between Frankenstein's monster and a triffid, and bearing no similarity whatever to Campbell's horror.

When I showed this verse to John, his only comment was: "Well, it's a hell of a lot better than The Thing."

Here's a tale of chilling horror
For the sort of guy who more or
Less thinks being an explorer
    Is the kind of life for him.
If he finds his life a bore, he
Ought to read this gory story,
For he'll find exploratory
    Work is really rather grim.

For the story starts by stating
That some guys investigating
The Antarctic are debating
    On exactly what to do
With a monster they've found frozen
Near the campsite they have chosen,
And the quarrel grows and grows, un-
    Til they're in an awful stew.

There's a guy named Blair who wants to r-
Eally check up on this monster
And dissect it. To his conster-
    Nation, everyone's in doubt.
So, of course, he starts in pleading,
And the rest of them start heeding
All his statements, and conceding
    That the Thing should be thawed out.

So they let this Thing of evil
Start to melt from its primeval
Sheath of ice; they don't perceive a l-
    Ot of trouble will ensue.
When the Thing is thawed, it neatly
Comes to life, and smiling sweetly,
It absorbs some men completely,
    Changing them to monsters, too!

Now we reach the story's nub, il-
Luminating all the trouble;
Each new monster is a double
    For the men they each replace.
Since it seems a man's own mother
Couldn't tell one from the other,
These guys all watch one another,
    Each with fear upon his face.

And so then the men are tested
To see who has been digested,
And who's been left unmolested,
    But the test don't work! It's hexed!
So each man just sits there, shrinking
From the others, madly thinking,
As he watches with unblinking
    Gaze, and wonders—*Who Goes Next?*

Now, they've found that executing
Monsters can't be done by shooting;
They require electrocuting,
     Or cremation with a torch.
When they find these Things, they grab 'em;
They don't try to shoot or stab 'em;
With high-voltage wires, they jab 'em
     'Til their flesh begins to scorch.

So the entire expedition
Eye each other with suspicion,
For they're in a bad position,
     And there's no denying *that!*
Now, to clear this awful scramble,
The ingenious Mr. Campbell,
Suddenly, without preamble,
     Pulls a rabbit from the hat.

Here's the way they solve the muddle:
They discover that a puddle
Of a pseudo-human's blood'll
     Be a little monster, too!
With this test for separating
Men from monsters, without waiting,
They start right in liquidating
     All the monsters in the crew.

Thus, the story is completed.
And the awful Thing's defeated,
But he still was badly treated;
     It's a shame, it seems to me.
Frozen since the glaciation,
This poor Thing's extermination
Is as sad as the cremation
     Of the hapless Sam McGee.

THE ADVENTURES OF "LITTLE WILLIE"

By Randall Garrett

ZAP!

Little Willie, full of fun,
Borrowed Daddy's proton gun;
He tried it out with great elation—
Now he's cosmic radiation.

BLAZE OF GLORY

Little Willie made a slip
While landing in his rocket ship.
See that bright, actinic glare?
That's our little Willie there.

HOT ARGUMENT

Willie and his girl friend, Bea,
While working for the A.E.C.
Got in a fight, and failed to hear
The warning of a bomb test near.
Their friends were sad to hear, no doubt,
That they had had a falling out.

INTRODUCTION TO
BENEDICT BREADFRUIT

By Grendel Briarton

In 2041, Ferdinand Feghoot successfully sponsored the perpetrator of these puns for membership in the exclusive Time Travellers Club, at their opulent rooms in King Charles III Street in London. He brought him in through the)(connecting the club rooms with any number of centuries, and presented him to the Members.

Old Dr. Gropius Volkswagen looked at him dubiously. "Why should we make him a Member?" he grumbled. "He does not even look as if he has genius!"

"I assure you," Feghoot said, "that he has. His puns are even more atrocious than mine. He is a dedicated writer—a veritable pen-addict."

"Maybe it is so," growled the old gentleman, "but how do we know he is a good, solid citizen?"

"I will vouch for him," Feghoot declared. "For generations, his whole family have emphasized their traditions and history. They have all been bred for roots."

"My dear fellow," put in the Club's president, Vice-Admiral Sir Trumpery Buckett, "is all this on the basis of your own intimate knowledge?"

"Absolutely!" said Ferdinand Feghoot. "After all, he was conceived in our garret!"

...Read 'em and weep.

THROUGH TIME AND SPACE
WITH BENEDICT BREADFRUIT

By Randall Garrett

I

On the ancient planet of Phogiu II, the natives were in a terrible tizzy. Their local god—a huge, intelligent lichen which covered a fifth of the habitable surface of Phogiu II, was dying. Naturally, they sent for Benedict Breadfruit. He took one look at the lichen and said: "It is obvious that the fungi part of this intelligent symbiotic organism is in good health. The other part, however—"

He gave it a shot of vitamins and a chlorophyll pill. The Great Lichen immediately spruced up and began delivering its deep pronunciamentos with the proper punctilio.

"What was wrong with it?" asked one of the natives.

"Nothing serious," said Benedict Breadfruit. "All it needed was an algae buttress."

II

The accepted method for removing space lice from the hull of a ship was by sandblasting, but the boys around the space docks noticed that Benedict Breadfruit's shiny hull was not pitted either by space lice or by sandblasting. Breadfruit used hydrogen cyanide to remove the pests, but he had never told anyone about it.

"Come, Breadfruit," said one of the spaceport officials, "'Tell

245

us how you remove your burden of pediculous pests!"

Breadfruit gestured at his HCN generator. "I gas 'em off."

III

"Father," said Benedict Breadfruit's son, Benedict II, "look at that robot over there! How can a machine in such horribly battered condition move about?"

Benedict Breadfruit looked sorrowfully at his offspring. "Haven't you ever seen junk amble, Junior?"

IV

"But what will they do with the robot when it becomes too decrepit to move?" persisted the boy.

Breadfruit pointed to a large vat of bubbling acid in the public square. "They'll throw him in the pool, yonder, son."

V

On the Planet Tenta I, plants of the melon and related families were so rare that the king himself had issued a royal fiat to protect them. Not knowing this, Benedict Breadfruit's young son started to pick a pumpkin. Fortunately, his father stopped him in time.

"But *why* can't I pick a pumpkin, father?" asked the child.

"It would be a violation of the Gourd Edict, son."

VI

"On the planet Toupher VI," said Benedict Breadfruit in his address to the members of the Institute for Twenty-First Century Studies, a group specializing in ancient history, "the natives keep time by means of cords which have knots tied along their length at precisely measured intervals. Since the material from which these cords are made is remarkably even in its rate of burning, it is possible to tell the exact hour by noticing how many knots have burned after one end has been lit."

"What is this remarkable contraption called?" asked one of the members.

"Why, naturally," said Benedict Breadfruit in his best British accent, "it would be a knot clock."

VII

The Black Beast of Betelgeuse, although horrible in aspect, was really a very pleasant fellow when you got to know him, as Benedict Breadfruit did. But because of his alienness he was forbidden to go to Earth by a Galactic Space Lines regulation forbidding tickets to be sold to "horrible monsters."

"It's an unfair law," said the Black Beast. "You're a man of some importance, Benedict; couldn't you do something about it?"

Breadfruit nodded. "I believe I can get the wretch anulled, *Bete Noir*."

VIII

The peculiar religio-sexual practices of the inhabitants of Hoogaht VIII are known throughout the Galaxy. One day a group of Hoogahtu called upon Benedict Breadfruit.

"We are," said their spokesman, "planning to build an old-fashioned Earth-type house for our group. The living quarters for the males and females will be on the first and second floors. The Temple of Love, as we call it, will occupy the top floor, just under the roof. Knowing your abilities with language, we would like for you to give us a name for our Temple."

"Orgiastic top floor, eh?" asked Breadfruit.

"That's right?"

"A hot-pants attic, as it were?" said Breadfruit.

"If you insist, yes," said the spokesman.

"A libidinous area just under the roof, one might say."

"That's what we said," agreed the Hoogahtu.

"In other words, a lewd loft?" persisted Breadfruit.

"Most emphatically," said the Hoogahtu spokesman.

Benedict Breadfruit shook his head, baffled for the first time in his life. "Gee, fellas, I just can't think of a damn thing."

COPYRIGHT DATA

About the Author:

Randall Garrett sold his first science fiction story to John Campbell in 1942. He was fourteen years old at the time, and in the Marines. Since that auspicious beginning he has published many books and stories, though even aficionados will probably not recognize some of the pseudonyms he has used: Darrell T. Langart (an anagram) for **Anything You Can Do**; Robert Randall for **The Dawning Light** and **The Shrouded Planet** (with Robert Silverberg); Mark Phillips for **The Impossible, Super Mind** and **Brain Twister**. He also wrote under the names of Blake MacKenzie and Seaton McKettrig. His best-known work, however, is under his own name: **Too Many Magicians**, part of the Lord Darcy series. Most recently, he collaborated with his wife, Vicki Ann Heydron, on the Gandalara cycle, published by Bantam Books. Another collection of humorous stories, **Takeoff, Too!**, will be published by The Donning Company in 1986.